Duwan had been spotted by the enemy, and now four Devourer guardsmen raced toward him, swords at the ready. Duwan gave ground till he reached a position that gave him some slight advantage against their numbers.

The first two warriors came at him, and Duwan parried an angry lunge with his shortsword, while measuring the skill of the second fighter with a feint of his longsword. With incredible speed, Duwan buried his longsword a hand's width into the heart of one foe and opened the throat of the other with his shortsword. Then he was springing back as the other two guardsmen moved forward. Duwan lunged and parried and spun away from the more skilled swordsman, and in his spinning, he sent his longsword hissing to decapitate the lesser of his enemies, continuing the whirling spin just in time to parry a lunge with his shortsword. Gaining ground, he paused to look upon his opponent, his eyes full of fire.

"Come," Duwan said, "Come to me, Enemy."

"Who are you?" the guardsman gasped.

"Your death. . . ."

SUNDRINKER

by Zach Hughes

DAW BOOKS, INC.
DONALD A. WOLLHEIM, PUBLISHER

DAW Book Collectors No. 718.

First Printing, August, 1987

2 3 4 5 6 7 8 9

PRINTED IN CANADA

COVER PRINTED IN U.S.A.

BOOK ONE

BOOK ONE

1

In the time of the long light Du, the source, circled low on the horizon. Warmed by the benevolent light, the air absorbed the steams of the valley to reveal, in all its glory, the purplish blue sky. Sheath ice, condensed from the vapors during the weary season of dims and darks, cracked, sheered away, fell in shardy cascades into dissolving heaps at the foot of the sheer cliffs.

The birds had been arriving since long before the celebration of the coming of the long light to soar over the valley, molting rainbow hued feathers, squabbling territorially over the choice nesting nooks on the rock faces. The valley's mobile young, their musical, piping voices singing the joy of the light, earned credit by collecting the fallen flakes of color and delivering them by the woven basketful to the looms of the matrons.

The bulky trappings of the season of dims and darks had been discarded, layer by layer, and Du poured his life-giving warmth in blessing, so that as Duwan the Drinker began his first scaling of the northern scarp, his mouth watering at the thought of his first feast of eggs, he had stripped away his torso covering and was dressed in the long light kilt, secured at his mid-section by a multi-colored sash of woven feathers, falling just above the articulation of his long, sturdy limbs.

He knew that he was rushing the egg season, for

on the lower cliff, where the source did not reach, ice still covered the rock, making it difficult for his horned toes and long fingers to find purchase. As he crossed the demarcation line between sun and shadow melting ice sheered away under his feet and only the strength of his hands, made powerful in grip by two opposing thumbs, saved him from sliding back. The tough horns at the end of his toes scraped away ice as he pulled himself upward into the full glow of Du.

For a long time he clung, legs spread wide, arms extended upward as his body adjusted rapidly to the full sunlight. He could feel the delicious energy of the source penetrating his yellow-green skin, could sense the arousal of chemical change in his blood. It was good. A clear, piping voice from below brought him out of his moment of worshipful reception. He looked down to see Alning. She, too, had shed layers of clothing. He knew that she had begun to flower during the season of dims and dark, but he was pleased to see the slim grace of her exposed torso, the surprising length of leg, the hint of new color in her face.

"Bring me an egg, Duwan," Alning called.

"Would I forget my little sister?" Duwan called back, as he reached for a new handhold. As he shifted his weight to find purchase with his toes his foot slipped and he dangled for a moment by his strong arms.

"Don't fall," Alning cried.

"Should I fall we will share and your new strength will graft my broken limbs," he said, with a laugh.

Alning's face showed yellow and her black eyes closed in embarrassment, for Duwan's light statement brushed the bounds of propriety, then she, too, laughed, and looked up at him saucily, her hands on her hips. In spite of her blush, she was pleased, for from the day of her first freedom she had admired Duwan.

"I will bring you a basket of eggs," Duwan said, as

he climbed strongly, feeling the power of the source in his blood as each of his cells knew the gift of Du. "But now, little sister, go away, for your presence distracts me."

He clung to the cliff face and watched her go. It seemed only a season since he had tended her, along with the other fixed young. He'd been only a new mobile himself at the time, earning credit by working in the young house, but he had noticed her, had been pleased by the freshness of her face, even then. It was a sunny face, was Alning's, and there was a sense of elan in her bright, black eyes. Of all that crop of young she had been the fastest learner. Now, in her first blush of maturity, her walk was graceful, still sinewy, but the sway of her walk spoke of things to come. He felt an odd gathering in his loins. He had suspected for some time that ripeness was coming upon him, and now he knew.

Suddenly, he was not thinking of the almost sensual pleasure of being in full sunlight, or of the anticipated feast of fresh eggs. He was in need of contemplation, and he had to force himself to climb instead of descending.

The rocks of the scarp had absorbed the warmth of Du and released it to him. He pressed his cheek against a flat area and watched the flight of the birds. He was nearing a nesting area. He could hear the harsh squabbling and, a lesser sound, the cooings of nesting females. He moved laterally across the cliff and a startled nester brushed his face with ruby wings as she burst out of a recess. There were three eggs in the nest. The shells were a beautiful bright green. He took only one. One did not rob any living thing of its all.

The area he had reached, some fifty feet above the topmost branches of a tall brother made lopsided by pressing closely to the cliff, was rich in nests. Eggs awaited his gathering in the sun on small ledges, in the shade of the overhangs, in small, cavelike cavities formed by thermal separation of the stone. Soon he had his egg basket almost filled. He needed only a few more. However, he had exhausted the resources of the nesting area immediately around him. Below him he saw promising irregularities in the face. He lowered himself carefully. His feet found a ledge wide enough for good footing. By moving along the ledge he filled the basket, decided that he had room for just one or two more eggs, and moved back along the ledge to the other end where a rounded rock protrusion hid a likely cavity at the level of his waist. Already tasting the feast, thinking of Alning's pleasure when he presented her with fresh eggs, he violated the cardinal rule of egg gathering; never put your hand into a cavity that has not been closely examined first.

The enormity of his mistake—the result of his source-induced euphoria, the hint of ripeness in his body that brought his thoughts back to Alning again and again, and the fact that he had his basket full and needed no more than two more eggs—came to him when his thumbs cupped an egg against his other three fingers and, instead of the warm, smooth texture he felt a leathery sponginess. His youth and his good conditioning, plus a lightning reaction time, saved him. Even as he realized his mistake and jerked his hand away from the false egg his arm was crushed from a few inches below his elbow. Had he not been so fast in his reaction the arm would have been caught in the maw of the rock sucker almost to his shoulder and he would not have had the freedom of movement that saved his life.

As the blinding, crushing pain weakened his body, numbed his mind, he felt his life being sucked out of his veins with a force that seemed to want to make his entire body collapse in on itself. He gave one sharp, bird-like scream as his right hand fumbled

with the hilt of his shortsword. Even as his mind
went numb as blood was sucked away from his brain
by the terrible force of the thing that held him, he
knew that he had less than ten seconds of life. The
sword rose, flashed, and he tried to aim it precisely,
for it was vital that he strike at the right place. The
blade flashed down, all the force of his strong right
arm behind it, and blood spouted greenish blue as
his arm was severed at the elbow. Then he was
falling backward, the clang of metal on stone ringing
in his ears, for the blow had been so powerful that
particles of rock fell with him as he tumbled.

For a moment all was blackness. He felt impact,
expected that to be his last feeling, but the force of
the blow that had severed his arm, his total terror,
had caused him to push away from the ledge as he
toppled backward so that he fell into the upturned
branches of the tall brother pressing closely to the
cliff. Twigs snapped, limbs clawed at him as the fall
carried him through the topmost branches. He
huffed as the wind was driven from his lungs by solid
contact with a larger branch that bent under his
weight and let him fall, more slowly, to other branches
until, with the blackness of unconsciousness dimming his eyes, he thudded to the ground.

He gasped, fighting for breath, found it, filled his
lungs. He paused only long enough to look upward,
to see the damage he'd done as he fell through the
tightly knit branches. "Forgive me, brother," he whispered, even as he forced himself into a sitting position and examined the stump of his left arm. The
stump was still gushing blood and now there was
another race against time for his life as he directed
the clotting juices to flow, willed the severed arteries
to close, watched, growing weaker, as his will gradually triumphed. When only an ooze of blood was
coming from the raw stump he looked around.

He was in the far north of the valley, in that

deserted quarter of hot, rushing springs. He was too weak to walk. To crawl back to the nearest house was a possibility, but as he began to move blackness came to him and when he once again saw the light through the mists of vapor from the hot springs, he knew that he was beyond his strength, that he'd lost more blood than he had imagined.

Alning. He had sent her away, after she'd followed him to the northern cliffs, but, perhaps, she had not obeyed. He called, but his voice was weak. He pursed his lips and used all of his will to put power behind a whistle. The effort brought the blackness back. When he saw again, he was still alone. Alning had, apparently, gone back to the village. His life was his to save.

A few yards away, over rough, rocky ground, a hot spring sent its steams into the warm air. His vision seemed to be distorted, but he was sure he saw a fat brother there. The fat brothers grew in the margins of the springs, bloating their stubby, multiple stalks with sap rich in the minerals of the spring. He began to crawl, slowly, slowly, painfully, for now the stump of his severed arm had regained feeling after the initial shock. He would never remember how many times blackness came to him, or how long that agonizing crawl of just a few yards continued.

He saw light again and the fat brother was near, squat, swelled with its gorging, skin glowing as it accepted the gift of Du. He reached it. He had never had the need to graft, but the instinct for it was in him, and as he prepared himself his weak voice begged understanding, saying, "Forgive me, fat brother, but I have need."

He willed, and felt a prickling sensation at his bud point, that little node in the center of his belly. Felt the opening, used his sword—he'd clung to it during the fall and had dragged it, in its sheath attached to his woven feather belt—to lance a small opening deeply into the skin of the fat brother, rolled to press his bud point, felt a stir there, felt the opening of himself and the first harsh entry of sap from the fat brother. His system, shocked, protested. His toes cramped and his fingers curled into painful knots, and then the initial harshness was overcome and he was adapting and it was as if he could feel the life flowing back into his body.

He judged the time of grafting by the wrinkles that began to appear in the flexible skin of the fat brother. The graft would cost the fat brother a sun cycle's growth. To cost the brother more was unthinkable. He had enough strength, now, to make it back to the village. He separated, felt his bud point contract.

"My brother," he said, in fondness, as he patted the fat brother's shrunken, wrinkled skin.

He had to rest often. When he was a short run from the village he encountered two newly mobile youths, gasped out his problem, and soon strong arms were around him, carrying him.

He felt the healing warmth of soil on his feet, opened his eyes. He was in the young house. The think vines had opened the ceiling to the light. All around him the new crop of young slumbered, not yet sentient. He felt the old, warm security of being a part of the earth. The soil of the young house, enriched by mulch, bird droppings, minerals collected from the accumulations in the springs, fed him through hundreds of small outreachings that had been engendered quickly by his regenerative organs. He was at peace. He slumbered, woke.

"Father," he whispered drowsily, for there was a familiar face close to his, a face full of love and concern.

"You have done well, my son," said Duwan the Elder.

"Sucker," Duwan said sleepily.

"Wake," The Elder said. "You must tell me."

Duwan struggled against the feeling of peace and sleep. "North," he whispered.

"A landmark, son. Give me a location."

"Must kill."

"Yes. We must kill the thing before it can divide. Tell me where."

"I kill when—" He could say no more. Peace and sleep held him. When next he awoke his head was clearer. Alning was watching. He opened his orange eyes and saw her face, full of concern for him. "Little sister," he said. "I fear that I broke all your eggs."

"No matter," she said. "You are safe."

A sudden urgency came over him, as he flashed back to that terrible moment when his arm was crushed by the strength of the sucker's maw. "Little sister," he said, and there was life and command in his voice. "Free me."

"It is not yet time," she protested.

"Free me, now," he insisted, trying to lift his own feet from the warm security of the rich earth without success. Alning, her face showing fright, ran from the young house. Duwan the Elder was there within minutes.

"Free me," Duwan said.

"Now you can tell me the location of the monster," his father said.

"It is high, and you will not be able to find it without me. Free me."

The Elder considered for a moment, looked closely at his son's eyes, burning with life, deep orange. "Yes," he said, reaching for a tool.

Duwan's feet, freed, were hairy with extensions. The rich soil clung, but showered off as the extensions withdrew into their almost invisible sockets and the pores closed around them.

A force of twenty warriors had been quickly gathered. Over Duwan's objection, he was carried in a litter. The force moved at a swift trot, for time had been wasted. There were those among them, old, hoary, skin beginning to harden, who remembered the first struggles with the monsters of the rocks, when there were so many that the cliffs were a no-man's-land of instant, waiting death and the suckers, things without brains, actually huge colonies of mindless, one-celled entities, came down from the cliffs to decimate all fixed life and to lie in wait for any unwary mobile. At any given time a sucker could divide, and divide rapidly, although it was the nature of the beast to avoid small divisions. That trait of the suckers had enabled the people of the valley to, it had been thought before Duwan's encounter, eliminate the killers.

It was simple to find the tall brother whose branches had broken Duwan's fall and saved his life. Tender twigs, broken, were already turning brown and the seriously injured larger limbs were being cut off slowly by a tightening ring of growth near the trunk of the tall brother.

The rock sucker had not moved. Duwan recognized it by its shape, saw the cunningly constructed cavity that was the thing's maw. It was a huge one, as well as they could judge, although the sucker imitated stone so well that it was difficult to determine for sure just how far it extended around the open, motionless maw.

Fire, that most deadly of friends, carried from the areas of eternal heat to the south, tended carefully, was coaxed into a blaze using the combustible, dead droppings of the tall brothers. Strong young warriors unslung their bows, saw to the stringing, tested, selected straight, strong arrows newly finned with fresh, multi-colored feathers. Duwan was standing, if a bit dizzily, longing to be able to take bow and send fiery death into the sucker, but he had no left hand to hold the bow. When all were ready Duwan the Elder gave the signal, and ten down-wrapped arrows

were ignited in the blaze, and at a further signal
went singing upward. Some bounced their metal tips
off solid rock, five embedded, and burned, and a
quivering began as the mindless beast's tissues began
to char and smoke. A second flight of burning arrows sang upward and the sucker, feeling pain, tried
to crawl, leaving behind a concave area of surprising
size. The target now outlined clearly, another flight
of arrows finished the job and the beast lost its hold,
fell to crash heavily through the branches of the tall
brother, dividing on impact with the ground into a
dozen small, writhing masses that were attacked immediately and mercilessly by torch-wielding warriors,
Duwan among them. He took satisfaction. He burned,
and charred, and left no single mass unbrowned by
fire and then refused to give up the search for tiny
survivors until his father took his arm gently and led
him back to the litter. Within a short time, Duwan,
weakened by the trek, was immobile again, hundreds
of tiny extensions drawing new strength from the
rich earth of the young house.

Watches were set on the northern cliffs. Roving
pairs of warriors scouted the entire rock face of the
valley. In the time of the long light rock suckers
were sometimes mobile, oozing over the rocks seeking new points of ambush for unwary birds.

Duwan sank immediately into a blissful sleep. The
raw stump of his left arm formed a crust, the texture
of which changed during the time he was immobile.
He was awake more and more, using his conscious
periods for meditation, longing for the mobility to
climb into the full warmth of Du. No more suckers
were detected. The young warriors climbed the sun-
heated rocks and all participated in savoring the
feast of eggs. Duwan had his share, brought to him
by Alning. When it was time he felt his extensions
withdrawing of their own accord, freed his feet, and,
walking with pride and strength, emerged into the

square to see life going on as it had done for generations. His stump drew stares and expressions of sympathy. He saw Alning running toward him and felt
the smile come to his face.

"You are well," she said, falling into stride beside
him.

"Yes, thank you," he said.

The square was invaded by a leaping, running
group of new mobiles. Duwan and Alning halted as
the youngsters crowded around, eyes wide as they
gazed at the stump of Duwan's left arm.

"Did it hurt?" asked one green-eyed little female.

"Fiercely," Duwan said with a loving smile.

"What will you do now that you are no longer a
warrior?" a young male asked.

Duwan frowned, pulled his shortsword from its
sheath. "Who says I am no longer a warrior?" He
brandished the sword, the well cleaned and oiled
blade hissing with the force of his motion.

"You can't pull a bow," the young one said.

"I have this."

"Don't worry," Alning said, as the young ones
rushed away in search of new fun. "Your right arm is
stronger than both in most warriors."

But there was a darkness building inside him. He
had, of course, considered the impact of losing his
left arm on his life. True, he could not draw a bow.
He would be able, he felt, to develop skills using one
hand. He had given thought to that, and felt that by
holding a shaft from the thin brothers of the hot
springs in his teeth he would be able to round arrows, and, perhaps, with a journey to the southern
end of the valley where the thin, hard brothers grew
taller, a shaft for a spear. A one-armed man could
use and throw a spear.

"Duwan," Alning said, her eyes unable to meet his,
"nothing has changed."

"Only my left arm," he said blackly.

"Nothing has changed in my regard for you," she said, her heart pounding at her boldness.

His mood became blacker. She was quite rapidly becoming the most beautiful one in the village, and she was the daughter of a warrior. She deserved better than a mate with only one hand. He was silent as they walked onward toward his father's house.

The village square was swept clean. The precisely placed houses lined it, lush and green as the think vines forming the walls drank in the light of the season. The houses, quite naturally, looked a bit scraggly, for the vines had been allowed to separate, to open the ceilings to the warm air and reach tendrils upward for the gift of Du. In one open and airy house a female was singing. A group of hard-skinned ones sat in the light, telling and retelling the stories of old.

"Duwan, you have not spoken," Alning said.

He heard the disappointment in her voice, glanced at her. Her head came to his shoulder. The delicate, multi-fronded pale green of her hair gave off a sweet fragrance. He wanted nothing more than to tell her that he was grateful, that his regard for her was unchanged, but the innocent questions of the young one had opened a chasm of blackness in his mind. A warrior without a hand was only a half-one.

Alning moved quickly from his right side to his left, put her hands on his upper arm. "I don't care," she said. "This doesn't matter."

He looked at her and saw a flowering face, a rich shade of yellow telling of her emotion, but there was doubt in him and he knew that her emotion could be pity as well as love. His pride swelled, filling him.

"As you said, Alning," he said, his voice sounding more harsh than he intended, "I have not spoken."

She flushed more, felt his rebuke strongly. He had not spoken. He had never spoken for her. She had been forward, lulled into it by her regard for him and by his near escape from death. She dropped her head, removed her hands from his arm.

Relenting, he said, "You are young."

She found no words. They were approaching the house of Duwan the Elder. Still she could find no words, but she felt the hot tears beginning to form in her eyes and, lest he see, she turned and ran with the abandon of the very young, ran from her shame, ran from his rejection. He raised his right hand as if to stop her, but did not call her back. Alning meant The Beautiful One. And the beautiful one deserved more than a one-handed lifemate. He turned. His mother was in the doorway, arms extended. Feeling quite young himself, he moved into her embrace.

2

Only a few had felt that incredibly deadly draining of blood into the maw of a sucker and lived to describe it. Death was not unknown in the valley, but it was rare. A warrior, too daring in his climb, fell from the top of the cliffs, crushing his head on the rocks below. A newly mobile young one fell into a boiling spring. The hardening took some old ones, but all in all death was a memory, a memory of the old days before the Drinkers came to the valley, when war was death. It was to avoid death that Duwan's ancestors had left the Land of Many Brothers and crossed the barrens, losing many to starvation and cold when the long light failed.

The valley was a miraculous oasis in the sterile, windswept emptiness. At its head it was no wider than an all-out dash without rest. In length it stretched two days' marching run, narrowing toward the southwestern end. When the wind came from the north, it brought with it the chill and the scent of the eternal ice. A southerly wind smelled of fire, and sometimes carried fine ash, an ash carefully collected to enrich the soil of the young house.

The valley was the Drinkers' only home in a cold, sterile land, land extending endlessly into waterless distances to east and west, and to fire and ice to the north and south.

Duwan, born with a full measure of curiosity, had explored, had felt the deadly cold of the ice, had pushed his horny toes farther east and west than any one in memory, had seen and smelled the eternal fires of the south, knowing the heat through the tough, hardened pads of his feet. He regarded his distant ancestors with respect, for try as he might he had found no path through the eternal fires and had, indeed, been frightened into turning back as the solid earth, itself, quavered and rolled under his feet to the accompaniment of the bellowing of count-less thunderous voices and in the near distance new fire had belched from the earth with a heat so great that it seared his skin.

Duwan believed. He knew the often told tales of the great journey by heart, and would, dutifully, pass them on to his young when the time came, but it was still hard to believe that Drinkers had actually made their way through that land of endless fire. On the evening following his recovery he found cause to reinforce his unspoken doubt, for the village min-strel had already composed the *Song of Duwan The Drinker*, and to say that it departed slightly from the truth was a kindness. As he listened, Duwan first smiled, and then had to hide his laughter, for the song made him so heroic, built his quick thinking actions into such bravery that he wondered anew if such stretching of the truth had not been applied to all the Drinkers' history.

For example, the old tales spoke of war, war and heroism, war and death, and yet no generation of Drinkers now living had ever experienced war. From northeast to southwest the valley was dotted with villages, none more than a swift dash without rest from the next, but no one had, in the history of the valley, raised an edged weapon against another. There had been times when Duwan wondered if the endless drills, the concentrated training, the mock battles had not been invented merely as a ruse to keep the growing energies of the young under control and to keep them out from underfoot. Still, the magic of the metalmakers gave one pause. To have the ability to know exactly where in the earth and rocks to find those scattered flakes, to know how to crush and wash and blend and then to fire the metal and shape it was an ability that could not have come naturally to any one there in the valley. And the quietly voiced tales of the old, hard-skinned ones rang with emotion, if not total truth, as they spoke of gushing wounds and death and the Enemy.

Perhaps, Duwan thought, as the minstrel, by popular demand, repeated *The Song of Duwan The Drinker*, there had been embellishing, stretching, and, if so, what harm? Perhaps, beyond the land of the eternal fires, there was an Enemy. If so, the years of training, the hard, muscle wrenching struggles, and the resulting skills with short and longswords, bow and spear and knife might yet be called upon one day. There had been times, when he was younger, when he had dreamed of the Enemy, had, in his mind, placed this Drinkerlike foe at the entrance to the valley to be met with metal clashing on metal, with blades sharp and deadly and with flying shafts of frightful penetrating ability. Thus, he had dreamed, he would prove himself and become legend. To have become a part of the lore by losing a hand was not to his liking, but he had, before the evening was far gone, become stoic in his acceptance. It was, it had been meant to be, and he would adapt.

The purpose of the gathering in the square, with all the village present, with the young ones bunched, wide-eyed, near the glowing fires, and the elders sitting in all dignity cross-legged on the warm earth, was to honor Duwan, who had used his wits and his sword with admirable quickness. Of course, in those wondrous days of the long light, almost any excuse was good for a gathering, with Du, the source, low over the southern cliffs to indicate eveningtime, but

Duwan took some satisfaction in knowing that he was well respected, and he stood to speak his gratitude only to find that his words froze in his throat. His father, chosen Village Elder long before his son's sprouting, was an accomplished speaker. Shamed, Duwan forced out some words, not really knowing what he said, but evidently he did not make a fool of himself, for his short speech was well received with coos from the females and a whistling hiss from the males.

The fermented juices of the narrow-organed short brother had something to do with the good spirits, as cups formed of half the shell of the nut brother passed from hand to hand with great laughter and small jokes and good will.

Alning was there, but she sat far back away from the cozy fires and refused to look at Duwan, so that he, hurt, drank more than his share to feel his head become light and his blood fiery.

Mothers began to coax their reluctant young away for sleep period. At a signal from Duwan The Elder the flowering young departed, Alning among them. Most of the mature females retired to their houses, leaving the warriors and the elders, who moved to congregate more compactly around the fires. Cups were passed. Duwan The Elder gave a contented sigh and sank back to lean on his elbows. The minstrel plucked the multiple strings of his instrument almost idly, but the sounds that came were soft and dreamy.

"We must consider the matter of my son," Duwan the Elder said at last.

Duwan's head jerked up. He'd been dreaming cozily of Alning, wondering how he could approach her to say that he was sorry for his harsh words.

The warriors and elders gave a hiss of assent.

"Who will speak?" Duwan the Elder asked.

For long moments there was silence, then Manoo,

the Predictor of Du, lifted a hand lazily. "Elder," he said, "we have spoken among ourselves. He is your son."

Duwan the Elder shook his head in sad negation. "No matter," he said. "The traditions are for my son as well as your son."

Puzzled, Duwan sat up, his right hand clasped onto his cocked knee.

"There is peace," Manoo the Predictor said. "Perhaps for once we can waive tradition."

"And when we waive all tradition, and we forget, and the Enemy comes?" Duwan the Elder asked. "No. He is my son, but he is of the Drinkers, and he will be governed by our laws."

"I will speak, then," said a tall, strong warrior, aged to his prime, skin just beginning to roughen.

"We hear, Leader," Duwan the Elder said.

Duwan looked at Belran the Leader with anticipation and respect. The hardy one, chief of all the warriors, was well known to all who had been trained, for each new warrior had to test his newly learned skills, quite often to his pain and chagrin, against the swords of Belran.

"He was," Belran said, "a warrior of great promise. Indeed, as my skin hardens, the warrior to become the Leader." Duwan felt his face flush and he swelled with pride, but the feeling did not last long. "I am saddened," Belran said, "but the shortsword is for parrying and the longsword is for killing and one without the other is wanting."

"I hear," Duwan the Elder said.

"Had the young one a calling," Belran said, "it would be easier."

Duwan looked down. He had undergone the trial periods with the metalmakers, and he had no skill for it. He had strained his brain listening to Manoo the Predictor and he could not come within days of stating the appearances of Du during the time of dims and dark. His calling was to arms, and without the shortsword in his left hand he had no calling.

"Young Duwan," Belran the Leader said, turning toward the increasingly concerned Drinker, "what have you to say for yourself? Have you, perhaps, a calling of which we are not aware?"

Duwan thought for a moment. "I have no calling other than to arms."

An old one, with hard, knobby skin, spoke in his old, strained voice. "I have seen young Duwan with the young. He has a good heart."

A keeper of the young? Duwan felt a deep shame. He rose. "The old ones speak of a Drinker, in the time of troubles, who lost his hand in war, and yet he fought, and slew the Enemy, and retained his honor."

"By severe test," Belran said. "Do you seek a test?"

Duwan swallowed his fear. "I do seek a test."

A young warrior rose quickly and ran to the community house, emerged with two sets of padded swords. Belran the Leader took all four swords in his hands, extended the hilts for choice to Duwan. Duwan knew the swords, for he'd wielded all in his training. He selected the one he knew was better balanced, and left three in Belran's hands. Belran handed back to the young warrior the odd shortsword and hefted the others.

"Am I to fight you?" Duwan asked. "Is that a fair test? You are the Leader, honored Belran. A fairer test would pit me against one of my own age."

Belran glared at him without pity. "My father's father, five times removed, was also a Leader, and strong, the strongest and the most skillful of his village. He faced the Enemy and was slain and, without protection, the village was destroyed."

"So be it," Duwan said, leaping to the attack, trying to eke out by surprise at least one small initial victory. His stroke was parried by Belran's shortsword while a counterblow of the longsword whistled toward

Duwan's stomach to be met by a swift move, a quick retraction of his longsword so that the padded instruments thudded together loudly.

Duwan's footwork brought hisses of admiration from the lounging warriors and elders, but from the first he was on the defensive for Belran had thought it to be kinder to end the uneven battle quickly. With a great leap, a feint of longsword and a sweep of shortsword he delivered a blow that would have, had the longsword not been padded, disemboweled Duwan. The strength of the blow sat Duwan down. He gasped for breath and rose to the battle, but Belran shook his head, turned, handed the swords to the young warrior who had fetched them and turned to shake his head sadly at Duwan.

"I will teach you the gift of storytelling," offered an ancient.

"The Watcher of the Fire needs no more than one hand," another said.

"Thank you, my friends and elders," Duwan said, "but I have not the memory for being a storyteller, and, as you well know, to watch the fire is a position of honor to be earned, not tossed to a disabled warrior as a sop to his pride."

"Drink," Duwan's father said, extending a cup. Duwan drank. He had to be carried to his sleeping pad in the small, private alcove of his father's house and he awakened much later with a bad taste in his mouth and the thunder of the land of the fires in his head. It was the time of the new greens, tender goodness plucked from certain low growing brothers without doing serious harm to them, and after he had accepted a dish from his mother and consumed it he felt better. He had not noticed, for she sat in shadows, that the old and hard and wrinkled figure of his grandmother was motionless in a corner.

"I saw you not, Grandmother," he said, "forgive me."

"I see you" the old one said.

"You see sadness and shame, Grandmother," he said. "You see a keeper of the young."

"I see one who escaped death." The old one rose with difficulty and moved jerkily until, with a creak of old limbs and a sigh, she sat on the pad next to Duwan.

"I don't know death," Duwan said sadly.

"It is not preferable to life," his grandmother said, as his mother nodded. "Perhaps, at this moment, you may think so."

"Never to climb into the gift of Du again?" Duwan said. "Is that not a form of death?"

"Walk to the south, go out of the valley, and bask in Du to your heart's content," his mother said.

Duwan made a motion of dismissal with his good hand.

The old one leaned down, her dimming eyes thrust close to the stump of Duwan's arm. Her rough, hard hands lifted his arm and put the stump even closer. She made a thoughtful, humming sound.

"It has healed well," Duwan said.

"Ummm," his grandmother hummed, as she lifted one crooked finger and tested the tender new tissue of the stump. Then, dropping the arm and looking into the emerald eyes of her daughter. "For your sake," she said softly, "I would not speak. For his?"

"Speak, Mother," Duwan's mother said, letting her eyes drop.

"I had a son," the old one said.

Duwan's interest was instantly aroused. He had never heard mention of a brother to his mother.

"He was of an age to you, my son," the old one said, putting her hands on Duwan's arm again. "And he, too, was of indecision between dishonor or death. At my insistence he chose to accept a false accusation. We will not go into details, for it is an old wound best left unopened. To ease my hurt, he chose against his inclinations. It was said that his fall from near the clifftop was an accident. I have never been sure. I do know that to prevent the risk of death he chose to abdicate his rightful position, as you have been asked to do, and I fear that, realizing his own mistake, he chose death with no hope."

"I am sorry, Grandmother," Duwan said, not knowing why the old one was telling him something that obviously gave her great pain.

"Ah," the old one said, "this does apply to you. Be patient."

Once again she lifted Duwan's stump to her eyes and felt it carefully with her fingers. Then she sighed. "Yes," she said, "the bud is there."

For a few moments Duwan had known a frail hope, wishing more than expecting an answer to his dilemma. Now his heart sank and he closed his mind as his grandmother continued, for she was voicing one of the most ancient and least believable of all the bits of lore.

"With the full strength of Du, it will grow," the old one said. "Not here, not in our valley, but far to the south, where the darks and lights are of equal duration, where Du is strong, it will bud, and grow. So it was of old. So it is still. We are different, my son, we Drinkers. It was this difference that drove the Enemy, this difference that he scorned and feared and made an excuse for a war of extermination."

"Oh, Grandmother," Duwan said sadly, for he had hoped. He knew that the wisdom of the very old ones was often filled with unexpected and surprising bits of esoteric knowledge, but this hoary old folktale?

"Do not the fixed brothers grow limbs to replace the lost?" the old one asked.

"They are fixed," he said.

"They are of the earth and for the earth," his grandmother said. "And of a blood to us, the Drinkers." She removed her hands from his arm. "It is up

to you to believe or not to believe. Better for your
mother that you disbelieve, for since we have lived in
the valley no one has returned from the south."

"They were burned in the land of the fires," Duwan
said.

"There is a way through the fires."

He wanted to believe. The mere possibility of belief had a perverse effect on him, bringing home to
him the extent of his disaster. To lose Alning, that
was certain, in spite of her protestations that nothing
had changed. She would change when she saw him
carrying, with his one arm, the nutrient containers
for the young, when she saw him mucking in the
soil, cleaning the insentient sprouts, when she came
to him to find him reeking of bird droppings. Not
that it was a job beneath his abilities, for he had, by
choice, participated, as did most, and a few had the
calling and were proud of their sure touch with the
sprouts, but his calling was to arms.

"Have you seen this thing with your own eyes?" he
asked.

The old one shook her head. "Nor have I seen the
old take root and become one with the earth. Here,
where Du is weak, we see the wasting disease, and I,
myself, feel it. But, nevertheless, in the south the old
do not die, and in the south new limbs grow to
replace those lost, unless the buds are damaged, and
your bud is intact. In fact, even in this place where
Du is weak and there is not the power, it has started."

She lifted his arm, traced the cone-shaped protrusion that had accumulated on the stump. He felt the
touch, felt a peculiar, stretching feeling in the skin of
the stump, and he almost believed.

"The way through the fires," he said.

The old one closed her eyes, as if that aided memory, and in a sing-song chant said, "Between two
smoking mountains Du shows his face at evening
over a lake of fire, but one mountain is broken, and

the fires drain not on the eastern slope, for there the smoking rock is cooled by springs. A layering of the skin of the needled brother smokes, but prevents the burning of the feet. A dash, a rest beside a spring, new layers of the skin of the needled brother brings one to the lake of fire where the skin pains and shrivels, but a turn to the west leads past the lake of fire into fields of cool, hardened ash."

"So it was said of old?" Duwan asked.

"So it was passed on, for your father's father, five times removed, planned to return once the Drinkers had rested, and had reinforced themselves by sprout with many warriors. He did not know the enervating effect of life without the full strength of Du, and that the dims and darks would limit sprouting, so that five generations have not replaced the losses in one."

"The ancient ones planned to return to the Land of Many Brothers?"

"So it was told, so it is prophesied, even now, among those who remember."

"I have not heard this prophecy," Duwan said.

"No, because it is safe here," his grandmother said. "Because there is no war. Females hold the tales of old. Females prophesy. And it is females who weep when their sons die in war. We choose to forget."

"And when I am through the land of the fires?"

"The time of the long light has just begun. You are strong. You will be in the land of snows while Du is long, but you must hasten until the small, scattered brothers become a great congregation, and even then you must not pause for rest, for the cold will be on your heels, chasing you from the north to bury you in snow. You will pass through a land of many waters, and if your pace has been swift, you will swim the iceless waters of the smaller waters, skirt the larger. Through dims and darks you will pass the congregated brothers, and there will be days shorter than the nights in the land of many waters. There you will first encounter the Enemy, but, perhaps, he has forgotten. You must remember that it is our difference that he hates and fears, and you must hide your abilities. When Du is just to the south of the zenith, and his rays are stronger than you have ever felt before, in a safe place, concealed from the Enemy, become one with the soil and let Du's power restore your limb."

"I will consider," Duwan said.

"Yes," the old one said. "Now I faint, I tire."

"I will help you to your house."

"Thank you, my son, but I am not yet helpless," she said stoutly, as she tottered toward the door.

"Mother, is it true?" Duwan asked, when the old one was gone.

"So it is said."

"Counsel me, Mother. You have always been wise."

There were tears in her eyes when she spoke. "I can offer only mixed counsel. My heart says stay, my son. My love for you, and my best wishes for you say go, and return to us whole with news of what has happened in the Land of Many Brothers during our exile."

He had never heard their condition called exile. He looked at her, wanting to ask questions. He was still, however, trying to digest the information he'd received from his grandmother. He knew that the old one and his mother were direct descendants of Alon, who had led the Drinkers to the valley, a man of renown, a leader of leaders.

"Exile?" he was forced to ask.

"A term,' she said, waving it away.

"Exile, mother?"

Her eyes hardened. "Once we were a great and populous people, living in prosperity and peace. The Land of Many Brothers was ours, and we became lax, became soft in our life of plenty. The Enemy from the south struck us a mighty blow before we could prepare, before we even suspected his existence. It was too late. Our warriors regained their old skills in defeat after defeat as we were gradually pushed to the north. For generations we fought, and grew weaker, and less numerous, until only a few thousand remained, pushed into the lands north of the waters into seasons of deep snows and bitter cold, and even then the Enemy was to be satisfied only by our total extermination, for he had found that we were different, that we could drink of Du, and communicate with our fixed brothers. It was your ancestor, the Great Alon, who explored to the east and the west and the north to find a great sea and the Enemy spread from coast to mountains and to find a hope, a small hope, here in the valley. The Enemy had not the secret of the way through the land of eternal fire, and presumed that we had been consumed."

"I will see this Enemy," Duwan said.

"I fear so," his mother said, with resignation.

"Perhaps, now, he has grown fat and weak."

"There is much preparation to be done," she said, "and each moment counts if you are to be south of the killing cold and impassable snows before the end of the long light."

"Guide me," he said.

3

Having fed and drunk until every cell of his body seemed ready to burst with stored nutrition, Duwan inspected the travel kit prepared for him by his mother and his grandmother. A pack, woven of feathers and fibers, rested snugly on his back, secured by woven belts around chest and shoulders. The pack bulged with the skillfully designed, padded, insulated clothing that would be vital to survival once the long light had passed and the ice sent its frigid breath southward. There was little space for food. A hollowed nut sealed with wax held an emergency supply of water. Dried tubers filled any small available space in the pack. At his left side rode the shortsword, at his belt his knife, and over his left shoulder the longsword. He would have no need for his bow, but aside from that, and his supply of arrows, he carried his total life possessions as he stood in the square and let his orange eyes appreciate the faces and the forms of his friends, his family. Alning was not immediately visible, but, at last, he saw her, back at the edge of the crowd of villagers who had gathered to wish him well.

Duwan the Elder, his father, came to stand before him, extended both arms. The entwining was incomplete, for the son had no left forearm, but it was warm and lasting, limbs twisted together in the age-old symbol of regard, loyalty, brotherhood. Then, one by one, he entwined with the warriors and the

old ones and brushed his one hand against both
hands of the females, except for Alning, who had
disappeared.

"Hear me," said Duwan the Elder, when the ceremony of parting had been completed. "The way is
long and harsh. To outdistance the wings of the
great cold will test you to the utmost. Strong warriors died during our journey to the north, their
cells crystalized and ruptured by the ice. You must
never rest, my son, not when the cold of the north is
upon you, for to rest, although it seems sweet at the
time, is death. If the brothers are in retreat, if there
are no life organs visible, cold is there or will come.
Move onward, onward, until tender life organs are
green with health, and then rest."

"I hear," Duwan said.

"Flee the Enemy," The Elder intoned, his pale eyes,
dimmed to weak yellow, fixed on Duwan's own.
Duwan felt himself stiffen. "Yes, flee, until you have
been restored, and even then remember that you are
only one Drinker amid hosts of the Enemy and gov-
ern your decisions with wisdom, not rashness, no
matter how great the temptation, how hot the blood.
For your journey is more than a personal seeking for
renewal and restoration, my son, it is for the Drinkers. The information you bring us will be of vital
import, and will have a decided effect on the future
of the ones in the valley. That is your primary mission. Your mission is not to kill one, or a dozen, or a
score of the Enemy, but to observe, to learn, to accumulate wisdom and live to impart it to your valley."

"I hear, father," Duwan said, bowing his head.

Duwan's mother stepped forward, two pairs of
sandals fashioned from the skin of the needled brother
in her hands. She lashed them to Duwan's pack and
pressed her petal fresh lips to his cheek before stepping back.

"Soak the sandals well," said his grandmother, in

her aged, croaking voice. "Remember, soak them well."

"I hear, Grandmother," Duwan said.

The minstrel had written a new verse to the *Song Of Duwan The Drinker*. His resonant instrument rang out, and his voice began to sing as Duwan, trying in vain to catch a glimpse of Alning, turned his back to the gathering in the square and paced away toward the southeast and the far tip of the valley. He felt swollen with his intake of nutrients, and his spirit was heavy, for he was aware of the dangers that lay ahead, and sore in the heart in his loss of Alning. He did not turn, nor did he look over his shoulder. He adjusted his pack for comfort and took long strides and the song of the minstrel faded, leaving echoes of the words in his mind, words telling of the courage of Duwan, words of the long way ahead. He was young, and he was hopeful. His heart could not stay heavy long. The time of the long light was too glorious, the birds too colorful, all the brothers of the valley too lush and green in their long light flush of health and growth.

Alning was waiting for him, half hidden in the heated, soft steam of a spring. At first he wasn't sure his eyes were being true, afraid that his desire to see her gave rise to visions, and then she stepped toward him, black eyes bright, hair moistened by the steams, her yellow green skin dripping attractively with moisture. He halted, and could find no words.

"You have not spoken," she said softly.

"No," he said.

"Nor will I, not until you return."

He felt a flush of happiness, and then reason regained its rule. "And if I do not come back?"

She looked away, black eyes misting.

"I cannot, in all conscience, ask you to wait for me," he said softly.

"Is it your desire to ask?" She locked her black eyes on his.

"I must consider you, Alning," he said.

"Be considerate, then," she said, moving toward him.

His loins tightened as his eyes saw the swift change of color in her exposed torso, a flowering, a glowing, and he had difficulty swallowing. She thrust her body to his and he felt her warmth.

"Be considerate,' she said. "Tell me that you want me to wait."

"Ah, Alning," he moaned, in an agony of indecision, wanting to do the honorable thing, knowing that it was very unfair to her to be left with any expectations.

"It is what I want," she hissed fiercely, and for delicious, long, heated moments he felt an almost painful heat on his graft bud as she pressed hard to him, her own bud swelling, softening. He leaned, drank the condensation of the steams from her smooth, heated skin, moaned in pleasure as she put her arms around him and pressed him tightly.

"I named you Alning, Beautiful One," he whispered. "I saw you as a sprout, and watched you grow, freed you from mother earth, laughed as you fell, and rose swiftly to fall and rise again. I have had eyes for no other. I will never have eyes for another, my Alning."

"There," she whispered, "was that so difficult?"

"But you will be alone, for Du knows how long, and—"

"Hush," she said.

His eyes went wide, for he felt a change in the contact of their graft buds, jerked away, looked down to see a scarlet ripeness at her waist. Indeed, from waist to loin she had seemed to swell, and he was thrilled as he'd never been thrilled in his life. She tried to push herself back to him.

"No," he said, holding her off with his good hand.

"Stay with me," she hissed, with an intensity that raised his temperature.

"I would, I would," he said, still holding her away.

"No," she whispered, as her color faded, and she seemed to regain some control. "I will not ask that of you, for, although I would accept you as you are, I want life to be full for you, and you must do this thing. Have no fear, Duwan, I will wait."

"When the ripeness is fully upon you—"

"I will burn," she whispered, "but I will endure, until you return."

"I, too, will burn, each time I feel the ripeness, each time I think of you." He put his hand on her cheek, lifted her eyes to his. "Hear me, Beautiful One. If, when the time of the long light comes and goes for the second time following this long light of my departure, I have not returned, you are to speak. You are to speak for another."

"No," she said heatedly.

"Do this," he said harshly, "or I will retract my words and give you a never word and that will end it."

She went pale.

"To think of you wasted would be a great sadness for me in Du's paradise," he said. "I would be handicapped, weighed down by this sadness. You must promise. At the first dim following the second coming and going of the long light following this long light of my departure, you will speak for another. Promise me this."

"At your insistence," she said, her voice very faint.

"Say it."

"I promise."

"Then entwine with me, Beautiful One," he said, extending his arms, feeling her smooth, rich softness as she wound her arms with his and then he pushed her away and ran, not looking back lest her beauty be a fatal attraction for him, lest he lose all his resolve and stay, a one-armed one, to tend the young and bask in her beauty and regard until she, after the initial intoxicating ripeness and grafting, came to hate him for his handicap.

He ran hard, slowing only to greet the Elder of each of the villages through which he passed, reached the narrow, always guarded cleft that gave access to the cliff-bound valley, saluted the warriors on guard and climbed the steep, narrow trail through a cleft in the rocks to feel the invigorating fullness of Du on his face. Du was to the south, at evening, and he ran at a steady, ground covering warrior's pace as the source made its great circle, swinging away to the west and moving behind his back only to appear in the east and swing gradually into another evening in the south. For a full long circle of Du he had kept the pace, and he felt lighter. Moisture respired outward to his skin, and was evaporated by the heat of the source and the dry, invigorating chill of the barrens through which he ran.

The only life within days of swift marching lay behind him in the valley. He ran over sterile rock, through swales of pebbles moistened by the unevaporated remnants of the snows that covered the barrens when Du disappeared over the southern horizon at the end of the time of the long light, up and over ridges where the forces of freezing and thawing had split away boulders, some as tall as the cliffs of the valley.

Now and then he would rest, sucking the moisture from the pebbles in the damp low areas, once chewing long and satisfyingly on a dried tuber. He slept after a respectable warrior's run of two full circles of Du. His pace was slowing only slightly after two more double circle warrior's runs and a sleep. He felt lean and fit, no longer heavy, and his pauses were more frequent as he sucked moisture. Ahead of him there was a change in the sky, a layer of what seemed to be cloud far away on the horizon. At times, now, his feet were padded by soft layers of fine sand in the swales. When he saw—as Du made circle after circle, the circles becoming a bit lop-sided, with the great source sinking lower and lower on the southern horizon—the first of the spiked brothers clinging to a dry pile of sand, he was heart-ened. The cloud formation now rose high in the southern sky, hiding Du in the evenings, bringing the gloom of twilight to the barrens. There were times when he smelled the smoke of the land of fires.

He had thinned down to his best fighting weight and his movements were effortless, strong, tireless. He added the soft, juicy pulp of the spiked brothers to his meager diet, being careful to separate a small finger carefully from the parent brother and, al-though the spiked brothers were far down the scale of development and dumb, politely thanking the brother for his contribution.

He was, because of his use of the warrior's pace, well ahead of his projected schedule. He slowed his pace, for now he moved through areas of fine ash which, if he ran, billowed up into clouds to coat the fine tendrils protecting his nostrils. He rarely saw the source now because of the billowing clouds of smoke, clouds that ranged in color from the blackest of blacks through grays and dirty yellows to odd, metallic greens and reds near the earth. Fitful winds began to blow, often bringing the smoke over him. Underfoot, the rocks had taken on a sharpness that tested even his hardened pads. The first steam vent he passed spewed forth boiling water rich in miner-als, strong tasting, but quite satisfying after it had cooled in the runoff from the vent. There he slept, warmed by the heat, soaking up liquid into every cell until, once again, he felt heavy. He had to wait for food until he had penetrated a deep valley of boiling vents and the spear canes began to grow. The tender shoots of the cane made delicious munching, and he carried a handful of green canes with him for sucking and chewing along the way as he climbed to the top of a ridge and saw, spread before him, the awesome land of eternal fires.

Fortunately, fire activity was at a low. Thermal currents caused winds to gust and eddy, sometimes lifting the smokes so that he could see, across a great rift, the outlines of the mountains of fire. Only once, as he crossed the rift and began to climb the cinders of the mountain slopes, did the earth shift under his feet, and then not too severely. However, he was beginning to feel the heat even before he reached the ash-covered saddle between two mountains of fire and saw, to both his left and his right, steams of molten rock pouring from the peaks. Although the ash-covered rock underfoot was warm to the pads of his tough feet, it was not yet time to put on the sandals. Both pairs of the sandals were well soaked, having been left in the runoff of a boiling vent during his last sleep.

Ahead of him a mountain belched and rumbled and fresh pillars of smoke rose into the sky. As he moved forward, he seemed to become surrounded by a ring of fiery mountains. Once before he had penetrated this far into the land of fires, and there had seemed to be no way open to the south. He remembered his grandmother's chanted instructions.

"Between two smoking mountains Du shows his face at evening over a lake of fire—"

Ahead, however, there were only fiery mountains and the eternal smokes. He squatted to rest, chewed on a cane. Which two mountains? There were many, spaced so closely together that their rolling, fiery belchings blended into one sea of molten rock. As

for Du, he was not to be seen through the thick
smokes.

He slept. It was a warm, secure sleep. Nothing
lived there in that acrid, heated, smoked, steamy
barren other than Duwan the Drinker. He awoke
with Du high in the northern sky and began to make
his way across the saddle between two mountains,
moving always toward the east, quartering the slope,
nearing the stream of molten rock that moved slug-
gishly down from the peak. It took a long time, for
the rocks were jagged, sometimes needle sharp. By
evening he was feeling the hot breath of the molten
rock on his skin, and then, as if by a miracle, the
smoke cleared for a moment and there was Du,
shining redly between two distant, smoking mountains. Beneath the kind face of the source glimmered
a huge lake of fire.

Encouraged, he moved forward to see that the
mountain's face was broken, that the stream of molten rock poured thickly and redly into a fissure.
Below that fissure he was able to leap across a chasm
at the bottom of which glowed the fires and now the
rocks began to burn his feet, so he put on a pair of
the sandals and ran toward the last sight of Du, the
sandals smoking as they absorbed the heat of the
stones.

He seemed to fly down the slope, taking huge
strides, his lungs pumping, for he had long since
used up the energy stores from the source. Ahead
he saw white, dense smoke and slowed his pace, but
the smoke was soft to his nose. Steam. A hot spring
poured out of the side of the mountain. Although
the water boiled and steamed, it cooled on contact
with the air and was rich, tasty. He drank and rested.
His sandals were burned all the way through. So far,
it was exactly as his grandmother had said. He put
on the second pair of sandals and ran until his way
was blocked by a lake of fire, his skin shriveling

under the impact of the fierce heat. He turned to the west, climbed a slope, and, on the last remaining layers of the sandals left the smoking, hot ground for a field of smooth ash that gradually hardened until he was walking on a rippled, hard surface warmed but not heated to painful intensity. The way to the south was open before him, only emptiness in the distance.

Once he stopped to look back at the land of eternal fires, the natural barrier that protected his valley from any enemy. Forbidding as the barrens over which he was marching were, the landscape to the north was far more terrible. For the first time in his life he could appreciate the courage, or the desperation, of the Great Alon and the ones who followed him. Had he, himself, been leading, not knowing what lay beyond those fiery, shaking, smoking mountains, he would never have mustered the determination necessary to enter that zone of fire. But then, he added, to himself, he didn't have the Enemy at his rear with sword and arrow and spear.

He had been on the march for enough circles of Du to make up a time of long light, and he had traveled far, and, to judge from the landscape of barren rock around him, he might as well have stayed near the valley. Only the attitude of Du in the sky had changed, the source now remaining below the zenith even in the morning, sinking out of sight below the southern horizon off to the west in the middle of the marching period.

He counted the dim and darks, but, not having the knowledge nor the talent of Manoo the Predictor, he could not relate those odd activities of Du to real time, so that he was not only lost in a barren, endless desert of cooling rock, he was lost in his sense of time. Only that natural ability, that sense of attraction in his very blood, made it possible for him to continue ever southward, never deviating from that line except to skirt impassable features of the land. It was always there, and he did not even have to think to know when he had his back directly to the north.

The standard valley day was measured by one full circle of Du during the time of the long light. He estimated that he had traveled for a length of days corresponding to one full period and to the middle days of another period of long light when he first began to know the chill during the times of dimness. Four estimated days after that, he donned dim-time clothing when Du was below the horizon, packed it away when the source came with his heat. Then, after more estimated days, Du was performing in an odd fashion, ducking below the southwestern horizon to reappear on the southeastern horizon in glory. He was beginning to be concerned, for his grandmother had said that he would be in a land of snows while Du was long. Nor had he seen any brothers, scattered or otherwise. Not even the smallest brothers were to be found growing on the warmed surface of the rocks.

He had no alternative. He pushed southward, running now, even though he was thin, honed to a fine tenseness of form. He ran in the light of Du and he ran in the dims, which became darks as the distance behind him lengthened and lengthened and then, after running through a dark, he saw, with Du's first rays, a dull green sheen on a rock ahead. Tiny brothers grew there, and he shared their life, careful not to disrupt their colony. There was new strength in him, although he needed water badly. On another morning he saw in the distance a spike of green and there was a small brother, so he knew that he was nearing a zone of life. He used the emergency water supply then, drinking it in one long, satisfying draft from the shell of the nut brother. Soon he was moving through a landscape of scattered soil pockets and scattered, small brothers, and still there was no snow.

He rested, and slept long, and woke with pain in every joint, the pain of cold. A heaviness was atop him. He tried to move and panic grew in him when he opened his eyes to see nothing, only an impenetrable blackness, and he was cold, so cold. Every movement was an effort. He shook, lifted his arms and legs against resistance, and then, with a scream of sheer terror of the unknown, he bunched his energies and exploded upward from under a fresh blanket of snow that had covered him during the night.

As far as he could see there was that deadly whiteness, but, when he had begun to move, trudging through a smooth, even snowfall that came halfway to his knees, his blood flowed and his cells were not ruptured by the ice and he knew that the cold was not a killing cold, as long as he kept moving.

There was food now. It was dry, tough, cold period fodder, but it was full of energy and the snow satisfied his need for water. He moved swiftly into a land of more and more brothers of one type, tall, thin, cold-resistant brothers who dropped dead limbs in profusion, making it easy for him to have a warm fire when he rested.

Never had he seen such darks as he saw when he entered a forest of tall brothers so dense that the glow of the sky's night fires, a newness to him, were hidden by the overlapped boughs. And the darks were long, and cold, and he had to travel through them, sleeping little, not daring to rest, for the cold was on his heels now, as he'd been warned, and to sleep long meant death.

He stumbled into the first of the waters. It was nothing more than a shallow, marshy pool, but it was water, and icy cold, and so delicious that, in spite of the cold he lay there where he'd fallen, gulping great draughts of it until he was bloated with its goodness. For a long period of lights and darks—Du was bright, but surprisingly distant—he waded, swam, skirted lakes, streams, bogs where delicious green brothers grew, until he began to notice that the tall brothers were increasing in size to assume, as he entered a great congregation and lost himself in darkness, sizes beyond his wildest imaginings.

The cold was becoming dangerous. Even when he found a sheltered spot and built a roaring fire he could not warm himself all the way through. So he moved, ran, walked, waded, pushed his way through drifts of snow, with Du a weak source in the sky and the cold always with him. He could not believe that he would see the Enemy there, for it was too cold, the snows too deep, the darkness among the tall brothers too complete.

4

A howling wind carried a cold unlike any cold Duwan had ever felt. Once, in youthful curiosity, he'd climbed out of the valley during the time of the long dark to find a world of crusted white. Then the barrens had been covered to a depth equal to more than his height in snow, and there was a still, quiet cold that gradually seeped into one's cells, but even that cold could not compare with the cold of the wind there among the tall brothers. And snow came with the wind, and there was no softness in the snow. It stung his face. It irritated his eyes so that he had difficulty seeing. The wind was so powerful that it blew him, hard, against a tall brother and the shock of the impact brought to him a sense of growing urgency.

The depth of the new snow sapped his energy. He sank to his knees, had to lift his feet high, had to struggle for each brief passage from tall brother to tall brother. The storm had dimmed the day, so that he had no sense of time. He was only beginning to comprehend that time had a different shape in this land of many tall brothers, far from his native valley. In the valley, time was measured by that lovely period when Du circled around the valley and gave light. The long dark, when Du left the valley, was merely a period of endurance, with time, itself, of little import. He knew only that the time of darkness was long, but bearable, made bearable by the constant output of the hot springs, a warmth so effective that snow melted as it fell to become a mist of dew that gave life to the valley even in the absence of Du. Now time was measured by short periods of light and periods of intense darkness longer than the periods of light and each dark seemed to become more deadly, for the cold intensified and seemed capable of attacking even the flames of his night fires. The cold seemed to impregnate the fallen, dry branches of the tall brothers, so that he had to use extravagant amounts of his carefully stored tinder to start the smallest twigs burning, and then they popped and cracked and smoked and burned only reluctantly.

The winds blew for days, and the snow continued until he was, at times, struggling through drifts up to his chest. His very skin ached. His blood seemed to move in his veins at a slowed pace. The necessary intake of snow for water allowed the cold to invade the core of his body, so that it seemed to seep outward as well as inward. For food there was only the dry, brittle, acidy needles of the tall brothers and, occasionally, dry fodder—if he had the fortune to find a spot where winds had cleared the snow enough to allow him to dig down to ground level.

By the time the storm ended his southward progress amounted to no more than an arrow's flight each day and he was keeping himself in motion only with the expenditure of all his will, and the memories of Alning, his father, his mother, and his duty to the Drinkers of the Valley.

From a sky washed clean by the storm Du gave him strength. He opened his multiple layers of clothing and let the life-giving rays do battle with the frigid air, and the net gain was negligible. One could not live in such cold. The cold froze small limbs on the tall brothers so that, in the stillness, broken only by Duwan's panting, the sharp crack of rupturing cells came, crisp and elear, echoing off the wall of tall brothers.

After a night of pain, when the cold seemed to turn to fire in his body, he struggled onward and paused, knowing not hope but astonishment, as the tall brothers ceased and a wide, level clearing lay ahead of him, so extensive that the tall brothers on the far side were dwarfed. He hoped that the clearing would make for easier travel, but there the soft, new snow was just as deep, and he came to realize that he was crossing a frozen lake, had just enough capacity for thought left to be awed by the sheer mass of water that lay under the snow and ice.

The winds came again when he was only halfway across, roaring down from the northwest with a suddenness that numbed him. Into the stillness came a distant mutter. The mutter became a roar and, looking over his shoulder, he saw a roiling mass of dark clouds springing up from the horizon, moving so swiftly that he could only stand and watch in fear as the storm approached with astounding speed.

The winds took him directly in the face, seemed to lance his skin. Then came stinging sleet and snow so that he had to cover his eyes. He turned his back to the winds and let them help push him forward, toward the distant line of tall brothers where there would be some protection from the icy wind.

By the time he reached the shelter of the tall brothers he was gasping in the cold air, feeling it chill his lungs. His clothing was covered with snow. Ice had frozen on his frondlike eyelashes and in the tendrils of his nostrils. His breath crystallized as he exhaled and became a miniature snowstorm that sometimes interfered with his vision. With his last resources of strength he made his way deeper among the tall brothers, too spent to notice that on the southern side of the frozen lake the tall brothers were different.

When he fell, he lay there on the snow for long

moments, his hands and feet making small, useless motions. He felt peace begin to come to his troubled spirit, felt a warmth begin to creep upward from his toes, thanked Du for it, then, in panic, he sat up, pushed himself to his feet, remembering his father's warnings that to rest in that cold was to die.

Overhead, the limbs of the tall brothers formed a solid canopy, and he could see accumulated snow there. Underfoot the snow seemed less deep. He found a sheltered spot behind a deadfall and began to dig down through the snow, found frozen earth. Fire. He had to have fire. He needed food badly, but his most immediate concern was fire, for that lack of feeling, that false warmth, was still in his extremities. He dug frantically, found cold-soaked limbs, broke away twigs, saw that his tinder supply was desperately low.

His first attempt was a failure. His fire rocks sparked, the tinder smoked, he blew it into a tiny flame, but the twigs, moisture laden and frozen, sizzled and the tinder was gone and there was no fire. He had tinder for no more than two to three more fires. He began to search for drier twigs and, hearing a soft plop, turned his head to see a newly fallen dead limb lying atop the snow. Another limb, with dry, brittle twigs, fell nearby. "Thank you, brother," he said aloud, although he knew that he was neither heard nor understood by the tall brother.

This time the fire smoked, blazed, and, as dead limbs continued to fall around him, blessed heat began to soak into his almost frozen feet and hands, and darkness was upon him. He gathered wood by the flickering light of the fire and tried the needles of one of the tall brothers. The taste was different, not at all unappetizing. He ate sparingly, found dead limbs to hold up his small night covering, basked in the heat of the fire, and was asleep without realizing it.

The density of the grove of tall brothers broke the wind. The tangled, solid canopy kept off the snow. The howl and roar of the winds overhead served as a lullaby and he slept soundly as the fire burned low, flickered, became a bed of embers. Loud cracks of sound, as the weight of new snow broke branches overhead, as the iron cold ruptured living cells, failed to wake him, for he slept the sleep of exhaustion, warm for the first time in days, and then warmed by the creeping death that failed, also, to waken him.

There was no ear to hear, for Duwan slept too soundly, slept that cold-induced sleep that is the prologue to death, as a whispering began, a soft, rushing sound distinct from the hiss and howl of the storm.

At first the whisperings had no shape or substance. Then they seemed to say, "Wan, Wan, Wan." And from the tall brother under which Duwan slept there fell a series of dead limbs to plop quietly into the snow, unheard by the sleeper.

"Wan, Wan, Wan."

He did not realize that his heart was slowing, that the cold was penetrating, that, already, cells had frozen on his outer skin, the liquids of life expanding to burst and freeze, forming a coating of ice on his feet.

"Wan, Wan, Duwan."

The whispering grew in volume, became a low, hoarse, steady hissing. "Duwan, Duwan."

A living limb cracked overhead, leaned, fell, struck Duwan at the waist. He stirred.

"Duwan, Duwan, Duwan."

He opened his eyes, felt a prickling pain in his feet, knew swift panic as he saw that the fire had burned down to embers, felt the frozen moisture at his eyes crack painfully.

He tried to stand, fell. He had no sensation in his feet. He crawled, gathered freshly fallen branches, built the fire into roaring warmth.

"Duwan, Duwan."

"Who calls?" he asked, looking fearfully around the small circle of snow lit by the fire.

Whispering voices seemed to compete with themselves, so that he caught only isolated words, "Cold. Storm. Snow."

"Listen, listen, listen."

He was still. His heart was beating strongly, awe and fear helping his half-frozen blood to circulate.

"Listen, listen."

"I hear," he whispered.

He saw nothing but the fire, the circle of light, the towering tall brothers, the snow.

"I am listening," he whispered, and there was a silence, as even the winds of the storm ceased for a few moments and the voices whispered softer, "Listen."

He tried. He cocked his head to one side and the other, and heard only the distant crack of a breaking branch, and then a picture seemed to form in his mind. He saw blocks of packed snow begin to form a circle. He felt warmth, safety.

A sprig of living needles fell into his lap and, as he listened with his mind, he munched them.

"Now, now," the voice whispered.

He used his knife. The packed snow abraded his fingers, sent the freezing cold into his being, but he was true to the pictures in his mind and the packed snow blocks circled him and then, after he'd raised two tiers of them, he dug out the packed snow and a rain of living branches began to fall, some missing him narrowly. He laid the living branches with their soft needles in the circle of packed snow blocks and then began to cut more blocks, working by the flickering light of the fire.

The dim light of dawn came, and aided him with the last tiers of packed snow blocks. Before him was a small dome of snow. Inside, the frozen ground was covered by fresh needles from the tall brothers. His fire was burning well, with no shortage of deadwood, for, as needed, it fell from above, although, he saw, as the day went on and he closed in the dome of his ice house, he would have to walk farther and farther from the ice house to gather the wood, for the tall brothers nearby had begun to clear themselves of dead branches.

The storm still howled. A section of the overhead canopy gave way not too far from his ice house and a cascade of broken branches and snow thundered to the ground. Duwan rested. He ate of the living needles from the tall brothers, considered his situation. The cold was intense, so that he had, continuously, to go back to the fire to be warmed. He was weak, in spite of the new supply of food, food more nutritious than that he'd found on the northern side of the frozen lake.

In early darkness he crawled into the ice dome and closed the opening with packed snow. It was cold, but, gradually, his body heat filled the small space and, covered by all his clothing, he slept. He awoke and pushed aside the snow that blocked the opening. The hiss and sigh and roar of the storm told him that there would be no traveling that day. He felt much stronger, alert enough to remember the strange events of the previous night, the whisperings, the pictures that had formed in his head and had saved his life.

He stood beside his rekindled fire and looked around. There were only the tall brothers, and the solid covering overhead. Had it really happened, those whisperings, his name being called, "Duwan, Duwan, Duwan?"

The legends said that in the Land of Many Brothers there was no death, until the coming of the Enemy. In the Land of Many Brothers Drinkers were of the earth and for the earth, there being no wasting disease, no hardening until an old one simply ceased to live. Could such things be believed?

"Brothers," he said, spreading his arms, "I thank you."

A small sprig of fresh needles fell into one of his outstretched hands, and he looked up.

"Brothers, did you speak?"

There was a warmness in his mind, and then a picture of vast distances and howling winds and iron cold.

Duwan fell to his knees and raised his hands. "I salute you, brothers, Drinkers of old. I praise you, and I give you my thanks. You have helped me. Now I need further help. I need guidance, brothers. I have far to go. Will I go now?"

A softness in his mind, a picture of his little snow hut, the taste of the needles in his mouth and something else, not yet identified, and then a sense of the passing of many days and a picture of the land without snow.

"I am to remain here, then?" he asked, and the soft, reassuring feeling came over him.

There was no more. He was alone. He left the fireside and walked toward the south and was assaulted immediately by the cold, a cold that caused his breath to freeze and tinkle in little icy crystals, a cold that sent a burning upward from his feet. Ahead was only the vast, unchanging forest. He went back to the fire, warmed himself, crawled into the ice hut and saw that wiry tendrils had grown upward through the frozen ground, making small cracks in the surface. He lay so as not to crush the tendrils and, as he mused, and wished that he was back with his own in the valley in the far north, he saw an ooze of liquid from the end of a tendril, touched it with his finger, sampled it to find it tasty and nutritious. Another drop of the liquid welled up at the end of the tendril and he bent to suck it away with his mouth, to savor all of it, and the flow became continuous.

There was no time. There was fire, and cold, and the endless storms. There were the fresh needles that fell as he hungered, and the constant supply, on his demand, of nutritious sap from the tendrils growing within his hut. He fattened, stored energy, exercised by taking brief walks. He discovered that the character of the tall brothers changed in all directions after a brisk, short walk, and became the same as those on the northern side of the frozen lake. His feelings changed, too, when he left the whispering grove. Within it, he felt safe and protected. Outside it he was alone.

Time. The days were growing longer. More and more often wet masses of snow fell, broken limbs mixed with it, to the forest floor. The iron cold abated until he could explore for a half day without ill effect. He was swollen with nutrition, eager to resume his journey, and yet there was the feeling that it was too soon. That feeling was borne out by one of the worst of the storms, a wind and snow that broke through the canopy itself and littered the ground with fallen limbs and piles of accumulated snow and sleet. He resigned himself, waited until the light of Du, penetrating through holes in the canopy, was bright, and made shining things of wonder of the drops of melt water that, as the days passed, made for an unceasing rain in the grove.

"Is it not time?" he asked, and a picture of distances came to him.

"My brothers," he said. "I believe. The tales of the old ones had foundation. I salute you, my ancestors, my brothers. Eternal life to you."

He heard the whisperings. He had not heard them

often during that long period of cold and darkness, but now he heard them and, instead of being disjointed, difficult to understand, the words were clear, simple words that caused him to thrill inside.

"All is one," the whisperers said. "We are all one."

"I hear," Duwan whispered. "All life is a oneness."

He covered distance with difficulty, at first. He walked through a cold rain as the snows of the canopy melted and made the footing mushy. He crossed another frozen lake with melting snow cold around his feet and with Du overhead, giving him more energy now than the cold could steal. He drank the rays, blessed them, and moved ever southward until the snows became only remnants in shadowed places and new, fresh green things sprouted in the thawing earth. He ate well, always thanking the food source and never taking enough to deprive a brother of health and life. He had no means of keeping count of the days. He knew only that as his strong legs moved him ever southward Du rose higher and higher into the sky, and he remembered his grandmother's words. When Du was just below the zenith at midday be would have reached his destination.

He was constantly on the alert now, for the land had changed. There were several varieties of tall brothers now, some of them putting out new, tender, delicious life organs after a time of bareness. He saw signs of life, but only in the form of animal tracks. From the songs of the minstrels and the legends of the old ones he remembered tales of animals large enough to be dangerous. Once he'd doubted such tales, but now, having known the whispering brothers, he doubted less. If one aspect of the legends was true, who could say what else was true? Still, he spotted no large tracks, saw only small, shy creatures so eager to avoid something as large as he that he had no clear picture of them, except for one little animal, the size of his hand, that lived in the tall brothers and squeaked excitedly when Duwan came near.

He swam a wide river, making his way through floating masses of melting, fracturing ice, spent a day drying his clothing and warming himself, and then was off again with the morning light.

He rested when Du was at the zenith, but still too low in the southern sky, and as he nibbled tender, green shoots he heard a distant crash and felt, unaccountably, a moment of sadness that was actual pain. Not long after he resumed his southward trek, he discovered the cause of the crashing sound. He heard, first, the steady rhythm of two sharp sounds. They echoed and reechoed among the trunks of the tall brothers. He began to move cautiously, came nearer. He heard voices.

Drinkers!

He increased his pace, but moved from cover to cover, carefully, until he saw, in a clearing ahead, a structure built of the split trunks of tall brothers. His heart leaped. Tall brothers had died to build that hut. He moved around the edge of the clearing, following the steady, rhythmic sounds, and froze into immobility when he saw, through the tall brothers, two Drinkers using chopping instruments to attack a tall brother. Even as he watched, someone yelled a warning and, with a groan, the tall brother toppled, the fall accelerating until the dying brother struck the hard ground with a smashing of limbs and the knowledge, shared by Duwan, that he was dying.

Duwan almost shouted, but his eyes had shifted from the two Drinkers who had killed the brother to the source of a harsh voice. A Drinker struck out at one of the choppers with a whip and the lash fell across the worker's shoulder. The worker yelled out in pain and Duwan reached for his longsword, but restrained himself as other Drinkers with weapons and lashes moved into the clearing and herded Drinkers dressed in rags to begin trimming the branches off the fallen dead brother.

Never had he seen such a thing. The Drinkers with weapons were dressed in leather and fur garments. They had, Duwan realized with a flush of anger, actually taken animal life to keep their bodies warm. His every impulse was to rush forth to punish this, the greatest of crimes, for the taking of life was the ultimate wrong. He held himself back, however, telling himself that he had been given a mission. He was not thinking, at that moment, of his missing arm, and the hope—a hope that had been growing ever since he'd discovered that at least a part of the old tales was true—that he could be whole again. He thought only of the dead tall brother, of the dead animals whose skins and fur warmed the killers, of the odd situation wherein one set of Drinkers forced others to work and struck them with lashes.

While uttering a prayer to Du for the dead, he circled far, returned to his southerly direction. In the days that followed he passed another settlement, this one boasting three huts made from the split trunks of tall brothers. Fortunately, the area was thinly settled. To the west was a snowcapped mountain range. A great river ran in a southeasterly direction, then turned east. Rolling, forested hills grew taller with each ridge to the south, and little cold streams made each valley a thing of delight, but there were no more settlements; at least Duwan didn't encounter any. All was green, and Du seemed to rise right up in the middle of the sky at midday now.

The sun was so warm that Duwan was all but intoxicated with it. He found that he could almost live on sunlight alone. He drank it and drank it and praised Du and wished that all of the Drinkers of the valley were with him for a celebration, knew, too, a sense of loss, for this, long past, had been their country. Why had not the old ones ever spoken of

this glory of heat and sun? But then, who, among
those who knew only the dim and distant Du of the
far north, would have believed them? Who would
believe him when he returned to tell of this land of
so many riches, of so many silent, fixed brothers, of
whispering groves, of Drinkers who killed?

On a morning when the sky was cloudless and Du
was climbing toward the zenith only slightly to the
south of the middle of the blue, he found his place.
It was a tiny clearing on the southern slope of a
ridge. Rocks thrust up from the earth, leaving a
pocket where no tall brothers grew, but with a space
of rich, grassy earth in the center exposed to the full
light of the sun.

He knelt, facing the north, and sent a prayer there,
greeting all those he loved by name, his father, his
mother, his friends, and, lastly, Alning. Then, eyes
closed, the warmth on his eyelids, he praised Du.

He secreted his weapons away from possible rain
in a cleft among the rocks, took one last look around,
stood in the grassy spot and began to bore into the
sun-heated earth with his horned toes. If there was
to be a time—when legend proved to be truth, the
time was now.

The earth cooled below the surface, but as tendrils
began to grow from his feet he felt and tasted the
goodness, the richness. It was loamy, enriched by
season after season of growing grass. He wiggled,
dug himself down until his knees were below the
level of the earth, used his hand to tamp down the
loose earth, leaned, looked up toward Du. He felt
the somnolent peace of the goodness of the earth
begin to seep into him, having that effect that is not
unlike sleep, but more total, more possessing. He felt
the tendrils extending downward and outward and
he knew that he was committed. The earth was taking him, and it would hold him, in that state much
like sleep, until it had done its work. In that time he

would be helpless, as helpless as one of the fixed
brothers who had not a brain to think nor sensitivity
to feel anything beyond the sweet earth, the soft
rains, or, perhaps, the sudden and searing pain of
death.

He could not let fear deter him, although it was
not too late to jerk his feet free, ripping away the
rooting tendrils.

Du would guard him. Du would restore.

5

Soft rains came, and growling, fast-moving storms that flashed and crashed and sent torrents of wind-driven drops. Mostly, however, the sun burned the eastern hills golden red on rising and blessed all with warmth. Small animals darted among the rocks, sniffed at the tall, growing thing with twin trunks planted deeply into the fresh, sweet, grassy earth. A tawny-purple quadruped reared and braced short, padded front feet on one truck of the growing thing and nibbled with the large, blunt teeth of the grass eater at tattered clothing, spit out the substance from which all nutrition had been removed in processing it into weavable cloth, sniffed, looked around alertly, pointed ears twitching, and lay down in the growing thing's shade, almost hidden by the tall grass.

A pale blue bird alit on the fronds atop the growing thing, twittered, peered at the ruminant still resting peacefully in the shade, jeered, flew, the beat of its wings disturbing the fronds.

The frond-like hair had grown rapidly. Two sources of nourishment were at work, with the light of the sun being converted directly into energy and with the rooty tendrils seeking out the minerals and moisture from the loamy soil. As days passed, and the rains came and went and the sun reached its northernmost position, near the zenith, the hair covered the growing thing's face. It swayed with the summery breezes, bent with the soon-passed winds of the thunderstorms. And from the pointed stub of the severed arm there appeared small, thin protrusions that became perfectly formed, three fingers and two opposing thumbs, tiny, almost ludicrous, but growing, soaking up a good portion of the nutrition provided by sun and soil. Yellow-green skin darkened in the full heat of the sun to a sheeny, rich, forest green.

He dreamed. The dreams were disjointed and distant, as if being observed through the deepest winter haze of the valley. Alning was there, her black eyes the most visible aspect of her, a hint of her femaleness, long legs, coloring torso; and whispers, insensate, wordless whispers of peace and goodness—the song of the growing grass, the purely sensory reaction of the nearer tall brothers to rain and wind and sun. He dreamed, now and then, that he was not alone, but that dream, too, was vague, and that oneness with the earth, that somnolency, made him little more than the grass, the nameless small fixed brothers, the tall ones.

The arm grew, now as large as that of one of the fixed young on the verge of mobility. Of that he knew nothing, nor did he see, for his eyes were closed, and covered with the fronds of his hair, that he, truly, was not alone.

She came from a valley to the east, climbing a ridge wearily, a tall, tired, rag-dressed female with thin, undernourished arms and pinched, hollow-cheeked face. She came with scufflings of feet, the movements of one not accustomed to traveling in the wilderness, with mighty pantings as she achieved the top of the ridge, rested, and then, with a fearful look over her shoulder, moved more swiftly down the slope toward the grassy clearing. Blood spotted the ground where she stepped with her left foot, and she favored it, limping, halting, as she reached the rocks near the clearing to sit on the sun-warmed stone and examine the left foot with concerned, purple eyes. She had tried once before without success to remove the long splinter that had entered into a softer area between her toes, and she was no more successful now as she sat beside the clearing.

With a sigh that was part sob she stood, gingerly put her weight on the foot, winced, and stepped onto the grass. The small ruminant that had been resting in Duwan's shade leaped, showing admirable ability to cover ground, and went flashing silently into the forest.

"Ahtol!" she gasped. Her eyes had been led to the growing thing in the center of the clearing. She turned to flee, ran a few steps with her left foot paining her, took a quick look backward, halted. Her initial panic gone, she realized that had he been a Devourer she could not have hoped to outdistance him on her painfully swollen foot.

Crouched and ready for flight, she crept back toward the clearing. *He* did not move, except to sway slightly in a gust of breeze. She came closer, closer, saw that *his* feet were buried in the earth to just above *his* knees.

"You," she said, "what are you doing?"

A tinge of red had been burned into Duwan's hair by the sun. It was long, longer than that of the female, and it gleamed with health, moved in the light breeze. She could not see his eyes, for they were hidden.

It came to her that this was some new form of torture invented by the Devourers. She twisted her mouth in sympathy and straightened to walk into the grass that came soothingly to the calves of her thin legs. Slowly, carefully, fearfully, she drew near. She saw that *his* chest was rising and falling, that *he* was breathing deeply, but oh, so slowly. *He* must be, she felt, near death. But she saw no blood, no great abrasions on *his* smooth, sheeny skin. Her eyes caught

the growing arm, now only slightly smaller than the
other, and they widened.

"What manner of thing are you?" she asked, and
was rewarded only by the call of a bird from the
nearby trees. She reached out a hand tentatively,
drew it back with a gasp as the fronds of Duwan's
hair moved in the breeze. Then, holding her breath,
biting her lower lip, she lifted the hair to see a face
in repose, in sweet sleep, a face of fullness and health
and no little beauty, the face of a young du, so
different from either pong or Devourer, and yet
familiar, a pong face idealized, perhaps. She let the
hair fall, examined him closely. His clothing was in
tatters, had fallen away from his powerful chest.

It puzzled her. She knelt, examined the points
where his legs disappeared into the moist earth, drew
on her courage to put her hands on his small arm to
feel warmth and smoothness, looked again at his
face.

A shocking thought came to her, a thought out of
hopelessness, out of whispered tales in the stink and
noise of the pongpens.

"Master?" she whispered.

*He will come from the earth, from the deep, rich, sweet
depths of the earth, and he will be mighty, and in his
strength and wisdom he will teach us, and deliver us.*

She had, until that moment, never believed the
hopeless, superstitious mutterings of the lost. Now
she sat on her haunches, ragged garment hiked up
onto her thin but still muscular thighs and pondered
this new thing, this—*being*—who seemed to be coming from the earth, growing as the trees, the grass,
the shrubs, the weeds, the flowers grew.

"Master?" she repeated, and then, with a sigh, lay
back to let the sun strike her full in the face. There
was something about the sun. In her days of freedom she had had little food. It was past time for the
berry fruits, and the nut fruits were still tiny, green

buds, and she had resorted to animalism, eating the
spongy mosses along the streams. Even that was forbidden. And yet, in spite of the emptiness of her
stomach, she did not always hunger, and seemed to
gain strength from the sun, or was it that she was
merely still euphoric at being away from the pongpens,
from the lash, and the endless drudgery?

She slept. She slept through the evening and the
formation of dew that glistened on her skin and
tattered garments, woke only once to see *him* there,
towering over her, to hear the snick-snick of small
tiny things grazing on the sweet, rich, new grass, to
see overhead the lights of the sky singing down upon
her.

With the morning she could not bring herself to
leave *him*. She went down the slope to the valley and
washed herself and drank deeply and nibbled on
spongy moss, wondering why—since she'd been eating it for a long time without ill effect—why the
Devourers so expressly forbade its intake, along with
most growing things.

She whiled away most of the morning playing in
the cool waters of the stream, soaking her hair, letting it dry in the sun, rinsing her ragged garment,
then, in the pleasant heat of midday, she climbed the
slope again and *he* was as before. She knew that she
should be moving on. They would be after her.
They punished escape with the most painful of deaths,
and, to keep order in the pongpens, they spared no
efforts to return an escaped pong. Yet she'd been
moving through these low, forested ridges for so
many days she'd lost count and there had been no
sign of pursuit. She felt an urgent need to know
about *him*.

As three more days passed, and she established a
routine of going to the stream, basking in the sun,
wandering the near areas, she thought she saw a
decided growth in that small arm. To prove it, she

tied a fragile vine tightly around the forearm and when, in just one day, it was broken and fell to the grass, she knew that a miracle was happening before her eyes and she fell to her knees, faced the northwest, the direction of the storms, and prayed to Ahtol, the du who made the lightning. She had chosen Ahtol as her personal du—for all dus were worthy—because he was, at least, visible and loud in his flashings and thunderings, even if he, like all dus, seemed utterly unconcerned with the plight of a mere pong.

Next day, as she lay on her stomach drinking from the cool waters of the creek, she heard a sound that caused her to leap to her feet and look around wildly. When the sound was repeated, from a point closer to her, she did not hesitate. She ran, heedless of the pain in her left foot, a pain that grew from day to day, a pain that made the swollen, discolored foot feel as large as the rest of her body. She leaped, caught the branches of a tree, lifted herself and, tearing her already ragged garment, climbed high.

The animal ambled out from dense growth to pause and sniff the air. It lumbered to the water, drank, tensed, catching her scent, cast around for a moment and then moved with frightening speed, head low, to stand below her. It was huge, standing one-and-a-half times taller than she when it reared, scratched the bole of the tree with long claws and opened its huge mouth to show discolored, deadly, sharp teeth. She could smell the feral scent of its breath as it roared up at her.

The animal was death. Omnivorous, savage, so powerful that the Devourers hunted it in groups, with the strongest of bows and iron-tipped arrows. But she was safe in the tree, although, for a moment, she considered climbing even higher.

After a long, long time, the animal went away. It disappeared downstream. She waited while the sun climbed to midday and began its descent before she climbed down and, all senses alert, scurried up the slope. *He* was there, unchanged. She did not like the idea of a farl being so near. If the omnivore decided to hunt the slope, if it came to the clearing, *he* would make a pleasant snack for the beast, and there would be no place for her to hide. She began to look around. The nearest climbable tree was too far way. However, there was a small cleft in the rocks just below the clearing, a narrow opening that was too small to admit the huge farl, but large enough for her to jam herself into and be out of the animal's reach. She tested it for size and discovered Duwan's weapons, wrapped carefully in his winter clothing. Musingly she tested the swords. They were of fine metal. She knew a bit about weapons, because her father had been a weapons maker pong before his death. The longsword was heavy. She could heft it, but wielding it was too much for her thin arms. She took the shortsword, buckled it to her small waist, and drew it, swung it. She had no illusions that she could kill a farl with a shortsword, but, if caught in the open, she could at least draw a bit of the beast's blood before dying.

She took both weapons with her when she walked back to stand musingly before *him*. "If you would only awaken," she said. "Your arms are strong and powerful." She touched them, one by one. The left arm was as large as the right now. "Wake up," she whispered. "Wake up."

She sat before him, longsword and shortsword at her side. She started from near sleep, for there was a movement, and for a moment she couldn't place it. She looked around, ready to flee for the cleft in the rocks. The movement came again and she caught it out of the corner of her eye. *He* was moving *his* left arm, flexing *his* fist. Muscles rippled as the arm lifted, lowered, lifted, flexed.

Eyes wide, more healthily purple than they'd been when she first encountered *him*, she backed away. The arm continued to flex and move, as if exercising, for the rest of the day, although *his* eyes did not open.

She slept restlessly, for *he* continued to move. With the morning sun, a glory of a sunrise, golden red and bursting over the hills to the east, she examined *him* closely. The arm was still.

The farl came shortly after sunrise, came silently at first, so that when it gave its chilling roar and charged it was almost at the edge of the clearing. She leaped to her feet, shortsword in hand, and, taking one despairing look at *him*, helpless, she chose her own life and ran. The movement attracted the animal and it moved heavily but with speed to close on her while the rock cleft was still beyond her reach. She smelled its fetid, panting breath, whirled, sword high, and made one powerful sweeping slash that laid open the farl's furry cheek and brought a scream of anger and pain before its weight thrust into her, sending her flying to land heavily, the animal leaping to stand over her, stinking maw dripping saliva mixed with blood into her face. She screamed.

Throughout the night Duwan's dreams had been more vivid. Those he saw were nearer. He dreamed that he was back in the valley in the time of the long light, lounging in the light of Du, Alning by his side, a sweet, summery breeze blowing in his face. Overhead were the lights of the sky, and that puzzled him, for when Du came the dim distant lights disappeared, but they were there and he was filled with a sense of well-being, a wholeness. He could use his left hand. He plucked at Alning's delicately colored fronds teasingly with two thumbs and a finger.

Du rose in blessed warmth. He needed to see. He was sleeping, and he couldn't open his eyes, and he needed to see, to praise Du. He felt the strength in his arms, flexed them. His feet were a part of him, but oddly distant. He tried to move and smelled the freshness of good earth as if he were in the young house again. He rested, felt the golden rays of Du on him, feasted, drank, felt himself bursting with nutrition. One eye cracked, and light dazzled him and he saw Alning, but changed, thinner—no, not Alning. There was a dazed, warm contentment in him. He took his time in opening the other eye. His hair was so long, falling in front of his eyes. He lifted his left hand and a surge of joy elated him, for he had fingers to push the hair back from his eyes.

Movement came suddenly. The female—not Alning—on her feet, running, a strange roaring, a feral sound, dark, flashing mass. He heard the female scream and saw her turn to face the thing, a thing unlike anything he'd ever seen, a thing out of legend, one of the great creatures of the past, of the Land of Many Brothers.

His right foot came free with a snapping and cracking and a sucking sound. Then his left. The female was fighting the animal, taking a rather admirable slash at it with a shortsword, and his longsword was at his feet. He jerked his left foot out and the female went down and screamed once more, the sound quickly drowned out by the angry roar of the wounded animal. He felt his tendrils trying to withdraw, but could not give them time, ran on tendril covered feet, longsword in hand. The animal slapped at the fallen female with one paw and great, bloody welts appeared on her bare shoulder. Duwan yelled warning. He had never taken life, but in that moment when there was no time for decision he knew his duty, for the life of a Drinker was more precious than the life of an animal. In this moment requiring action his training took over, training so well drilled into him by Belran the Leader that it was instinctive. He knew nothing about the anatomy of the animal, knew of it only from legend—and this was one more instance where it was being proven to him that the tales of the old ones had not been fabricated. He raised the heavy longsword and, positioned himself slightly behind the huge beast's head, a head that was lowering, mouth wide, teeth dripping, to engulf the head of the female. He struck, felt the blade hit bone, heard a loud snapping sound. The beast fell heavily directly atop the female, its spinal column severed at the neck. Frantic movement, uncoordinated, did some damage to the female underneath, leaving claw marks on her exposed legs.

Glorying in his strength, in his wholeness, glancing in awe at his left arm, complete once again, Duwan had to exert all his strength to push the animal off the female. She was alive, breathing, but she was unconscious. Still a bit dazed, Duwan looked around, remembered the stream at the foot of the slope, lifted the female. She was quite light, all skin and bones. He took only an instant to wonder why she was starving in a land of plenty.

Her clothing had been further damaged by the attack of the animal, and clung to her by shreds. To determine the extent of her injuries, Duwan removed the garment. She lay on moss at the brink of the stream. He cleansed her wounds. They would be painful, but not fatal. The worst claw gashes were on her shoulder. Her skin was pale, not as rich and smooth as his own, or as that of Alning. She was thin. Her bud point was enlarged, and, although he had never seen such—drinker females who had grafted were modest—he knew that she had performed, with someone, that act of which he had dreamed often of performing with Alning.

He had finished cleansing the shallower wounds on her legs when he noticed her left foot. It was discolored, festering, inflamed, quite nasty looking, an old wound. He examined it, saw that it needed lancing, used the point of his knife and narrowly escaped having the accumulated putrescence jet into his face. He squeezed out the rest of the bad juices and saw the black tip of the splinter, cut away dying flesh, exposed the soggy wood, drew it forth and it was followed by bright, fresh, healthy blood. He closed the wound with a pulped mixture of two tissues from fixed brothers growing along the stream, applied the same healing mixture to her other wounds, and sat down to wait. Her swollen, exposed bud point held a certain fascination for him, so he covered it with her torn garment.

She awakened with a start, jerked her head upward, moaned and fell back to be comatose for a few minutes longer. The next time she opened her eyes Duwan said, "Be at rest."

Her eyes, he saw, were purple, like an evening sky before a storm. They examined him, wide, searching.

"Master?" she whispered.

"You are not hurt badly," he said. "I have treated your wounds."

She raised herself on one elbow, groaned as her injured shoulder pulled, tossed aside her garment casually and examined herself.

"The farl?" she asked.

"Farl? The animal that attacked you? It is dead."

"Good," she said. "Now we will have real food."

Shocked, Duwan was speechless.

"The haunches are best," she said, trying to sit up. "There will be so much of it that we won't be able to eat it all before it spoils, but, ah—"

"You would eat flesh?" Duwan asked.

She looked at him. "Who are you?"

"I am Duwan the Drinker."

"An odd name."

"And you? You are Drinker."

She looked puzzled. "I am Jai."

"You are Drinker," he said, for as he had worked

on her injured foot he had seen the small pores from which would grow the tendrils, should she have need to return to the earth.

"I don't know what you mean," she said. "Until I ran away I was pong in the city of Arutan."

Duwan shook his head. She spoke as a Drinker, but her words were, occasionally, misshaped, slightly askew, and he did not know the words pong, and Arutan.

"I have been starving," she said. "Please, please, cut a great slice of meat from the haunch of the farl. As hungry as I am I can almost eat it raw."

Duwan reached for a life organ on a particularly succulent fixed brother, breaking it away carefully. "If you are hungry, here is food," he said.

Her eyes went wide. "It is forbidden."

He took a nibble of the leaf, thrust the rest toward her mouth.

"Must I, Master?" she asked.

"Eat," he said. "You will need your strength to heal your wounds."

She closed her eyes, swallowed, took the leaf and began to chew it. Her eyes opened. "Good," she said, reaching for the fixed brother, which was quite near her, tearing away several leaves.

"No, no," Duwan said. "Gently, and carefully."

She would have stripped the fixed brother had he not restrained her, gathering more for her from other fixed brothers, taking only a small portion of their life, thanking each as he did.

"At least I will die with a full stomach," Jai said, as she munched.

"I think," Duwan said, "that we have much to learn from each other. When you are rested, we will talk."

6

It soon became apparent to Duwan that the female, Jai, was not the most articulate of Drinkers, that, indeed, her ignorance was astounding. Nor was he the most experienced of interrogators. His curiosity was great, but satisfying it was complicated by Jai's tendency to throw in words with which he was not familiar, words that did not have the sound of the only language Duwan had ever heard.

"Slowly, slowly," he said. "You speak of pong. What is or are pong?"

"I am pong."

"You are not Drinker, female?"

"I know not this word, Drinker."

"I am Drinker. All are Drinker."

"You have the basic form of pong, but more beautiful," she said. "Yet you could pass for Devourer."

"Again," he said, "I know not that word." Unless, he thought, it also meant Enemy. "Are the Devourers the Enemy?"

"Enemy?" She mused. "Does that mean one who is against you?"

"One who kills, who takes."

"They kill," she said, "so I suppose they are enemy."

Duwan sighed and looked up at the sky. "Long, long ago this Land of Many Brothers was the home of the Drinkers. The Enemy came from the south. You cannot be of the Enemy, for you are Drinker."

She looked puzzled. Irritated, he lifted her good

72

foot and pointed to an area of many small pores. "This shows that you are Drinker," he almost shouted. "Do these Devourers have such pores on the bottoms of their feet?"

"I have never had occasion to examine feet," she said.

Duwan reached for a tasty life organ from a nearby brother. Jai's eyes followed the movement of his hand. He sighed, plucked another life organ, handed it to her.

"You act as if the weeds are alive," she said.

"Alive? Of course they are alive."

"But not as we are alive, surely."

"All life is a oneness."

She looked away, moved uneasily.

"That troubles you?"

"Master," she said, "I cannot think in such lofty terms. I see myself, and then I see a weed."

"But this small, fixed brother," he touched a life organ gently, "feels, drinks the sun, and it can die."

She shrugged. "I am trying to understand."

"Both you and I and this small brother are of the earth and for the earth."

"At any rate," she said, "I am your pong."

"Just what does a pong do?" he asked.

"We work for the Devourers."

"Not for yourself, not for the group?"

"We are allowed to grow enough food to keep us alive, that is all we do for ourselves."

"To the north I saw ones who looked Drinker beating others who also looked Drinker with a lash," he said. "What way is that?"

"The way of Devourer and pong."

"Have you been beaten?"

"Not often," she said. "No more than three times. Once I was beaten unjustly, for something I didn't do."

He frowned. "Are you implying that it was just the other two times you were beaten?"

"I had erred," she said calmly, without resentment.

"The Devourers drive pongs to do their work for them, beat them. Why don't these pongs simply rise up and slay the Devourers?"

She laughed. "Impossible."

"Are there so many more Devourers than pongs?"

She looked puzzled. "No. No. We are many, but— Well, you simply don't understand. They are—mighty. They are—" She took a deep breath. "It is impossible."

"Are the Devourers immortal, cannot they be killed?"

"Oh, they die. I once saw a Devourer crushed by a falling tree."

"And was he not as dead as the animal I killed on the slope above?"

"Yes, but—"

"The pongs are many, the Devourers of lesser numbers and yet pongs do not fight."

"We have no weapons. They have the seed from which we grow our food. They control the animal pens from which we get our meat. We work only under supervision. We are alone only in the pongpen, at night."

"But you escaped."

She nodded.

"Have others done the same?"

"So it is said. I know of no one in my lifetime who has. One tried. He was caught and peeled and left to die slowly tied to a post in the central compound of the pen."

Gradually, Duwan began to piece together a picture of life in the Land of Many Brothers. The Enemy, called Devourer by Jai's people, lived mainly in cities built of stone, lived on the hard work of those called pongs who were, if they were like Jai, with pores in their feet, Drinker. It has been thus forever, according to Jai. It was the will of the dus— and this concept amused him, for there was only One Du, great, kind, life-giving Du—that it be thus, that the dus-favored Devourers enjoy the fruits of pong labor, living well off the bounty of the rich land.

Of the great truths of life Jai knew nothing. She did not even know that she drank life from Du, although it became obvious, after long questioning, that she had eaten nothing more than some rather tasteless and relatively unnourishing moss for many days. She knew that she felt good basking in the rays of Du, but she had no concept of why. Pongs, at work, covered themselves with poor garments woven from the poorest of material, under orders from their overlords that the rays of the sun, being harmful, were to be avoided. The main food, aside from flesh, that was consumed by pongs came from, if Jai's description could be believed, a grass-like brother that seeded hard, bland-tasting kernels that were then ground, mixed with water, and baked over fires. The plenty that existed around them, everywhere, in the fixed brothers, was forbidden to them, poisonous. Such teachings were drummed into all pong young at the hands of lash-wielding Devourers, and to taste of the good fruits of the brothers, except for certain berries and nuts, was punishable by death, if, indeed, the poisonous, forbidden things did not kill the unfortunate pong first.

Jai had seen pongs die of the poison. It occurred, she said, usually at the time of the new growth, when the land greened, and the sun warmed.

"They die badly," she said. "Just at this time, when there was still a hint of cold, and the green things were beginning to break through the earth, one was tossed into the pongpen, after having eaten green. He writhed and screamed and died with noxious discharges coming from his body openings."

"Did you see him eat the green brothers?"

"No, he did it in secrecy," she said, "for had anyone seen him he would have been reported."

"Yet you have eaten green and you are well."

"It is because of you, Master."

Having been at his frustrating questioning for most of a day, Duwan was restless. His thoughts kept going north, past the land of the waters, across the great barrens, past the land of the fires. "Tomorrow," he said, "you will take me to this city of the Devourers, so that I may see for myself."

Great tears sprang to her eyes.

"Du," he exploded, "why do you weep?"

"If you say that I am to die, it is well," she said.

"You will not die."

"I will die if we go to the city."

"I will see that you live."

"You are great, Master, but one against so many?" She sobbed. "I will be peeled. My skin will be tossed into the animal pens, and I will be suspended on a pole, and when I am dead I, too, will become slop for the animals."

"I must find someone who can talk sense," Duwan said to himself. He watched her weep until she subsided. She had heard his muttered comment, and it had given her hope.

"It is said, whispered in the pens at night, that those who have escaped in the past traveled far to the west, and that they live there, how I do not know, but that there are no overlords there. They would talk sense."

Duwan considered. Perhaps it would be too dangerous to visit a city. The Devourers he'd seen in the land of tall brothers to the north had appeared to be strong, capable, well armed. Yet, he had to know more than he could learn from this empty-headed female.

"Sleep," he ordered. "We will travel with the first light of Du."

Truly, the Land of Many Brothers was a land of promise, a land of plenty. He gorged himself on a variety of food that pleased him, and, as the days passed, he saw that Jai's frail, thin limbs were filling out, for she ate more constantly than he. She refused to accept the fact that the good, green, growing brothers were not poisonous, but continued to express her conviction that the magical powers of Duwan kept her alive after doing the forbidden. Duwan gave up trying to convince her.

She had no conception of brotherhood with living things. She knew nothing of the legends of immortality for Drinkers, of a life, different but full, of fixed contentment after a return to the earth. She listened respectfully when he spoke of such things, and once, in a whispering grove, he tried to get her to hear the unspoken, almost alien thoughts of old ones who had grown tall with endless years of sun, and wind, and rain.

"Almost I hear them," she said, but the look on her face told him that she was lying.

Jai's favorite topic of conversation was how she had guarded him while he slept, at one with the earth, how she'd climbed the tree to escape the great beast, and then how she'd fought it with Duwan's sword—all to protect him. It was as if she needed constant reassurance that, since she'd served him well, he would protect her. Almost every time she started to eat she would look at him, her purple eyes imploring, and say, "You have made it good?"

After several attempts to explain, once again, he gave up and merely nodded, or said, "Yes, it is good."

Although a variety of growth was the rule, the overall aspect of that good land was of many tall brothers, rushing streams, small hills. Twice they skirted isolated settlements, Jai trembling in fear when they came close enough to see Devourers driving their pongs. As they traveled toward the setting sun, day after day, Jai began to glow with health. She halfway believed Duwan's explanation that her body drank energy from the sun, and took to traveling without even so much as the tattered garment that scarcely covered her now. Time and again Duwan found his eyes going to her marked bud point, but he became accustomed to her lack of modesty.

Ahead, the low mountains began to rise into heavily covered mounds, each ridge reaching higher toward the sky. There, in a little valley, Duwan killed his first Enemy. As they followed a stream, now walking on mossy banks, now in the shallow, cool waters, he heard the telltale sounds of cutting tools and led Jai into the tall brothers to skirt another settlement. They crossed a well-traveled path after Duwan had looked carefully both ways and had listened, and they were into the cover of the forest again when he detected the sound of running footsteps. He told Jai to hide, and remain motionless, made his way silently back to the trail in time to see a young female, not many years past mobility, running toward him along the trail. She had large, green eyes that were widened in panic. Duwan's first impulse was to stop the female and find out what had frightened her, but he held back, for, just behind her, there ran a male, broad of shoulder and sturdy of body, a great longsword clanking at his thigh as he ran.

The trail opened into a small clearing on the bank of the stream and, as the running female entered it she tripped on a stone and fell heavily, could not get to her feet before the running male was on her, fell beside her, grasping her arms and holding her to the ground. Duwan growled in his throat and his right hand was on the hilt of his longsword.

"Don't be frightened, little one," the male said, and the words stopped Duwan.

The young female said, "But I do fear it, master," she said.

"It will hurt only for a little while," the male said, as

he ripped the female's scanty garment away to reveal a closed, young bud point that was scarcely visible.

Duwan relaxed. He did not approve of what was happening, but it was not unheard of for a male to indulge in play with an unripened female. Some couples, who had spoken for each other while very young, did, indeed, occupy the same dwelling in the valley, reveling in touching without grafting until they both ripened. He had, he felt, stumbled into such a play, and although the young female seemed to be frightened, he was sure that no harm would come to her.

He chilled when the male exposed himself and, with a grunt of effort, threw himself atop the small, young female. A piercing scream caused him to shiver in rage. From between the naked bodies he saw a quick, rich flow of blood, and, with a roar of outrage, he launched himself into the clearing. His roar brought the powerful, large male to his feet, and sent him lunging for his sword. Duwan took one look at the female and sick revulsion came. To force an unripe bud point was a crime that had never even occurred to him in his imagination.

"Ho, brother," the male said, sword in hand. "You startled me. Are you from—" Duwan did not catch the last word.

"Animal," Duwan said. "What have you done?"

The male looked puzzled. "This pong wench?"

"This female."

The male's sword came up. Duwan leaped. There was a clash of iron that caused sparks and then it was over, for the skill of the male was no match for Duwan's long training. His blade smashed bone, exposed the spongy brain and then he turned. The young female was bleeding badly, rich, vital blood gushing. But even as he ran to kneel beside her, to try to staunch the flow, the rush became an ooze and she was still.

"I mourn for you," he whispered.

He found Jai cringing in her hiding place.

"I heard the fighting," she said. "I feared for you."

Duwan, still feeling revulsion and pity, said nothing, started walking. She ran to catch him, saw the grimness of his face. "I heard a female scream."

"You do not want to hear," he said.

"The scream of pain that comes with bud opening," she said. "Am I not right?"

He looked at her in astonishment. "That animal forced her bud."

"Yes," she said.

He couldn't speak.

"How else?" she asked. "Otherwise, they would have to wait until nature opened the bud, sometimes many years."

Duwan swallowed. "You?"

"I was fortunate. The master who opened me was kind. And he was not large. When a master is large the female sometimes dies."

"I will go home," Duwan told himself. "I will tell them that we want nothing from this land of barbarism. I will tell them that we are best off where we are, even if Du visits only for a short period. I will tell them that immortality is not an end to seek, that returning to the earth is, indeed, a splendid wish, but not as vital as being civilized, not as important as loving one's fellows, as working together, as honoring Du, and as loving one's spoken choice."

"Did you kill a master?" Jai asked, later.

He nodded.

"They will follow."

"Let them," he said, thinking that it would be pleasant for his sword to drink the blood of creatures who beat and killed their brothers.

"They will have smellers to follow our trail, and they will be many and well armed."

"What is a smeller?"

"They are small, but have sharp teeth."

"Du, female, speak straight. Answer my question," he roared.

She cringed away. "They live in the houses of the Devourer masters and eat scraps and sometimes, when a pong is difficult, they allow them to chew upon the pong's feet and legs—"

"Animals that can smell our trace?"

"Yes, yes," she said eagerly. "We must find water, and walk in it for a long way."

Duwan mused. The settlements had been small. He estimated that no more than four or five could be mustered for the chase, and if they were no more skilled in weaponry than the one he'd killed—"We will leave a trace to be followed easily," he said.

He saw his pursuers from the top of a ridge early the next morning. They were moving fast, following a scrambling pack of small, lightly furred animals restrained on leashes. He spent the next few hours selecting his spot, and chose a pass between two sheer slopes, where no more than two of them could face him at one time. He rested there, after drinking his fill at a stream, and positioned Jai among rocks high on the side of the hill.

"The sniffers will find me and bite me," she wailed.

He gathered stones the size of his fist and piled them in front of her. "Should an animal try to come to you hit him with a stone."

She seized a stone and held it with both hands. "We can still run. We can follow the stream. The sniffers cannot follow us if we walk in the water, for the water washes away our trace."

"Peace," he said. "You have a view of the approach. When you see them coming, make this bird sound." He demonstrated the cooing sigh of a bird of the far north and, after a few attempts, she made an acceptable imitation. Then he went below, sat on a large boulder, and examined the cutting edges of his swords.

It was growing late when he heard Jai's first attempt, and then heard her succeed in making a cooing sound that would not have fooled the youngest Drinker in the valley. He rose, stood with his feet spread, his weapons hanging at his side. He heard the careless, scrambling approach from below, and as the pursuers neared, he counted four males and six of the small, snarling animals. He wished for a bow and a quiver of arrows, but when he'd left the valley he'd had only one hand and no need of a bow.

He had been spotted. The four below were surprised. They halted and stared up at him and consulted among themselves. Duwan stood motionless, his swords in their sheaths. One of the males below bent and, one by one, released the sniffers, pointed, barked an order, and the six animals began to slink up the hill, following the trace left by Duwan and Jai. When the leading sniffer spotted Duwan the fur raised into a crest on its back and it leaped forward with a whining snarl. The others followed. Duwan's swords flashed as he drew them, and he met the first sniffer's leap toward his stomach with flashing blade, caught the next in midair with the backswing, stabbed deeply into the barrel chest of a third. The fourth managed to sink sharp teeth painfully into his lower leg as he dispatched five and six with both hands working in perfect coordination, and then the chewer whined for only a moment as iron bit into its spine.

Startled shouts from below. The four Devourers rushed toward him together, and then, as they reached the narrow pass, the two larger took the lead, swords at the ready. Duwan gave ground until he had reached the pre-chosen position which gave him some advantage. The two enemy had to come at him face on, unable to split up and get him between them. He parried an angry lunge with his shortsword and measured the skill of the second man with a feint of his longsword. The clash of metal echoed off the hillsides. Behind the two fighting Devourers the other two yelled encouragement. Duwan buried his longsword a hand's width into the heart of one, opened the throat of the other. Two dead lay at his feet and he retreated a few steps so that there would be no danger of stumbling over the dead as the other two fighters moved forward, their dark eyes shifting, a new caution upon them.

One showed himself, immediately, to be more skilled. Duwan concentrated on that one, while holding off the other with his parrying shortsword. This one had a dangerous straight lunge that followed a feint with the shortsword, and Duwan was forced backward as metal clashed on metal. He gained a new respect for the Enemy. He knew that he was going to be hard pressed, for the pass was opening, and soon the last two could pin him between them. He had to make a move. He lunged and parried and spun away from the more skilled swordsman and in his spinning sent his longsword hissing horizontally to decapitate the lesser of his two enemies, continued the whirling spin just in time to parry a lunge with his shortsword. Then he gained ground, looked upon his foe with his orange eyes full of fire.

"Come," he said, "come to me, Enemy."

"Who are you?" the other gasped.

"Your death," Duwan said, leaping, feeling a great shock in his right hand as his mighty blow was parried, but with quick, instinctive movement, half falling, thrusting his shortsword to its hilt into his opponent's stomach. He narrowly avoided a downswing of the fighter's dying, last stroke, and then all was quiet.

"Duwan, behind you," he heard Jai scream, and he spun, bringing up both swords to the ready, to see so many others that, at first, his heart quailed, then rallied as he lifted both his swords high.

"Du," he roared, using his full voice. The sound

echoed and reechoed from the hillsides. "Du, be with me."

"Peace, warrior," a male cried, holding up both of his hands, empty. "Peace."

Duwan's chest was heaving. His orange eyes lanced fire.

"We are not the Enemy, warrior," the man said, his hands still exposed in a plea for friendship. "Who kills the Devourer is not our enemy."

Duwan panted, his eyes took in the ragged, scarecrow ranks of the males who faced him, more than twenty of them, crude bows on their shoulders and, in some cases, in hand, but no arrows pointed toward him.

"Who are you, warrior?" the spokesman asked.

He was full of elation, his heart still pounding with the heady joy of the fight. They had called him warrior, and warrior he was. In the back of his mind he called out to his trainer, to Belran the Leader, a great, unspoken shout of thanks, and then, because he, at last, had discovered the reason for all those long, long hours of drudgery in training, he lifted his face to catch the last red rays of a sinking Du and roared, "Duwan! Duwan! I am Duwan the Drinker."

His roar echoed, became a loud, slowly diminishing growl of sound that reverberated, then sank into a murmur and then silence.

A small, emaciated male stepped forth from the ranks of the newcomers, fell to his knees.

"Lord," he said. "Master."

And then, one by one, the others followed suit.

7

The ragged, emaciated group of males shifted uneasily in the face of Duwan's triumphant roar. Only one stood, a bit taller than the others, thin but with stringy, powerful muscles in his arms and legs. When the others fell to their knees he was the last to kneel, and even then his face was up, his dull gray eyes wide.

"Rise," Duwan ordered. "There is no need to kneel to me."

The tall one rose, stepped forward. "Master, we wish no harm to you, nor to anyone."

The newcomers had no weapons other than the obviously inferior bows. "Who are you?" Duwan asked.

"We are free runners. I am Tambol, called The Hunter, for the accuracy and strength of my bow."

"Let me see the bottom of your foot." Duwan said, stepping closer, both hands still filled with his bloodied weapons.

Tambol did not look surprised. He stood on one leg and lifted his left foot. Duwan saw the telltale pores. "Are the others like this?"

"How, Lord?"

"With the small, dark pores, thus," Duwan said, brushing the sole of Tambol's foot with the tip of his longsword.

"I—I—don't know," Tambol said.

"Have them sit upon the ground and lift their feet," Duwan ordered, and it was done, and he saw the pores on all and then stood, facing them. "You have escaped the slave pens of the enemy?"

"Only a few living have," Tambol answered. "Most are sons of those who escaped long ago."

"Are you many?" Duwan asked.

"No, not many, Master," Tambol said.

"And do you kill the Enemy?"

Tambol shivered. "No, Master. In fact, we must run from this place, but first we must bury the masters, and their sniffers, hoping that they will never be found, for to kill a master brings the army of Farko. This has not happened in my lifetime, but once it did, and only a few free runners survived."

Duwan looked thoughtfully at the sky. Du was nearing the midpoint. "Do it, then," he said. He walked to the slope and called up to Jai, who descended nervously. The runners were busying themselves in digging. Tambol, seeing Jai, came hurrying to bow before Duwan and cast suspicious glances at the female.

"This is a pong female, Master," Tambol said.

"This is a Drinker female," Duwan said.

"She was being chased by the masters with sniffers," Tambol said. "We are in great danger. We must run, and we will have to abandon our homes to flee farther into the west."

"I escaped long ago," Jai said. "Those whom my master killed were not chasing me, but him."

"Master," Tambol said, "I know not who you are. Now I think you are Devourer, and again not. You are mighty, and I beg your mercy. There are those among us who fear that you are a pong-catcher, and that your actions are designed to trick us, to influence us to lead you to our homes so that all free runners may be taken to be peeled on the stakes of Farko."

"He came from the earth," Jai said, "as in the prophesy of old."

Tambol's eyes widened.

"It is true," Jai said. "For as he grew from the earth
like a divine flower I guarded him, and even kept
him from being devoured by a farl. Is this not true,
master?"

Duwan hid a smile. "It is true."

Tambol bowed low. As the digging to hide the
bodies of the Devourers had begun, he had received
much whispered advice. "We must kill him," he'd
been told. "Obviously he is a Devourer," another had
said. "That he has not killed us means nothing. He
waits to ensnare all, our females, our young."

"And who will face one who can kill four masters
with such ease?" Tambol had asked.

"All will leap upon him at once," someone said.

"And many will die," Tambol had said.

Now the bodies were buried, branches had been
used to erase tracks and the signs of struggle, and
the free runners were moving uneasily toward the
point where Duwan and Jai faced Tambol. Tambol
turned to face his fellows. "We will run swiftly now,"
he said, "to put distance between us and this place of
death."

Duwan and Jai found it easy to keep the pace set
by Tambol. Behind them, however, the weaker members began to straggle, so that when Tambol called a
halt, in a hidden valley where there was water, it
took some time for all twenty of the free runners to
join the main group.

"Now I will speak to you," Duwan said, standing
on a rock beside the stream. "You need not fear me. I
am Drinker, and I come from far to the north.
There we, too, are free. I am not of the Enemy."
He lifted one foot. "Look. See the small, black pores
that mark the Drinker, then examine your own feet.
We are of a blood, you and I. There are secrets I will
tell you, secrets hidden from you by your masters,
the Enemy. Listen to me, and hear me with an open
mind, and you will no longer be hungry. Listen to

me and it may be that in the future we, the Drinkers, will fight side by side with the free runners to take back this Land of Many Brothers that was once ours."

"Madness," someone muttered.

"I have learned much about you in this short time," Duwan said, "merely by observation. "You hunt in a pack of twenty for the small, helpless animals of the forests. You take life, and get in return only enough food to keep you weak, and thin, when you could be swollen with the goodness of the earth, of which you are, for which you are."

"Would you have us eat the green poisons?" Tambol asked.

"Only in your own minds are the good things of the earth poison," Duwan said. "For you have been told this by the enemy, with one intent, to keep you ignorant of the fact that you, Drinkers all, could live on the bounty of the land without depending upon the Devourer's seeds, and his cultivated fields, and his animal flesh."

A low moaning began and spread through the group. "Master," a quavering voice moaned, "if you mean death for us, make it swift, as you made it swift for the masters, not slow and painful from the poison."

"He has magic," Jai said. Duwan motioned for her to be still.

"Who will trust me?" Duwan asked. When there was no volunteer, he turned to Tambol. Tambol lowered his head and was silent.

Duwan, frustrated, glared out at them. Jai whispered at his side. "Show them a magic, Lord, and they will believe."

"I have no magic," Duwan spat. He turned to Tambol. "Do you know nothing of your origin?"

"Yes Master," Tambol said. "We are children of an unholy union between Aang the Devourer and the animals of the fields, and we are called unclean, although we had no choice, for it was Aang, father of the devourers, who sinned and soiled the earth with his lust. It is the punishment of the dus that Aang lives atop the high mountains and looks down each day to see his unholy children working to atone for his original sin of lust."

"So you were told by the Enemy?" Duwan asked.

"So it is written," Tambol said.

It was evident that the free runners were as ignorant of the true nature of things as Jai. The Enemy had, indeed, done a skillful job of indoctrination. Further questioning revealed to Duwan that, as in Jai's case, all had been taught from childhood—in the case of the free runners not even by the Devourers but by their own parents, for so strong was the indoctrination that generations of free runners had perpetuated the myths—that to share the sweet food of the green brothers brought sure, painful death, that the rays of Du were harmful, and that the body was to be protected from the rays at all times.

Tambol and his fellows wore ragged, dirty garments that covered all portions of their bodies save hands and feet. A loose hood half-hid the face.

It was also evident to Duwan that he was not trusted. He saw fear and something else in the faces and eyes of those who stood before him.

"I will speak with your wise men," Duwan said, "your elders, your Predictor."

"So be it," Tambol said.

The free runners lived within the earth. In a narrow, hidden valley, accessible without great effort only through a narrow, steep-walled canyon from which flowed a small stream, they had burrowed into the hillsides like animals, concealing the openings to their caves with brush and stones. Males with bows that would have been almost useless against anything larger than a tree animal guarded the canyon. As the hunting party marched up the valley, heads appeared

from the caves in the hillsides, and soon a crowd
followed. The hunters carried only a few small, furry
carcasses, and some females, seeing the scarcity of
food, began to wail. A scuffle broke out as one hunter
left the party to join his female and his young and
others tried to take his prize, one small, pathetic tree
animal.

"We have done wrong in coming here, master," Jai
whispered. "These live like animals."

Duwan kept his right hand on the hilt of his
longsword. The runners were thin and weak, but
they were many, and the presence of Duwan and Jai
among the hunters left in their wake a buzz of talk.

Tambol, in silence, led them onward, as the other
hunters dropped off one by one to be met with
rejoicing or weeping depending on whether they
carried flesh.

The way led to the head of the valley, where the
stream dropped from high rocks to fall with a roar
into a broad, clear pool. There, facing a sheer rock
wall, Tambol halted. "I will inform the elders of your
presence," he said, and then disappeared into a natural stone cave. Jai clung to Duwan's arm and looked
around fearfully.

"Master," she whispered, as males began to drift up
the valley toward them, bows in hand, "we can run.
You are mighty, and you will have to kill only a few
of them and then they will not try to stop us. We can
go far away and live fatly upon the good green that
you bless of its poison."

Duwan did not answer. He, too, had noted the
approaching males, and he feared their puny bows
less than their numbers. If they were determined
enough, if enough of them would die, they could
overcome him by their sheer mass.

He heard a tapping sound from within the cave
and tensed, thinking that perhaps attack would come
from two sides, but an ancient one appeared, his

eyelids massed into wrinkles, squinting at the sun, his hair long, sere, and his body stiffened with the hardening disease. The tapping had come from the walking stick he used. He seemed disoriented at first, his watery eyes looking everywhere but at Duwan. Behind him there appeared other oldsters and behind them Tambol.

"I am Farnee, Eldest of the free runners," the old one said. "Come closer, warrior, for I see you but dimly."

Jai held tight to Duwan's arm as he stepped closer. "I bring you greetings of the blood of the Drinkers from the far north," Duwan said.

"How?" Farnee asked, cupping a hand to his ear.

"He says he is from the far north," another of the old ones shouted into Farnee's ear.

Farnee nodded ponderously. "And yet we are told by Tambol that is it said you come from the earth."

"We are all of the earth and for the earth," Duwan said. "Perhaps, honored one, we could be seated, where you will be more comfortable."

After that suggestion was imparted, in a shout, to Farnee, he nodded and, without speaking, turned and hobbled back into the cave. Duwan followed, and the others fell in behind him and Jai. Farnee seated himself on a stone covered with patched, stitched furs, leaned on his stick, and blinked in the dimness, lit by an open fire. The others ranged around the stone in a circle, surrounding Duwan and Jai.

"Now," Farnee said, "who has seen this one come from the earth?"

"I," Jai said defiantly.

"And you are?" Farnee asked, at last finding her with his eyes.

"I am Jai."

"You are not a free runner, by your dress, female," an elder said. "You expose your hide to the sun as the Devourers do."

"I escaped from the pongpens of the city of Arutan," Jai said, "many months past. I saw this lord, growing from the rich earth, a divine flower. I saw this with my eyes, and I have seen, since, his magic, for he eats, and makes it possible for me to eat, the green poisons and grow fat."

"Ha," someone grunted.

"Enough," Duwan said. "I am Duwan the Drinker and I have come from the far north, past the land of fires, through the lands of the iron cold and the snows. That is all you need know of me, except that I come in friendship to all who oppose our Enemy, who wrested this land of Many Brothers from us in the time of the Great Alon."

"Alon," someone whispered. "He speaks of the du."

"I speak of Alon, the Great Leader, who took our people to the north to escape the all-devouring enemy. I come to determine the strength of this enemy, to find those who would stand by our side as we reclaim our land."

There was a buzz of talk among the seated elders. Farnee raised one hardened hand and made a sound in his throat and the elders fell silent.

"What do you know of our ancient legends, strange one?" Farnee asked.

"Enough to call ignorance and enemy lies by name when I am told that Drinkers are unholy offspring of a Devourer and animals of the field," Duwan said.

Farnee nodded gravely. "That is the teaching we allow our young to hear until they have reached an age of wisdom," he said.

Behind the elders, Tambol stirred uneasily.

"Yes, my son," Farnee said, pointing his stick at Tambol, "you, too." He looked back at Duwan. "To tell the young the truth would inflame their spirits, and then there would be war and death, death for all free runners in a war we could not hope to win."

"And what is the age of wisdom?" Duwan asked.

"When the hide hardens, and the fires of youth are cooled," an elder said.

"That is to say when one has reached the age where fighting would be impossible," Duwan said, and Farnee nodded.

"If you have come to stir our young ones to war, we will not allow it," Farnee said.

"Father," said Tambol, moving to stand rather belligerently inside the circle of elders, "if we are not spawn of Aang, than what are we?"

"You see what you have done?" Farnee asked.

"All this land was once ours," Duwan said. "The Enemy came from the south, and we were a peaceable people, without skill in arms, so that by the time we learned we were overrun, and it was then, to save enough of the race to regenerate it, that the Great Alon led the Drinkers to the north, fighting a rearguard action all the way, losing many."

"Enough," Farnee said. "I will speak." He rose unsteadily and gazed at Tambol. "This is for your ears only, my son. I trust, although you are still young and your hide has not begun to harden, that you will have gained enough wisdom from me, your father, to heed my words after you hear."

Farnee seated himself, gazed at the smoke-colored ceiling of the cave. "It is as the strange one says," he said softly. "We were called, although I know not why, Drinkers. We were, the legends say, many. And we lived in peace and plenty. We could not stand against the invaders, for they had weapons of iron. But there were wise men among us, and those wise men sought peace, for it was better to live as pongs, they said, than to die on the sharp points of the masters' weapons. That is all. The rest, uttered by this strange one, is invention."

"But when this Duwan mentioned a name you knew it," Tambol said. "This Alon?"

"One of the many minor dus," an elder said. "Du of death. An unpleasant du, and thus, largely forgotten."

"Hold," another elder said, rising. "Some things we have kept within the circle of elders, but we have never lied overtly to our young. I will not lie now."

"Be quiet," Farnee said.

"No," the standing elder said stoutly. "Tambol is soon to be a member of this circle and he will know then, so I think he should be told all now."

"Tell him," another elder said.

The standing elder looked directly into Duwan's eyes. The elder's eyes were pink with age, but still clear and alert. "We whisper this legend among ourselves, the elders. It speaks of the free Drinkers who fled the wrath of the masters, fighting, slaying the invincible, but being slain themselves. The legend has no name for a leader. You say Alon, and if that, indeed, was his name then it is understandable why he has come to be called a du of death, for the bodies of Drinker and Devourer littered the land leading northward."

The old man paused and looked around the circle. "When I was but a new mobile, in the pongpens of Arutan, my mother whispered this story to me. In the lands of ice, to the far north, there are free ones, fierce warriors, ones who escaped, and from them will come a new master, one of supernatural abililty who will lead all pongs to freedom. You have all heard this legend."

"And more," said another elder, standing. "I note that this female maintains that the strange one came from the earth. All elders have heard this prophesy, for it, too, was whispered among the hopeless in the pongpens of old. *He will come from the earth, from the deep, rich, sweet depths of the earth, and he will be mighty, and in his strength and wisdom he will teach us, and deliver us.*"

"He is mighty," Tambol said. "I saw him kill four Devourers. This I saw with these eyes." He faced Duwan. "Are you this new master, sent to deliver us?"

Duwan was slow to answer. He wished for opportunity to consult with his father, with Manoo the Predictor, with other wise ones among the Drinkers. But he was alone. He was beginning to get a picture of the state of things in the Land of Many Brothers, and he did not like what he saw. According to the free runners, the Enemy was many, was invincible, and yet he'd killed the Enemy without being sorely tested. He longed for home, longed for the welcome sight of the beautiful face of Alning, and the feel of his father's limbs entwining in greeting. He had information. Should he not ease the minds of these poor, deluded ex-slaves? Should he not assure them that they were best advised in keeping to their own meager lifestyle? They would hunger, and grow old before their time, in the midst of plenty, but who was he to try to erase generations of superstition? That would best be left to older, wiser heads, if, after his return to the valley, it was decided to return to the Land of Many Brothers. And yet there was doubt in him. The Devourers were many, and lived in stone cities. The Drinkers of the North were few. He could not afford to risk the loss of potential allies.

"Are you this new master?" Tambol repeated.

"Only you have used the word 'master'," Duwan said.

"But did you come from the earth?" Tambol insisted.

"There is no simple answer to that question."

"Is it true that this female, Jai, saw you with feet and legs implanted, that you remained thus for weeks, that you then came from the earth when a farl attacked the female?"

"That is true," Duwan said.

"He is the Master," Jai blurted. "For he also speaks with the trees, as to the spirits of the departed."

This had to be repeated, loudly, for Farnee. Around the circle elders were whispering to each other.

"I am surprised," Farnee said. "For that bit of

superstitution is as old as the race, and long since discredited. It is said that you eat of the the green, growing things. If you, as this female hints, subscribe to that ancient, dark, barbaric belief, why then, as it is reported to me, do you eat of the so-called green brothers?"

"I, too, eat of them," Jai said, "for they are made clean by his magic."

A sign came from the gathered elders.

"Do you have powers unknown to us?" Tambol asked.

Duwan again thought carefully before answering. "Unknown to you, yes, but not peculiar to myself, for all Drinkers have the same powers. All of you can grow fat on the green plenty of this land. All of you can draw sustenance from the blessed rays of Du. You can become one with the earth, with filaments that will grow from the pores in your feet. You can be healed by the good earth, and you can even regenerate a missing limb, as I did, when this female watched me as I was a part of the earth."

There was a general gasp of shock and disbelief.

"This, too, is true," Jai said, "for when I first saw the master his left arm was the size of the arm of a newly sprouted young one. It grew and became strong, as you see."

"Superstitious nonsense," Farnee said. He rose. "I have decided. This strange one, this who calls himself Drinker, and Duwan, has been affected by the harmful rays of the sun to which he exposed himself. And so it is with the female, for you see, yourselves, how she is colored by the harmful rays. That he knows some of the secrets of the elders is his only claim, and I know not how he came into such secrets. Perhaps by contact with other free runners, for it is said that there are other groups, farther to the west. At any rate, I reject his claims."

Duwan nodded. "Then I will go as I came, in peace," he said.

"Wait," Tambol protested. "The Council of Elders has not voted."

"You are not yet a member of this council," Farnee told Tambol. "It is not your place to call for a vote."

"We will have a vote," one of the elders said.

"So be it," Farnee said. "All who vote with me, Eldest of the free runners, will stand."

All but two of the elders stood.

"So be it," Farnee said. "Go in peace, strange one. You are doomed to die, doomed to be peeled by the Devourers, and I warn you, on pain of action, not to remain in our land, lest, in your delusion, you lead the Devourers to us. Is that understood?"

"May peace be with you," Duwan said, although he was bristling at the threat. He took Jai's arm and she looked up at him wide-eyed. He turned, stepped over the legs of a seated elder, and made his way into the sunlight. Before him the males of the runners were gathered, some with bows in hand. With a snarl, he drew his weapons.

"I came in peace, to give you hope," he said. "I am cast out. It is up to you whether or not I go in peace."

He thrust Jai behind him and holding his two swords at the ready, moved forward at a swift walk. The males of the runners melted from his path in silence. As he exited the valley through the narrow, rocky cleft, walking on stones protruding from the streambed, a volley of crooked, ineffectual arrows fell to his rear, causing Jai to scream in fear. Duwan, who had seen the runner males creeping among the tall brothers, did not even glance back.

8

Duwan sat moodily on a carpet of fallen needles. A storm was brewing, and its advance winds sighed through the upper branches of the tall brothers. The fire flickered and eddied in the gusts. A dead limb fell quite near the fire and, although she had seen before how certain trees seemed to give to Duwan of their deadwood, Jai started. They had halted only with the coming of darkness, having by then put several ridges and valleys between them and the valley of the free runners.

"Master, are you angry with me?" Jai asked.

Duwan shook his head without looking at her.

"You have not spoken to me, have not called my name since we left those weak ones."

"Forgive me," Duwan said. "I have much to ponder."

Jai broke up the fallen limb and placed some of it on the fire. From a distance came the warm, sweet smell of rain. "We will have a wet camp tonight," she said.

Duwan had not spread his sleep covering. Jai lifted his pack and began to unfold the material. Duwan remained silent, staring into the flickering flames, as she used dead sticks to form the covering into a canopy.

"There," she said, "you will sleep dry."

A patter of large drops made a soft murmur on the trees. It was a whispering grove, and the distant, sighing communications of ancient Drinkers mixed in Duwan's mind with the sound of the wind, the patter of raindrops. Then the storm was upon them. Jai cringed with the flash and rumble of it; and the rain penetrated the overhead foliage and began to wet them. Duwan, aroused from his thoughts, crawled underneath the canopy. Jai sat huddled by the hissing fire as it fought to survive in the increasing rainfall.

"Come," Duwan said, motioning to her to join him. She came gladly, curled herself, being careful not to touch him.

"You will have a wet backside," Duwan said, with a chuckle, as he observed that her rear protruded into the rain. She moved closer to him and they touched.

"Forgive me," she whispered, drawing back.

"Come," he said, putting his hand on her waist to pull her into cover. She edged closer, felt his body heat on her flank.

She was shivering. He could feel it as his arm lay loosely across her waist. "You're cold," he said.

"Yes, Master," she whispered, although her shivering was not from cold.

"We must think about getting some proper clothing," he said.

"Yes, Master," she whispered.

"Give me your back," he said, pushing her into turning onto her side. "I will warm you." He pulled her to him, spoon fashion, and held her tightly with his arm. "Better?"

"Thank you, Master," she said.

"It is time we made something clear," he said. "You are no longer a slave. No one is your master. It does not please me to be called master."

"Yes," she said, still shivering. Then, to distract her mind from his closeness, "If you will kill animals I can make us garments from their fur. I have never done it, but I noted that the women of the runners wore such garments and perhaps I can learn to make them."

"We will not take life," he said.

"As you will it," she said.

"You're still cold?"

"Yes." Then, after a pause, "No."

"No?"

"Your touch—the feel of your body—"

Duwan felt his face grow warm. He started to push her away, but did not. "These things affect you?"

"You are very beautiful, Mas—" She paused. "Do you feel it?"

"I feel the warmth of you," he said.

"Shall I make you feel more?"

"This is a newness to me," he said. "I cannot will the heat of ripeness."

"Ah," she said.

"And you, is the feeling of ripeness with you always?"

"Not always."

"But you can graft without the ripeness?"

"With the ripeness, there is fruiting. Without the ripeness only pleasure."

"Very strange," Duwan said.

She turned in his arms, lay facing him. Her soft arms went around him. "You saved me," she whispered, "and I have nothing to give you in return except myself. If I can give you pleasure—"

He felt her bud point swelling, opening, a ripe, warm, soft pressing against his stomach. He felt his body stir and his blood sing in excitement. He told himself that it was the custom among these strange Drinkers in the Land of Many Brothers. He was alone, far from home. He was discouraged. He was warmed by her, and he felt himself begin to open and then, as if by signal, the whisperings came to him from the ancient brothers, a mixed, incomprehensible murmuring that grew and grew until, not in words but in pictures, he saw a flowering land of virgin green, saw Drinkers, strong, active, happy, and he knew that he was looking into the distant past.

Then, as his body burned, as Jai pressed herself closer, as her face touched his and her lips were warm and moist on his, he saw a vision of the endless tall brothers of the far north, and, as if he were a bird, he was soaring over the land of the snows, the land of the big waters, into the barrens and in the distance he saw the smokes of the land of fires and soared past them, high, to look down into the valley in the time of the long light. There were his father, his mother, his grandmother, all the Drinkers. And there, sitting alone, was Alning.

He clung to the vision and communicated with his mind. "Brothers," he said, "who among you has seen this? How can you show me this?"

And from the whisperings in his mind there emerged a clear voice. "None have seen save you, brother."

And then the whisperings were incomprehensible again and he was gently pushing Jai away. "You have offered me something of great value. Do not be insulted."

She, trembling, tried to touch him at the bud point and he caught her wrist and held her hand away. "Sister," he said, "I do not reject you, for you are sweet and precious. I reject an act that is against my code, my teachings."

"I understand, Master," she said, trying to pull away.

"No," he said, "stay. Give me your back so that we can share warmth, for after the rain the night will be chill."

He awoke with the light of Du strong, with birds singing in the tall brothers overhead, but it had been a noise not in keeping with the grove that had awakened him. Jai lay by his side, facing him, one of her legs thrown across his thighs. He pushed her away gently so as not to awaken her, rose silently, reached for his weapons. Again there came the sound, and he flowed in smooth, silent motions toward it. Someone was coming toward him, not being too careful about being quiet. He hid himself behind a large tall brother and waited. The intruder was walking swiftly and as he neared Duwan sprang out, longsword raised. He halted the downstroke in time to avoid splitting the head of Tambol the Hunter.

"Master," Tambol gasped.

"You have narrowly escaped death," Duwan said. "In future, should such a need arise, it would be best to announce your coming."

"Forgive me, Master," Tambol said. "I have traveled hard, and throughout most of the night to overtake you."

"For what purpose?"

"I will go with you," Tambol said. "I will hunt for you, prepare your food for you."

Duwan laughed. "Would you have me become as skinny as you?"

Tambol lowered his head. "I can but do my best, Master."

"So you will go with me," Duwan said. "And yet you know not where I go."

"No matter. I am sick to death of hiding. I will fight by your side. I will die as a Drinker, for after you left I questioned the elders and now I am convinced that you speak the truth, and that this land was once ours."

"Perhaps it will not be necessary to die," Duwan said. He motioned Tambol forward, and they joined Jai, who was just awakening. "Sit, and we will eat," Duwan said. He gathered food, came to sit facing Tambol and Jai, placed the good, green life organs in Jai's outstretched hands, then gave a portion to Tambol. "To be with me," he said, "it will be necessary to open your eyes and your mind, to cast off the misinformation that the Enemy has used to poison your thinking."

Tambol's face went slack. He lifted a bit of food and sniffed it, saw Jai eating eagerly, watched as Duwan munched. He lifted his face and was, obviously, praying to some du. Then, eyes closed, he ate. Surviving, he obeyed Duwan's orders, as the day's march got underway, to expose portions of his body gradually to the rays of the sun. This death, he thought, would be slow, but he had decided to put himself into the hands of the Master.

Still alive, and sampling tidbits of green as he marched, Tambol saw that the way led toward the east. He remarked on this in the middle of the afternoon. Duwan nodded. "My mission is to assess the strength of the enemy, to learn his habits and his methods of warfare. To do this I must go among him."

"We will be in the area of settlements soon," Tambol said. "Instruct me, Master, so that I may kill the enemy at your side."

Duwan took Tambol's bow and flexed it. "This would prick a warrior just enough to make him angry," he said.

Tambol's face fell.

"Soon we will obtain proper weapons for you," Duwan said. "And clothing."

It was two more days' march before they saw signs of settlement. Now Duwan marched carefully. When he heard the distant sound of axes he instructed Jai and Tambol to move silently behind him. As they neared the sounds of activity Duwan heard a moan, a cry of despair and pain, and his skin crawled.

"Did you hear that?" Jai whispered from behind his shoulder.

He turned to look at her in surprise, for the moaning cry was the death sound of an ancient Drinker who had gone back to the earth. "You heard?"

"I think I heard," Jai said. "It was not a sound as a sound is usually made—"

He smiled. "You *are* Drinker," he said.

"I heard nothing," Tambol whispered.

Duwan led the way forward. He saw a typical Devourer settlement, a hut made of the living boles of tall brothers, a clearing, fields growing the tall grass with the small, brown nut, a single Devourer overseer, lash in hand, standing by as two pongs began to trim the fallen tall brother. He strode boldly into the clearing and was seen, first, by one of the slaves. Then the Enemy turned and gazed at Duwan in puzzlement. The Enemy hailed him in his own language. Duwan walked with long strides toward him. The Enemy spoke again.

"I know not your barbaric tongue," Duwan said.

"Halt where you are," the Enemy said, in words that Duwan understood. The overseer's sword seemed to leap into his hand. Duwan drew his weapons. With a snarl, the Enemy charged forward, sending what was intended to be a decapitating blow toward Duwan. Iron clashed and Duwan's shortsword drew blood. The two pongs fell to the ground, moaning, prostrating themselves before Duwan. Tambol emerged from the trees.

"Watch these," Duwan said, turning to walk toward the hut.

The door was open. Odd smells came from within. Duwan peered inside and almost lost his nose as a blade hissed down just in front of his face. He swung backhanded with his longsword and the blade split the belly of a female who had been hiding beside the door. Duwan saw her fall, saw the spurting of blood, and, although he was saddened, turned away to examine the interior of the hut. There were a crude table and chairs, a bed, an open fireplace in which hung a black, iron kettle. The odd smell seemed to be coming from the kettle. He walked across the small room and tilted the pot with his sword and his stomach rebelled, pouring bitterness upward into his throat. Stewing in the white sauce were the arms and legs of an infant. He turned and ran from the room. Jai was there in the front yard. Tambol waited with the two pongs.

"What ails you?" Jai asked.

Duwan was unable to speak. Jai pushed past him and went into the room. She came back quickly, the shortsword that the enemy female had wielded in her hand. "I now have a weapon," she said. Duwan stood, stunned. "Is it that you have killed a female?"

He was silent.

"You need not be concerned," Jai said. "When I was among them, I dreaded working for the females, for they are worse than the males. Her sword was in her hand. You did right in killing her, for she would have gladly killed you."

"In the pot—" Duwan said.

Jai looked thoughtful, disappeared back into the hut, came back gnawing on a tiny forearm. Duwan screamed in rage and the back of his hand sent the forearm flying, and sent Jai spinning to the ground. He stepped toward her, his outrage causing him to see the light of Du as seething crimson. He raised his sword, for it was his intention to end this abomination, this creature who would eat the flesh of her own kind. He did not see that Tambol had hurried across the yard and as his sword fell Tambol clung to his arm and deflected it so that it sank into the ground with the force of the blow.

"Master, Master," Tambol cried, as Duwan tossed him aside with a sweep of his arm and jerked the sword from the earth. Jai was crawling away, screaming silently.

Sanity returned to Duwan. He lifted his face to the sun and an anguished roar came irom his throat. Jai froze. Tambol picked himself up and looked fearfully at Duwan.

"Animals," Duwan hissed, looking first at Jai and then at Tambol. "You are animals."

"Master," Jai sobbed, "what did I do to offend you?"

Duwan slumped. "The fault is mine," he said.

"Master," Jai said, "is it that I do not eat enough of the green? Is it that I am not to taste the savory flesh of a Devourer sacrifice?"

"Tell me this new horror," Duwan said, still tasting bitterness in his mouth.

"The sacrifice dinner is eaten at the change of the season," Jai said, her sobs lessening as she saw Duwan grow calmer. "It is in praise of the du of plenty, and if the sacrifice is not made, and the meal not eaten, untimely rains will rot the crops, or the sun will burn them, or the snows will come late and kill the tender shoots."

Duwan looked in revulsion at the small forearm, now covered with dirt and small twigs after its roll along the ground.

"I had never had the opportunity to sample this sacred food, being pong," Jai said. "Did I do wrong?"

"The young one, pong or Devourer?" Duwan asked.

"Pong," Jai said.

Duwan sighed, voiced an urgent prayer to Du in his mind, looked around as if he were just awakening. "We need clothing," he said. "Jai, go into the hut and find something for yourself. Tambol, we will wear the garments of the enemy. You, female, bring me garments, for I will not reenter that place."

Jai came back quickly and watched with approval as Duwan donned the blouse and kilt of the Enemy. She, herself, was reveling in luxury, as she tried the garments of the dead female. Tambol was standing by, waiting a chance to speak. When Duwan was fully dressed he saw that Tambol had done nothing. "Why are you waiting?" Duwan asked.

"Master, if I may speak. We are in the area of

settlement, and it is your stated intention to study the Devourer close at hand. You can pass for Devourer, but we—" He waved his hand at Jai, who was wrapping herself in a fur mantle. "This one would not pass for Devourer. Her looks, her speech. Nor would I. If we are to go among the enemy we must go as pongs and master."

Duwan nodded. "You speak with wisdom, Tambol."

"No, please," Jai wailed.

"I will take the garments of one of these," Tambol said, waving a hand toward the two pongs who still crouched near the fallen tall brother, awed and fearful. "Female, if there are no pong garments for you, use a pong tunic from the other male there."

"Master," Jai wailed.

"One day you will have fine garments," Duwan said, taking the fur mantle from Jai's shoulder.

Jai resigned herself. "Master, if you are to be Devourer, your hair must be trimmed."

"This is so," Tambol said.

"How will this be done?" Duwan asked.

"I have some experience," Jai said. She disappeared into the hut once more, came back with cutting instruments, seated Duwan on the stump of a tall brother and, for the first time in his life, Duwan felt his hair being severed. There was no pain, but he felt oddly light when it was finished and Jai held up a mirror for him to see a face that looked odd and strange without its mantle of fronds.

"Now you are a proper master," Tambol said. "All that is needed is this." He handed Duwan the dead enemy's lash. "It is, when not in use, worn coiled over the left shoulder."

Duwan grimaced with distaste, but allowed Tambol to position the lash.

"Master, we are ready," Jai said. She had dressed herself in an all-covering, robelike garment she'd found inside the hut. Tambol had taken the smock of one of the pong males and had, on Duwan's orders, sent the two pongs traveling toward the west, to join the free runners.

"There is one thing more," Duwan said. He strode to the fallen Devourer, hoisted the body effortlessly and threw it into the hut. "That," he said, pointing toward the tiny, pathetic forearm that was being attacked by ground-crawling insects. Without hesitation, Tambol picked up the arm. "Toss it inside, too," Duwan ordered.

Duwan forced himself to enter the stench of the hut once more. He took down a lamp, poured its oil over the heaped covers on the bed, drew a burning branch from the fireplace, threw it into the pooled oil, and stood there muttering a prayer for the dead young one as the flames leaped high and began to fill the hut with smoke.

He stood in the yard for a long time as the flames ate their way upward and burst through the roof and then, as if in one giant explosion, began to consume the hut. Without looking back, without a word, he started toward the east.

As the days passed, settlements became more frequent. Usually Duwan avoided them, but, to test his pose as a Devourer, he choose to pass through one two-hut settlement where he saw only four Enemy males. There was one problem. He did not speak the language of the Devourers.

"That doesn't matter," Jai told him. "They will think nothing of your speaking your own language, although some of your words do sound odd. You must tell them you are from a far place. Actually, the masters mostly speak as we speak even when they are speaking among themselves."

"You speak the Enemy's tongue, do you not?"

"I do," she said.

"Listen, then. If something is said in the Enemy's tongue that is threatening, warn me."

As they walked into the settlement clearing, Jai felt new importance, and she walked, perhaps, with just a bit too much pride for a pong, but the enemy males driving slaves in the gathering of the grass nuts took no notice of her, past a glance. Their eyes were on the tall, impressive figure of Duwan.

"Greetings," Duwan said. "I have traveled far."

"Welcome," one of them said. "Cool yourself at our well. And be our guest at the evening meal."

"You are kind," Duwan said. "I will accept your offer to cool myself at the well, but I beg understanding for we have far to go and must continue our travels to cover as much distance as possible before darkness."

"You come from the west?" another of the enemy asked.

"From the southwest," Duwan said, for both Tambol and Jai had told him that it was said that to the southwest were unknown lands leading to a great, waterless desert.

"The unknown lands?" one of the enemy asked. "We would hear of these lands," another said.

"There are mountains, and there the great farls roam," Duwan said. "And then the land where the sun bakes the earth into a dryness and there grow only sparse, dry things." He'd never seen a desert, so he was picturing in his mind the approaches to the land of fires.

"Odd and terrible," said a Devourer, shaking his head. "Stay, friend, and tell us more as we celebrate the sacrifice. Our females are even now preparing it."

At that moment Duwan heard a cry of terror and pain from one of the huts and his hand shot to his sword hilt. Tambol, seeing this reaction, came forward.

"Forgive me, masters, may the female and myself have water?"

Duwan forced his rage to die, to be swallowed.

Another life had been taken, but he told himself that he, alone, could not stop the customs of the Enemy. He reminded himself of his mission.

"I beg understanding," he said, bowing, and backing away. He saw Tambol and Jai drawing water. "Drink your fill quickly," he yelled, "or feel the bite of my lash."

Now they began passing through small villages. Duwan was discovering that the Enemy was, indeed, many in number. And he was becoming more confident. He found that if he pressed on, moving with purpose, his head high and his gaze forward, he and his companions were not bothered as they made their way past more elaborate dwellings, through the dusty streets of the villages.

And everywhere he saw the misery of the Drinkers, the pongs, the enslaved ones. Each village had its slave pen and there the pongs huddled when not working, barely sheltered from the elements with crude coverings, eating greedily of the meager ration of food allowed them by the masters. And in one village he saw the raw, obscenely naked body of a pong, peeled and hung on a post by lashed ropes that cut into the exposed, tender, bleeding flesh. He had to fight to hide his shock and disgust.

"You," he said imperiously to Tambol, "ask some pong what this one did."

Tambol talked with a cringing local pong and came to report. "He was caught stealing food, master."

"Thus should he be served," Duwan said, for two Enemy males were within hearing. "Remember this example, pong, lest it be your carcass that hangs there."

Away from the village, on the open road that led toward the city of Arutan, capital of the Devourer king, Farko, Duwan walked with his head high, his eyes closed to the brightness of Du, and prayed for guidance, for strength, for the ability to continue to control his desire to draw his weapons and slay the Enemy. For in his anger and anguish Duwan longed to make the dusty streets and roads run with blood until, at last, he, himself, overcome by numbers, lay there at peace, no longer tormented by the pain that came to him because of the waste of Drinker life.

From a distance, the city of Arutan exploded into view like some unnatural growth on a plain of high, green grass. Roads radiated toward the city from all directions, and they were well traveled. Outward bound groups of pongs, laden with bales, packets, baskets, labored under the lashes of the Devourers. Groups traveling toward the city carried the produce of the forests and the fields.

The city was gray. Around it a wall, built of the stones of that region, rose in dark threat. Behind the wall the gray, grim buildings reached into the sky like some supreme insult to Du, not of the earth, not for the earth, but ripped from the earth, dug from the earth to leave gaping holes, stones as gray as the inside of the caves of the free runners.

Outside the walls peddlers hawked their wares. Food, drink, garments. It had been a long and thirsty walk across the plain surrounding the city. "How does one obtain something to drink?" Duwan asked Tambol.

"Would my Master like the wine of Arutan, or some fruit juice?" Tambol asked.

"I know neither."

"Wait, Master," Tambol said, moving toward a vendor. He returned with a cup of something that, to Duwan, was sweet and delicious. "Fruit juice, Master," Tambol said.

"Have you none for yourself?"

"Water is good enough for pongs," Tambol said.

"How did you obtain this fruit juice?"

"With coins."

"Coins?"

Tambol reached into the folds of his garment and withdrew a purse of leather. He looked around, saw that no one was watching, and showed Duwan a handful of round, flat, metal objects. "The coin of Arutan," he said.

"How did you come by this coin?"

"Forgive me, Master," Tambol said. "I did not want to trouble you. It is not unusual for a pong to carry his master's coin purse, lest the master be soiled by trade."

"Where did you get it?"

Tambol hung his head. "From the hut in the forest where you killed the Devourer male and female."

"You have done well. I know nothing of such things."

"We are not rich, master, but we have enough to take decent lodgings within the city, and to purchase food and drink."

"I am in your debt, my friend," Duwan said, putting his hand on Tambol's arm.

Tambol sprang away, then leaned forward in a bow. "Never, never touch me, Master, when others can see. It is not done. Touch me only with the lash."

Duwan nodded. "Both of you must watch me closely, and keep me from committing other errors."

"We will, Master," they said together.

"Now," Duwan said, "let us see this city of the Devourers, this city of Arutan."

9

Duwan's first impression of an Enemy city was as an assault on his senses. His nose quivered as rank odors rose from a gutter running with sewage. A chatter of voices, a clash of metal on metal from a worker's shop, the wail of a female slave as she was lashed in a casual, matter-of-fact way by a Devourer female, the scrape of horned feet on paving stones; a movement of masses unlike anything he had ever seen.

The avenue leading from the gate was wide and it was crowded. Slaves carrying bundles of firewood, huge sacks of grain, and various other loads walked near the gutters, rank, full of human waste. The overlords walked in the center, many of them dressed in colorful garb. Here and there the backs of slaves were bent under the weight of a portable chair in which lolled a disdainful Devourer female.

"Master," Jai said, "follow the street until it enters a large square. Turn to the right and you will see a building on the corner of the next street with a sign showing a picture of an eating bowl and a bed. Take lodgings there."

Duwan walked in the center of the street, eyes looking past and through those that he met. He noted Jai and Tambol slinking along abreast of him, sometimes being pushed into the gutter by laden slaves.

The stone-paved street opened into a square of impressive dimensions. It, too, was crowded. Across

the square, rising stern and stark, was a stone building that reached higher into the sky than its neigh-
bors. He noted that Enemy males in long, white
robes stood in conversation on the steps, and went in
and out of the high, wide entrance to the building.
Elsewhere, blank-walled stone buildings lined the
square. He turned to the right, looked back to see Jai
and Tambol keeping pace with him, and soon saw
the sign of the eating bowl and bed. Tambol came
scurrying up to him, bowing, with Jai just behind
him.

Before Duwan could speak to Tambol, he heard
the sound of rhythmic, marching feet, turned to see
a group of about thirty Enemy males dressed in
identical, tight, smart uniforms, come striding into
the square. Each man was armed with a longsword
and a curved dagger at his belt. They marched in
perfect coordination. A voice rang out and the unit
halted, slapping the hilts of their swords.

"Who are these?" Duwan asked.

"Members of the High Master's guard," Jai whispered.

Duwan watched with interest. Orders were bawled
and swords flew from their sheaths, gleaming in the
sun. The guards, spacing themselves smartly and in
perfect unison, went through an impressive exercise,
swords whirling overhead, lunging, slashing. Duwan's
eyes narrowed. He had killed Enemy, true, but he had
not encountered any Enemy as skilled with a sword
as these.

"How many like these?" he asked.

"I cannot say," Jai said. "At times there are more in
this daily ceremony."

Duwan watched with great interest. The weapons
were well kept, gleaming, obviously well sharpened
and well constructed. The guards were of a size,
strong and young. He could tell by the exhibition
exercises that the guards knew the capabilities of

their weapons. When the ceremony was over and the guards had marched smartly away, he turned. Apparently the daily ceremony was old stuff to the residents of the city, for it had not attracted more than passing attention.

"That building across the square," Duwan said.

"The temple of the dus," Jai said. "The dus dwell within, high up, and they are fed and served by the priests."

"Those in white robes?"

"Yes," she said. She made a face. "Never cross the priests, master. They have the ear of Farko, and they are powerful. And the screams one can hear coming from the temple tell that they are not of kindly disposition toward those who dispute their power, or the sacrifices."

"Do they, too, kill the young ones?"

"The dus feed on pongs," Jai said. "Occasionally, for a meal of more quality, a Devourer is sacrificed, but he or she is always taken from the prisons."

"Let us see more of this place," Duwan said.

"Take lodgings first," Jai said, "before the rooms are all filled. Tambol, go to the Devourer behind the desk and tell him you want lodgings, lodgings of quality and cleanliness, for your master. He will ask you for five farks. You must, very respectfully, tell him that five farks is too much, and that your master will pay three."

Tambol approached an aging Devourer male, not without some nervousness, and it happened as Jai had said, a room was assigned, and Duwan walked imperiously up the stairs, Tambol and Jai cringing behind. The room was small, the bed smelled strongly of unwashed bodies.

"Tambol will sleep on the floor, guarding the door with his body," Jai said. "It is acceptable to have a female slave to warm the bed for a master, but I, too, can sleep on the floor."

"We can sleep when we have returned to the earth," Duwan said. "We will now see more of this city."

There was a sameness about the streets. Away from the main avenues and the square they were narrow, always shaded from the blessed rays of Du by the overhanging balconies of the crowding stone buildings. More than once Duwan had to move quickly to avoid being splashed as house pongs emptied slop pails from the balconies.

"It is a bed of ground insects," he told himself, as he walked through the streets, having to step aside quite often to avoid colliding with an Enemy male. "Are all Devourers so rude?" he asked Jai, who was walking a step behind him.

"I have hesitated to mention it, master," Jai said, "but it is the custom for Devourers to play a game of domination."

"When I step aside I am showing that I have been intimidated?"

"Yes, Master, but perhaps it is best. After all, you do not want to call attention to yourself."

But Duwan was young enough to feel the injury to his pride. If it was a question of dominance, he had seen no one for whom he would step aside in willing admission that he was the lesser. The next time a Devourer male came striding toward him he looked the fellow in the eye, his orange eyes seeming to glow with fire, and, at the last second the Enemy stepped aside. No more did Duwan give way.

On the south side of the city, beyond the great square, sprawling in squalor just under the defensive wall, were the slave pens. There the stench was greater, the air thick with it. Inside the wooden barrier Duwan saw ragged females cooking over open fires, children swaddled in all kinds of cast-off rags standing or sitting listlessly.

"That was my home," Jai said, with a shudder. "My shelter was there, directly against the wall." She pointed and Duwan felt a great wave of compassion for her, and for all the Drinkers, so ignorant of their true nature, who were herded into the crowded, filty pens each night after a day of slave labor in the city.

Aside from the smartly uniformed guards who had paraded in the square, he saw no evidence of defensive capability, save for the stout walls. He was feeling optimistic. The well trained warriors of the valley Drinkers would each be a match for five of the enemy. All Enemy males went armed, true, but he saw evidence of neglect of weapons in the form of rusted hilts and frayed sheaths.

"I have seen enough," he said. "We will sleep, and then we will leave this place with the first light of Du."

Jai knew the city well. She guided them back toward the inn through narrow streets where there were fewer encounters, and they were almost back to the central square when a tall, well-built Devourer in the uniform of the High Master's guard seemed to fill all available space in the narrow street. Duwan's first impulse was to give way and step aside, but he had seen the sword exercises of those smartly uniformed men and he was wondering if their skill would be effective in serious fighting instead of parade ground show. Then, too, he was Drinker, and he was in the land of his ancestors, and he was young and prideful. He narrowed his orange eyes and marched directly toward the oncoming guardsman.

"Master, Master," Jai was whispering from one pace behind him, a bit of panic in her voice.

Just as it appeared that the two males could walk directly into each other, when one more pace on the part of either would have resulted in a nose to nose collision, both halted, faces inches apart, eyes locked. The guardsman had pale green eyes.

"You have the space of one breath to move aside," the guardsman said.

"Does the law of this city give the High Master's guard the right of way?" Duwan asked, his voice low and polite.

"This gives me the right of way," the guardsman said, patting the hilt of his longsword.

"Then I will be breaking no law if I contest?" Duwan asked. "I am a stranger, and I do not, of course, want to break any laws."

The green eyes of the guardsman narrowed. "I see that you are armed in the ancient manner, in the manner of our ancestors. I seldom find it necessary to use two swords, one being quite adequate."

"I can understand that," Duwan said. "It is rare that one has the skill of hand to handle both long and short swords."

"Since you have stated that you are a stranger and do not want to break any of the laws of Arutan, I will explain to you that dueling in the streets, while not unlawful, is frowned upon."

"Perhaps there is an isolated place?" Duwan asked.

The guardsman's eyes shifted, examined Duwan from head to foot. "Do you refuse to give way?"

"Unless I am breaking some law, yes."

Jai drew near, cringing. "Master, Master, beg forgiveness of this officer."

Duwan ignored her. The guardsman nodded.

"I will turn and make my way back to the square. We will settle this matter there, if that is your wish." the guardsman said.

Duwan nodded. The uniformed enemy turned and walked away, back stiff.

"Master, don't be foolish," Jai begged. "You will have to fight him in the center of the square, and every eye in the city will be on you."

"And if I kill him?"

"The weapons will be padded," Jai said, "but whether you win or lose, Master, great attention will be focused on you. Can you risk discovery?"

"I'm curious," Duwan said. "These guardsmen seem to be the finest warriors of the enemy. I will test this one's abilities."

By the time Duwan reached the square, with Jai and Tambol following behind him, a crowd was beginning to form in the center. The guardsman was there, and white-robed priests were filing down the stairs of the temple. Duwan took his place in the open area. The crowd stared and pointed and there was a great deal of wagering going on, most of the bets being placed on the guardsman with the odds against Duwan. A priest walked to stand in front of Duwan, padded sheaths for weapons in his land.

"The captain allows you to use both your weapons," the priest said.

"Will he use only the longsword?"

"Yes," the priest said.

"Then if you will hold my shortsword for me I will be grateful," Duwan said, extending his longsword for the priest to cover with the padded sheath.

The two combatants faced each other at a distance of a few paces. "There is still time to give way, stranger," the guardsman said.

"My sword arm needs exercise," Duwan said.

The guardsman came in a rush, and the muffled thud of blade on blade came time and again. Duwan held up on offensive thrusts, wanting to determine the extent of the warrior's skill, and he was not disappointed. The guard captain seemed in a hurry to end the bout, his blade seemed to be a living thing, thrusting, slashing, hammering. So skilled were both men that gasps of admiration went up from the crowd, and Jai noted that the odds against Duwan kept going down until, as the shadows of the sun moved by inches and both combatants were drenched in sweat and no blow of either had penetrated the other's defenses, it was even money.

After a lightning series of thrusts, all parried by

Duwan, the captain stepped back. "You fight well, stranger "

"I have never faced a more worthy opponent," Duwan said.

"Is your sword arm as weary as mine?" the captain asked.

"I fear so," Duwan said. He tossed his sword, caught it deftly by the hilt in his left hand. "But, since I fight in the manner of the ancients, I have a spare."

The captain's face went grim and he came to the attack with a renewed fury. However, he had gauged himself to Duwan's right-handed technique and so, as he faced a left-handed attack, with Duwan unleashing all his offensive tricks, he had to give ground. Duwan was now eager to end it. He pressed his attack, going for the guardsman's head, for if there was a weakness in the captain's defense it was at head level. He saw his opportunity, sent a great smash downward, felt his padded blade thud into the enemy's skull but even as he felt the shock of impact his breath went out of him in a great huff as the captain's padded blade took him in a full slash on the stomach.

The guardsman went down, dazed, and Duwan fought to get his breath, felt a great wave of weakness as he could not breathe, fell to his knees, gasped and finally got wind into his lungs.

The officiating priest stepped forward. The crowd was screaming in delight. "You are both dead," the priest said. "Let me commend you on a display of swordsmanship seldom seen in these peaceful days."

"Stranger," the captain said, getting to his knees, "you've addled me properly."

"And you have given me a blow I will feel for days," Duwan said.

"When we meet again in the streets," the captain said, "I suggest that each of us take one half-step to the side."

"A sensible suggestion," Duwan said. He was reviewing the bout in his mind, trying to remember places where he could have applied this or that technique.

"If you seek a place in Arutan, come to the guards quarters and ask for Captain Hata. Your sword would be a valuable addition to the High Master."

For a moment Duwan considered accepting the invitation. How better to learn all of the Enemy's secrets than as one of them? But then he reconsidered. He had enough information. "I am honored," he said. "But I am a wanderer."

"So be it," Hata said, giving a polite little nod of his head. Duwan returned the nod. The crowd began to disperse, still haggling over coins. Jai came to stand behind Duwan.

"Are you hurt, Master?"

"I will ache for a while," he said. He started walking toward the inn. He was tired. When his way was blocked by an ornate portable chair carried by four gaunt pongs, he started to walk around it.

"You," said a feminine voice from behind the lacy curtains of the chair. "Come here."

Duwan's inclination was to ignore the command, but he felt his tunic being tugged by Jai, who whispered, "Master, you must obey. The chair bears the royal crest."

Duwan stepped close. The slaves stood, heads hanging, panting. The lacy curtains were pushed aside and he saw a female half-reclining on luxurious cushions. She wore a garment unlike any he'd seen, a thing of smooth and gossamer construction that showed the shape of her, the swelling of her bud point emphasized by a circular pattern of lace.

"Who are you?" the female asked, in a soft, inviting voice.

"I am Duwan."

"She is to be addressed as High Mistress," Jai hissed.

"Please!"

Forgive me, High Mistress," Duwan said. His only desire now was to get back to the inn, rest, and then start his journey to the north. "I am a wanderer, strange to your city and your ways."

"So, Duwan," the High Mistress said. "I have not seen such swordplay since my father was a young one. You will present yourself at my residence at the time of the evening meal." She tossed a ring toward him, and Duwan caught it in the air. "Present this to my guard." The curtains closed and, after a soft command, the chair moved off at a trot.

"We must flee now," Jai said. "For that was the daughter of Farko, himself. She will find you out, master. Let us not even return to the inn, but make our way to the gate and put a night's distance behind us."

"I am tired," Duwan said.

"If you stay and do not obey her orders she will have the entire guard out looking for you," Jai said. "If you go to her, she will see through your stories of travel to the southwest, for she has access to all information as the High Master's daughter."

Perhaps it was only pride that formed Duwan's decision. He was young, and he'd held his own with one of the Devourers' finest swordsmen, and he was convinced that had the swords not been padded, had he used both his weapons, he would have killed Captain Hata. Perhaps it was just that he did not feel like running, that he was weary. He led the way to the inn, washed himself, brushed his rather soiled clothing, and, as Du sank beyond the western walls of the city he followed Jai's directions, walking into a section of the city enclosed by a separate, interior wall, into a place of wide, lush gardens and stone mansions with painted decorations that provided unexpected color amid the uniform grayness of the city.

Uniformed guardsmen flanked the gate leading to one of the more impressive mansions. He showed his left hand, on which the High Mistress' ring gleamed, and was admitted. He was escorted by two guards to an ironbound, high, thick door and then he stepped into brightly lit luxury.

Bowing, smiling slave girls guided him down a long hallway whose walls were decorated with carved and painted things of considerable beauty. Another great door was opened by a male slave. The room beyond was large enough to be spacious, small enough to be cozy, and there, at its center, reclining on brightly colored, fur-covered cushions, was the High Mistress. Before her was a table laden with dishes that sent a variety of odors into the air of the room. She motioned Duwan to come forward, indicated that he was to sit beside her. Her gown was even more revealing than her apparel of the afternoon. It seemed to float near her rather than bind her, and through the gossamer thinness of it he could see that she was either naturally dark or that she exposed herself to the rays of Du. Her long, shapely legs were positioned attractively. Her bud point was enchantingly visible through one single thickness of the material. Her eyes, he noticed, were the red of the molten rock in the land of the fires.

"Your earlier efforts, have I trust, left you with an appetite?"

"Yes, High Mistress."

She waved one graceful hand. "Here in privacy we waive the formalities. You may call me Elnice."

"Thank you," Duwan said.

"Your weapons show great care, but your apparel—" She reached out and fingered the crude cloth of his tunic.

"I am but a wanderer, High Mistress." At her frown he smiled and said, "A wanderer, Elnice."

"A body as well formed as yours should be adorned," she said. She clapped her hands and two pong females scurried from behind hanging material. She gave orders in the language of the Devourers. Within minutes, the females were back, carrying fine garments.

"Your kindness is great," Duwan said. "Where shall I go to change."

"Go? Are you so modest?" She smiled. "Help him," she ordered, and Duwan was pulled gently but insistently from the couch by the two females who, gigglingly, began to divest him of his clothing. He saw the flame red eyes narrow as his powerful chest was exposed. He felt his face grow hot as his lower garment was removed and he stood, naked, with the flame red eyes sweeping him. Then a kilt of soft, comfortable material was fastened at his waist and a loose, luxuriously made tunic pulled over his head.

Elnice clapped her hands again and the two females began to serve. There was fruit and flesh and various dishes of green things and, of course, dishes made from the staple of the Devourer diet, the nuts of the tall grass.

"The meat is special," Elnice said, as Duwan refused a serving.

He looked at it in doubt, wondering if it was the flesh of a Drinker young one.

"My own hunters range far," she said. "This is the flesh of a grass eater and it is brought to me from far beyond the plain of Arutan. Do you have an aversion to eating flesh?"

"I do," Duwan said. "In my wanderings I have acquired odd tastes."

She shrugged, and the motion gave her upper body so much grace that Duwan felt a flush of pleasure.

"Then drink to new friends," Elnice said, lifting a cup. Duwan raised his own cup. The contents smelled like the fruit juice he'd once tried, and as the female drank deeply he did the same. The taste was fruity, but there was a tang, a tartness, that he'd never experienced.

He did well by the food, for he was hungry, and the cooked dishes of green things and the bread made from the grass nut were delicious.

"Tell me now of your travels," Elnice ordered, although her voice was soft and sweet.

To be safe, Duwan stuck to the truth, telling of the north, of the vast tracts of trees—he'd learned enough not to call them tall brothers—of the snows and the frozen lakes. His detailed account seemed to bore the female, so he paused.

"How do you like our city so far?" Elnice asked, arching her back, smiling at him.

"I am overwhelmed by the numbers," he said, "and by the odors of the streets." He smiled. The fruit juice, he was finding, tasted better with each glass. A female stood behind him and filled his glass each time he emptied it.

"Do you not find it beautiful?"

He cued himself from her little frown. He was finding her to be quite transparent. If it was a compliment she wanted . . . "I find, in this room, great beauty," he said.

"Do you?" she asked. "Is it my furniture, my works of art?"

"If I may be so bold, it is you," he said.

"Ah." She rose, came to take his hand. "Come, then."

The room seem to roll as Duwan arose. She put her arm around his waist, pressed her soft, female flank against his, guided him through a doorway into a chamber which seemed, to Duwan's eyes—and there seemed to be just a little something wrong with his eyes—to be nothing much more than a huge, luxurious, covered bed.

"Since you know beauty," she whispered, releasing him and stepping away. Duwan's eyes went wide as, in one graceful motion, she denuded herself, leaving the gown heaped on the floor. "Make yourself comfortable," she told him, guiding him toward the bed, pushing him down. He felt a bit odd, so he allowed this, and sat there leaning against a pile of cushions as she stepped back, and began to do things with her body that seemed almost impossible. She moved in sensuous waves, arms striking poses that showed her at her best, hips undulating. As she danced she made a low, humming sound and her fiery eyes never left his.

One of the serving females came in, left a pitcher of the tangy fruit juice on a table beside the bed and, to cover his confusion, Duwan drank deeply. He was wondering what was happening to him, for he felt his body as he'd never felt it before, felt his bud point swelling.

When she came to him, swaying, a picture of such beauty that he was breathless, he made no objection as she took his kilt, his tunic, and lowered herself to him, lips to lips, bud point to bud point. He felt the heat, the moist union, felt himself extending and then entering and after that only an excitement that made his brain spin and his blood race. That it was his first grafting was lost to him, for his movements were instinctive, and as he rolled, putting his weight on the female whose beautiful face was pressed to his, as he knew her bodily juices with his mouth and that other part of himself, she was making that soft, humming sound that, to his ears, was the most pleasant noise he'd ever heard.

They lay, joined deeply, the after-pleasures coursing through their bodies. Duwan slept, and so skilled was the female that when he awoke, in darkness, she still held him within her and the fire rose up in his blood again so that she was awakened and began that low, musical hum of satisfaction.

With the light of day, with his brain pushing against

his skull in painful throbs, he wept quietly as Elnice of Arutan still held him within her and, his mind clear, if pained, he knew what he had done.

"Alning," he whispered. "Ah, Alning."

The sound roused her and, to his shame, her lips, her arms, her movements kept him there.

"This weapon," she said, touching him, "is used as skillfully as you used your sword. You will stay with me, Duwan the Wanderer."

"High Mistress," he said, "I am honored, but my business—"

"Is to please Elnice of Arutan," she said, with a hint of metal in her soft voice. "Now we will eat."

He found that a few cups of the fruit juice stilled the throb in his head. The bed was soft, the female soft and her commands irresistible.

"How long will you allow me to stay?" he asked, putting the question as tactfully as he could.

"Until I cool that fire in you," she smiled. "You act as if I am your first female."

He felt heat in his face, but he did not admit that she was right. "Am I so different from others?" he asked.

"Some can make it through one night without cooling," she said.

He resolved to make his own fire dim, and to his chagrin it roared higher. Her touch was enough. The next morning he knew that he would stay as long as she would have him, for his body controlled his mind now.

"Elnice," he said, "I have two pongs at the inn. I would send for them. Can you house them here?"

"Don't concern yourself with two pongs. They'll be taken to the pens."

"I have these two trained to serve my needs," he said. "It's such a nuisance to have to train others."

She laughed. "I know. When I had a serving pong peeled for spilling food on a new gown it took months to train a new one. Sometimes it is better to put up with the stupidity of the pongs one has than to train others. I will send for them." She reached over and pinched him painfully on his bud point. "But you will have no use for the female."

Three days and three nights were spent without either of them leaving Elnice's inner quarters. But now there were more periods of talk, as they lay joined, and Duwan used that time to learn more about the enemy.

Elnice's father, Farko, a direct descendant of Farko the Great, who, in antiquity, had led the Devourers out of the steamy, dense jungles far to the south, ruled the lands from the western mountains to the eastern sea. In his realm were twelve major cities, Arutan the queen of them. Thus it had been for generations. Of the lands to the south and the west Elnice knew nothing, so it was safe, at the rare times when she questioned him, to make up lies about the southwestern desert and the mountains of the far west. It was when he was telling a tailored version of his encounter with the great animal, the farl, that he garnered some interesting information.

"In your travels to the west did you encounter any of the escaped pongs?" she asked.

"Of course not. Had I done so I would have killed them."

"Captain Hata continually advises my father to mount an expedition to the west, to exterminate those escapees."

"I don't think there are many," he said. "And what can pongs do against our blades?"

She mused for a long moment. "In the guards quarters, once each full moon, it is required that all guards hear of the past," she said. "The telling is done by a priest of Ahtol, and it is to remind those whose responsibility it is to guard the throne that pongs were not always docile and stupid."

"I would like to hear this telling," he said.

"It bores me," she said, reaching for him, "but if you so desire, I can arrange for a priest to give you a private telling."

"It would please me," he said.

True to her word, a priest came to her quarters at midday, and Duwan had to admit that he was a bit relieved to part from her for some brief time. He left her lying in graceful beauty among the colorful cushions, her bud point swollen attractively and invitingly.

The priest was an old one, with wrinkled skin. Duwan, politely asking the priest's age, was amazed to hear the number of years, and it was then that he learned another difference between Devourer and Drinker, for Devourers did not harden as did Drinkers, but seemed to crumple in on themselves, judging from the old priest.

"When Farko the Great led the people to the north the rich, cool lands were teeming with a population that seemed, at first, to be like our people. They were not warlike. They lived on the bounty of the land, eating the green things that grew so plentifully. It was Farko's first intention, with conquest so easy, to integrate these native peoples into our own, but soon it was noted that there were basic differences. This was first discovered when a living bed of young ones was discovered. The barbarians' of this land, after sprouting young, actually planted them, like grass, in the earth, and roots grew from the young ones' feet to feed on the things of the earth.

"The first major differences among the two peoples grew out of the barbarians' superstitious regard for any living plant. When our settlers cut down trees for building, the barbarians protested, calling the trees brothers. Among them it was believed that the trees contained the departed spirits of their dead, who, when their skins began to harden, planted themselves in the earth and were magically transformed into trees.

"From these differences there arose conflict, and at first the barbarians fell by the thousands to our iron blades, but then there arose opposition. The barbarians learned the use of our swords, and across the land there roared war, a war of extermination, for Farko the Great had decreed that the alien difference between our people and the barbarians made living together in the same land impossible. It was not an easy war, for our soldiers had to carry food, while a barbarian could live off the country and, indeed, take nourishment from the sun itself.

"He was able to go for days with nothing more than water and the rays of the sun, and this made him a formidable opponent.

"The war lasted for the lifetime of Farko the Great, and into the reign of his son, and his son's son, and then there arose a great barbarian leader called Alon, who led small forces that made individual raids on our towns and settlements, never pausing to do battle with an equal or superior force, but slashing and hitting and then disappearing into the forests. Life became painful in this land, and it was decided that an all out effort had to be made. The land would not contain both our people and the barbarians. We mobilized totally, and our great armies swept the length and breadth of the land and, at last, cornered Alon's forces in the forests of the northland, where the snows are deep and the cold bites like an animal. There Alon made a stand, and it was apparent that all his forces, and all his females and young ones, would be exterminated. To avoid this, he fled into the snows, and it was thought that none could survive. Our armies guarded the forests for the winter, with much hardship, and parties went out in the summer to find, far to the north, a land of fire, an impassable land, and there had been seen the moldering, animal-gnawed bones of barbarians, males, females, young ones, all along the way.

"But all of the barbarians did not manage to die with Alon in the land of the fires. Here and there across the land remained small pockets of them, and those who were not killed were forced to work in the mines, or in the clearing of the forests. From these, who were, obviously, made of lesser stuff than those who followed Alon, came the pongs of today."

"These pongs," Duwan said, "do they have those odd differences, too?"

The priest nodded. "This is why we must remember our history. The barbarians called themselves Children of Du, or Children of the Light. They were prideful, and they were dangerous opponents, once they began to adapt to the use of our weapons. We, the priests of Ahtol, are constantly warning that the potential for violence exists now, since we have allowed the growth of the pong population."

"They seem harmless enough," Duwan said. "I have had pongs. I own two now. They know nothing of getting nourishment from the sun, for example, but cover themselves head to foot to avoid its rays."

"Yes, because they are taught as young ones in the pens that the sun kills, just as they are taught, with vivid lessons—a pong is fed poison and dies rather painfully—that the green, growing things are poison. However, should one desperate pong disregard our teachings, should he discover that he can grow fat eating the green things and drinking of the sun, then, with their numbers—there are more pongs in Arutan than masters—they could become dangerous, especially since our prosperity has made it unattractive to follow the profession of arms."

"They seem too stupid to figure out these things for themselves," Duwan said.

"Yes, they are animals," the priest said. "But in the pens, at night, there are whispers. There members

of a mystical society tell of free Drinkers in the far
north. They know so little that they can actually
believe that Drinkers could survive the cold and could
pass through that land of fire. The myths speak of a
master who will come from the north to lead all
pongs to freedom. We've peeled a few of the mystics,
and their eagerness to talk as their hides are removed a strip at a time tells us all. It's nonsense, but
it is a hope for the masses. We waited too late to be
able to eradicate this hope. We should have destroyed
every pong in Arutan when it first arose, this myth.
And our greatest fear, among the priesthood, is that
the escaped pongs carried that myth with them and
that they have rediscovered their abilities to live off
the land."

"Well," Duwan said, "a conspiracy of slaves would
give occasion for some exercise of the sword arm."
He laughed. "I think, priest, that you make too much
of the danger."

The old man shook his head. "So do they all," he
said, "and I pray to Ahtol that they are right."

Duwan, having seen the pongpens, and having
seen many of the slaves, doubted that any uprising
could ever happen. Perhaps, with a free Drinker
army in the field, pongs could be recruited to do
labor, to carry supplies, but it would take much to
turn any of them, even such as Tambol, into a fighting Drinker. He was a bit discouraged, but full of
thought, as he went back to Elnice's quarters to open
the door to her bedroom. His blood was already
running hot, and his conscience cold, when he opened
the door to see Elnice's lovely backside protruding
into the air as she squirmed atop a muscular male.

Duwan halted in surprise. He felt a flash of anger,
then of relief. He made a sound and, without stop-
ping her graceful, sensuous movements, Elnice looked
over her shoulder and gave him a flashing smile.

"I take it, High Mistress," Duwan said, "that I am
now free to resume my business?"

"As you will," she said. "Go. Wander. When your fires are rebuilt sufficiently, come back to me."

Duwan found Jai and Tambol in the slave quarters. They both looked well fed, and each had new slave clothing. When Duwan had led them out of Elnice's mansion, he halted in a little traveled place.

"Jai, in the pongpens, did you hear talk of a deliverer, a master who would come from the north to free the pongs?"

"Yes, it was whispered. From the earth, some said, as you know."

"Should such a master come, would pongs fight?"

"With their hands?" Tambol asked.

"If that was all they had."

"Some would," Tambol said.

Jai shook her head. "Not many."

Duwan had made his decision. "Tomorrow we will leave Arutan," he said. "For the rest of the day, and as long as you can find pongs to talk with tonight, I want you to wander the streets, whispering this myth, telling any who will listen that the Master is coming, that he is coming with an army, that he will free all, and that he will provide weapons for any who will fight at his side."

He had given the idea much thought. The risk was that a pong would tell what he had heard and that the enemy would, forewarned, begin preparations. However, his observations, his talk with the priest of Ahtol, made him believe that this, too, would be ignored by the complacent enemy as just another myth among the pongs. He could not seriously imagine a man like Captain Hata fearing a pong uprising, or even believing that such a thing could happen. The chances of the story doing any good were slim, considering the totally downtrodden state of the pongs, but if it encouraged even a few, and made them ready to learn to fight, then it would have been worthwhile.

While Jai and Tambol wandered the city, Duwan spent his time in the inn, where he drank a little of that tangy fruit juice that had been his downfall in Elnice's house. He questioned travelers about Devourer cities to the north. When, as Du peeked up in the east, he led his loyal pongs out of the city, he had his route planned. It would take him to three of Farko's cities, one on the shores of the great eastern sea, before his way led him into the thinly populated forests of the north.

It was growing late in the year, and he knew that he would have to winter somewhere to the north, and then make his dash for home as Du's renewal time moved up from the south. He had told Alning to wait for two passings of the time of the long light, and then speak for another. That thought, now, now that he knew the goodness and sweetness of grafting, now that he knew the joys that would be his with his own Alning, was a pain, and he was tempted to travel as quickly as he could and risk being caught in the iron cold.

He kept Tambol and Jai with him as he visited the city on the sea, to find it much like Arutan, but smaller, and with a less impressive garrison of uniformed guards. The other two, farther north, were still smaller, and even less well defended. He would sweep down from the north, taking villages and cities as he came, and then, his forces swelled by recruited pongs, he would face Arutan.

The chill of the change of seasons forced him to use coins, somehow always in supply, thanks to a skill for confiscation developed by Tambol, to buy furs, and he told himself that the animals were already dead, that he had not killed them, and that their hides were serving a good purpose. Their lives had been lost, but he would avenge them, and, the Land of Many Brothers in Drinker control again, there would be no more killing of green or animal brothers.

With the first snowfall, he was in the changing lands, the deep forests of tall brothers not far to the north. He found a cave in a rocky canyon, stocked it, with the help of Tambol, with firewood and dry, preserved foodstuff, and then, as Tambol shivered and longed for the warmer lands to the south, he told both of them that they were to leave him now, to rejoin the free runners in the western hills, there to await his summons when he returned with the Drinkers. Tambol was only too eager to go. Jai wept, but obeyed, and he sent them off dressed warmly, and went into his cave to think of home, of Alning, of how he would tell the wise ones of his people all of his knowledge of the enemy and of the beauty and bounty of the Drinkers' native land.

He awoke to find that snow had covered the ground to ankle depth. He walked in the crisp, cold air and discovered that the tall brothers in the canyon floor were whisperers, and, being few, that their unspoken words were partly to be understood. He opened his mind.

"Brother, brother, brother," they seemed to be saying, and they dropped dead limbs for firewood as he walked among them.

And there came into his mind pictures, the past, the happy Drinkers living in plenty, and a sense of desperation and loss and pain as death came, and then, insistently, an urge to move, to climb out of the hidden canyon.

"Tell me, brothers," he said. "What is it?"

Pictures almost formed in his mind. Alning's image was confused with that of the beautiful Elnice of Arutan, and there was a sense of urgency. He wrapped himself well and climbed out of the canyon into a quiet, cold, blinding snowstorm and, obeying the impulses, hearing the whispering, scouted the trail he'd followed up from the south.

She was crawling when he saw her, weak, cold, her skin already hardening on her extremities.

"Jai!"

"Oh, Duwan—"

She went limp in his arms. He carried her back to the cave and warmed her by the fire, covered her with furs after rubbing her feet, legs, hands, arms to restore circulation. When she opened her eyes they went wide and then she smiled weakly.

"What happened? What of Tambol?"

"Tambol is well. He moves swiftly toward the south." Duwan frowned. "And you?"

"I ran away. I could not leave you, Master. Forgive me, but I would as soon be peeled as leave you."

Her presence complicated things. And yet, with the coming of the change, the renewing, he could still send her south. The journey through the land of forests, water, barrens, fire, would be a long one, and he would be eager to make as much time as he could.

But her presence would not be unwelcome during the long, cold, dark nights that lay ahead.

"I should use the lash on you," he said.

"If it pleases you, but don't send me away, please."

The snow fell, soft, quiet, all covering. The entrance to the cave was all but blocked, and the snow barrier made it cozy inside, if a bit smoky. They rested, and talked, and ate of the dried food, and slept together for warmth—or so Duwan told himself, that very first night, until, as he held her closely she turned to face him and his hands moved as if of their own accord to bare their bud points.

Then the winter did not seem long.

Interlude

In the early winter, after the first invasion of frigid air had moved down through the forests, bringing a clean, fresh, cutting wind from the great ice caps, there came to the fringe settlements of Kooh, northernmost of the cities of Farko, a priest of the minor du, Tseeb, he of the clear skies. The worship of Tseeb was not a popular cult, for followers of that fair-faced du took vows of poverty. The priest was dressed in a bundle of cast-off things, torn pieces of Devourer dress, tattered slave wear, and he shivered with the cold as he called on outlying settlements, begging permission to give a message of piety to the pongs.

Pongs, being an inferior sub-species, stupid and gullible, were especially susceptible to the fair-skied belief in a du of kindness and goodness. Masters had no objection to the practice of a religion that taught acceptance of one's lot in life, of obedience to authority, in hope of the promise of a better life in the afterworld, so the ragged priest was welcomed, and was allowed to share the meager food and squalid quarters of the pongs.

So closely was the priest bundled in his rags, so nearly did he piously cover his every body part, that no master saw that he was sleek, well-nourished, almost, in fact, pleasingly fat. Nor did any master bother to listen to the priest in his teaching, thus no master saw that the priest did not partake of the pongs' grass nut bread or the meager portions of animal flesh.

Upon the departure of the priest, for a while, at least, the pongs seemed to perk up slightly, but, the masters noted, they soon fell into their old, slovenly ways.

Through storm and crisp, clear, brittle days the priest tramped the snow, visiting dozens of settlements, villages, and came at last to the city of Kooh, itself, where, upon application to the City Master, he was given permission to spend time in the pongpens. There, among more sophisticated Devourers, the priest was a source of shame, for, although priesthood in a dozen or more cults was a socially accepted way to earn one's bread, to lower oneself to the level of the pongs, to live among them, was going, masters felt, just a bit too far.

Most Devourers who had property, or power, or wealth, looked upon the various religious cults as necessary evils. The powerful priesthood of Ahtol actually shared power with civil authorities and served an excellent purpose in keeping an eye on the masses, and keeping down any possible disquiet among the majority of the ruling race who had no direct say in policy, government, and other matters of importance. Only naive fools really believed in an afterlife. Most Devourers were advocates of Ahtol, if only because the priests of Ahtol, with their sacrifices, put on a stirring show, helped, by the use of pong young, to hold back the redoubling of the pong population, and were generous with the surplus flesh used in sacrifice. The tiny temple of Tseeb was, in that northern city, hidden away near the wall in a cul-de-sac surrounded by pongpens, and the three ancient priests who served the tiny temple often had to share pong food in order to survive. That winter, however, they had received what was, for them, a munificent gift from a wealthy Devourer and, well fed, they built up their fire and sat before it feasting and drinking the summer's wine, letting their small following, mostly among the pongs, serve their own spiritual needs. They did not hear of the visiting Tseeb priest, and even if they had, they would not have left the warmth and comfort of their fire.

During the shortest days of the year the ragged priest moved south to Seman, spent weeks in the outlying settlements, then a short time in the main pongpen within the city. Next he betook himself to Tshou, and there by the cold sea he taught his message.

As the days began slowly to lengthen he was in and around the capital, Arutan, and there, where the population of pongs was greatest, he found his largest audiences, pongs gathering around him, huddled against the cold, to hear a message that had preceded him, carried by the pongs of masters who had come to Arutan from the other, more northern cities.

His message, in essence, was a brief one, and could have been summed up as follows:

"The Master has come. He has seen. He has judged. He has gone away to counsel with his father (who is not, by the way, the du of clear skies, the insignificant and rosy-minded Tseeb, but an ancient, forgotten du, who manifests his image daily in the skies as Du, the sun), but he will return. With him comes freedom."

There was, of course, more to the message, for the priest knew well that the minds of pongs tended to be simple and doubt-filled. What right have the hopeless to hope? So he elaborated. He offered personal testimony.

"I have lived and traveled with the Master. I saw him come from the good earth." In this, of course, he was stretching the truth, but he *had* talked with one who had seen the Master come from the earth. "I have seen him prove his bravery and his strength in killing a great beast of the forests, and in besting the finest sword of the Devourers. I have shared his magic, as I demonstrate now." At this he would eat of some delicious growing thing, and there would be fearful gasps and exclamations and some laughter, for all expected him to fall down, writhing in his death agonies as did those who, with regularity, ate of the deadly green each spring and died.

"For generations," the priest told his incredulous audiences, "the enemy has deprived you of your heritage, your land, and the du-given ability to live off this land of plenty. In all life there is a oneness, for we are of the earth and for the earth, and all that grows from the earth is good, and the brothers of the fields and forests share willingly."

By this time he had lost most of them.

"Moreover, we were once called the Children of the Light, for the good one, Du, sends down the power to create energy from nothing more than his own goodness, and this, too, has been stolen from us by the Devourer teachings that our own Du harms us."

If a few younger pongs looked up at the sun, as the season changed and there was warmth coming from the fiery "Du," that was, at first, the only tangible result of the teachings of the priest. Yet he was tireless, and now and again he would see, as he returned to the outlying settlements, a pong push back his hood and feel the good warmth of Du on his face.

He had much ground to cover. There were nine more Farkoian cities, hundreds of thousands of pongs, and many, many weary marches through the growing warmth, the spring rains, and the days of wind and dust.

A westward detour occupied weeks of the priest's time. In the mountains he found the free runners, thin and hungry after a long, cold winter, still trying to use their weak, inaccurate bows to feed themselves from the sparse animal life.

"You have seen and heard the Master," he told them sternly. "You have seen him sleek and fat and full of life as he lived off the plenty of the earth, and drank in the sun's goodness. You saw the woman, Jai, follow the Master's lead, and you see me now. Am I starving, as you are? No, because I eat of the earth's plenty. Listen to me, runners, listen. The Master is returning. Eat of the plenty. Strengthen yourself so that you can join his holy, victorious army."

"Tambol," they said, "you have exposed yourself to the sun too often, so that the deadly rays have baked away your reason. Leave us with your madness."

"I cry out truth and only the wilderness hears," Tambol said sadly, setting off toward the southeast.

After Tambol's preaching in the city of Arutan, momentous events had taken place. A winter fever had taken the High Master, the hereditary ruler, Farko. At his funeral four hundred female slaves were sacrificed, a disobedient male pong was ceremonially peeled and left screaming on a pole in front of the temple. Young Devourers found that the story was true, that the flesh of a pong, when peeled, was so soft that a straw, thrown just so, would embed itself. The feast was generous. Four hundred female bodies made much meat, and females were tenderer than males. Moreover, using the females as sacrifice helped in two ways to ease the population pressure created by the pongs, who, it was generally known, spent all their nights in breeding activity.

A Devourer, who had stolen, was sacrificed by the High Priest himself, and choice cuts were delivered to the table of the new ruler, Elnice of Arutan. She ate in company with her strong right arm, Captain

Hata. As he gnawed a rib bone, Hata, his mind actually on the body of his ruler, a body that was beyond description for its sweetness, talked idly.

"When they peeled the pong today it was rather amusing."

"I can't stand the stench," Elnice said.

As the priests took the first strip of hide he yelled at them defiantly. He said, 'You kill only my earthly body, for I will join the Master in paradise.' Then, with the second strip, he yelled, 'The Master has come, and he will return to avenge me.'"

Elnice was savoring the soft, sweet flesh from the dead devourer's bud. She chewed thoughtfully for a moment. "The Master has come?"

"The prattlings of a dying pong."

"What else did he say, as they began to really get down to it?"

"He started screaming in pain, of course, and between screams he begged for a quick death, promising to tell all about the Master, and how he was going to give freedom to all pongs."

"In going over the law and order reports last night," Elnice said, "I noticed that more than twenty pongs have had to be lashed for exposing parts of their bodies to the sun, and that only in the last few days."

"Indeed?" Hata asked, around a mouthful of solid rib muscle.

"It's probably coincidence," the new ruler said. "Peel a few at random and see what they say."

"Shall I save their buds for you, High Master?"

She laughed. "It is a rich diet. A few. But when it comes to buds, I prefer to pick and choose and take them internally in another manner. If you have finished your duties, come to me early tonight."

"With the greatest of pleasure, my ruler," Hata said.

BOOK TWO

BOOK TWO

1

Duwan struggled through deep snow, his arms laden with choice, tender needles from tall brothers. He had tired of dried foods, and had ventured into the dim sun of the short, cold, winter day to gather greens. He noted, as he neared the cave, that Jai, too, had ventured out, and he was concerned until he saw that there were two sets of her tracks, the second leading back to the cave. He entered, placed the tender green needles on a rock ledge where the food was stored, and then stood in puzzlement watching Jai using freshly gathered boughs to prepare a bed on the opposite side of the fire from the bed they shared.

"Tonight, and for some nights to come, I will sleep here," she said matter-of-factly, as she patted the boughs into place.

"I think we will both be cold," he said, still not understanding.

"It is necessary," she said.

"Perhaps you will find time, since much of the winter is ahead of us, to explain why it is necessary."

She turned to face him and laughed. Her full face, in laughter, was a thing of great beauty to him. He remembered her as he'd first seen her, thin to starvation, hair unhealthy and lank. She looked the proper Drinker female now, full and fat, even on winter fodder, and the thought of not having his arms around her at night was painful to him.

"You really don't know?" she asked.

"I am but a simple male."

She opened her outer garment, pulled up the undersmock. He gasped. Her bud point had bloomed overnight. The fleshy petals had swollen and colored so that that most intimate part of her flared, gleaming in hues of the rainbow.

"Hold," he said, as she started to cover herself. He had never seen a female in full bloom, and the wonder of it awed him. "Come to me."

She walked toward him, her eyes downcast. "We have a long journey ahead," she said, "and although I would be honored to bear your young I will not burden you in your journey with a female with a fat stomach and, perhaps before we arrive, a new young."

He knelt, held back her clothing. From her flowering came a perfume that made him dizzy. He felt his own body began to change, felt his heart beat faster, and felt a swelling beginning far inside him.

"Beautiful, so beautiful," he whispered.

"The air is cold, even with the fire," she said, but she was smiling.

"Lie with me, let me see this wonder," he said, and she went with him to the bed, lay down, allowed him to arrange her clothing until she was fully exposed. He stared for a long time, unable to get his fill of the beauty of that flower of femininity.

"Stop," she whispered weakly, "or you will color, too, and then—"

"I think I color already," he said, pulling at his garments. It was true; he was pink, and the petals were expanding, and his bud was exposed, and even as they both watched, and Jai giggled delightedly, the color reddened to a flame and his breath was short and quick.

"I am going to run to the other side of the cave," she said, pulling away, "and I'd suggest that you go roll in the snow." She smiled wistfully. "Unless you want me to bear your seed, Duwan?"

"It would be *my* honor," he whispered, and, almost, he was ready to graft with her and take the consequences. However, good sense prevailed. The journey ahead was long and hard. Only he knew just how hard. He would not, under any circumstances, weaken her with the extra weight of a growing seed. He covered her with a sigh and hid himself, but would not let her go. "You will not sleep across the fire. We will sleep here, but you will sleep with your back to me."

"As you will," she said.

It was by far the most difficult thing he'd ever done, keeping himself from entering that flower of rainbow hues, that perfume-scented orifice to bliss. But he held her and talked to her. He tortured himself by uncovering her during the short days, when the dim light of Du helped illuminate the cave, and even as his eyes and nose loved her, he talked, and she talked, and told him of her young days in the pongpens, and how a master had forced her when she was still unopened, and how, after that, until she became gaunt and thin as she grew, more than one of the masters used her. And of the pain. And as she spoke he clenched his fists and hated.

"And of our kind?" he asked. "Have there been many?"

She clung to him. "Not many. Nights are long and cold in the pens. We sleep together for warmth, and it happens sometimes."

"You've never been fertilized," he stated, hoping for the answer he wanted, wanting not to think of her carrying another's seed.

"No, the masters who owned me did not want young, and I would fight pongs when I was flowering."

"If, someday, you could grow my seed—"

"I want that."

He was moodily silent, and guilty, for his thoughts went to Alning, for whom he had spoken, conditionally, if he returned within two cycles of the time of long light. He would. Their journey would begin with the first warm days and he would be in the valley before Du retreated to the south again.

"I hate it when you leave me like this," Jai said.

"Leave you?"

"You are far away in your thoughts."

"I admit it."

"You were thinking of her, of the female you left behind."

"True, Jai. That is true. It troubles me. I am a mere male and although I have erred here in this land of the enemy, I like to think that I am an honorable male. Yet I don't feel that it is wrong to graft with you. How is that? And how is it that I can love two females?"

She cupped his face between her hands and kissed him. "It is not love you feel for me, but the love of pleasure, and that is good, and natural, at least in the world as we know it. In an ideal time, perhaps, the code your people follow is good. But pong females are forced, quite young, and used without reservation by any master who desires it, and the pleasure we get with other pongs is the only pleasure in our lives. How can you love two? I have loved not many, but several, and yet I chose no mate, lest I love too deeply and he be taken from me by the Devourers, sold or traded away. The only love you have is the love for your Alning. Don't be concerned. When we arrive in your valley I will be your loyal slave, nothing more."

He did not see, in the dark, that tears were wetting her cheeks. "I will always count myself blessed that I have had you for this little time, and if, later, you choose to give me a seed that I may nourish it and grow it and love it, and raise it in the freedom that you will give to all our people, then I will thank that Du of yours, and all the other dus."

"There is only one Du," Duwan said.

"As you will. I will thank him, and demand nothing more."

In his desperation, but with good sense still overcoming nature's strongest urge, the urge to graft when two Drinkers colored together, he found that the perfume of her flower tasted like nectar and that his mouth gave her exquisite pleasure, and then the coloration was gone and she was his.

Drinker does not live by love alone, and in the long months remaining he taught her everything he knew about Drinker history, and she taught him the language of the Devourers, and then the snow began to melt and they marched northward, sometimes sinking up to their knees in mud, swimming cold, swollen rivers, finding, as they slept in whispering groves, that Jai was now more sensitive to the whisperings.

One day they encountered two of the Devourers, males, and, being challenged, Duwan killed both with ease. They took fresh clothing and Jai took weapons, a longsword and a shortsword.

"Teach me," she said, brandishing the weapons rather dangerously near Duwan's head.

He laughed and said, "First lesson, don't decapitate your teacher."

She insisted, and in the light of campfires he taught her the basic strokes and thrusts. She was good with the shortsword, her left hand being quite nimble, but rather weak with the longsword. However, as the long trek continued, as they passed out of the land of the tall brothers into the marshy, grassy, seemingly endless tundra where flowers brightened the dull landscape as the strength of Du moved northward, following them, her right arm began to develop muscle so that she could truly swing the longsword. She was now dressed in male clothing, taken from the dead Enemy, and he called her his warrior maiden.

The time of the long light had come when Duwan finally saw he smokes of the land of fires in the distance, and it was passing as he led a frightened Jai through the seemingly deadly fields of molten rock. He was eager now, and he set a pace that left them both exhausted at the end of the long days. Ahead were the barrens. He began to recognize landmarks, and, after an extremely long and tiring march, saw the rock formations that told him the valley was but a day's march ahead.

He slept fitfully. If Jai noticed that he seemed bemused and distant she did not remark on it, nor did she try for closeness as he slept on his back, not touching her.

2

Belran the Leader had always taken his role seriously, but since Duwan had departed he had intensified the training of the young warriors to the point where no Drinker of fighting age was without bruises. Belran had awaited the coming of the second period of long light eagerly, and, as the beautiful time came, and lengthened, he found occasion often to go to the lower end of the valley, climb the narrow vent, and gaze out over the barrens.

It was pleasant to be alone for a change, away from the respectful but exuberant, young, would-be warriors. He stood on a high, rounded boulder and looked away across the barren landscape to the south. Du was growing weaker, sinking ever lower in the sky, and soon the long darkness would begin and the Drinkers would accept the limitations put upon their activities by the long winter, made bearable only by the many hot, flowing springs that warmed the valley with their steams. The think vines would be directed to close in, to make the houses airtight with their closely locked bodies and cold-resistant life organs, and during that long darkness a few new ones would be sprouted to be entrusted to the good earth in the steam-filled young houses.

There was no sign of movement within his eyesight. Du's dimming light gave the bare stones and pockets of sterile sand a melancholy aspect, and he turned away sadly. He'd been fond of Duwan, who had been one of the most promising young warriors he'd ever taught, but it was not only the thought of Duwan being dead that made him sad. With Duwan died hope, even that weak, reluctantly rekindled hope that had come when, at last, one of the Drinkers traveled to the south. He thought of going south himself. Perhaps it had been too much to expect that a youth with only one arm should be able to overcome the vast distances and the unknown dangers and return.

Soon the long darkness would end all hope, and then—

He was not willing to face the people feeling as he did. He felt a sense of guilt as he walked into the valley, chose a spot near a spring where Du touched the hungry earth and lay down, exposing his chest to the sun. He felt warm and languorous with Du feeding him, and his eyes closed.

He awoke with a jerk, his ears searching for the sound that had awakened him. His sword seemed to materialize in his hand as he leaped to his feet to face the ragged, bundled apparition that stood before him, longsword pointed at his belly.

"Greetings, Belran," the apparition said, "I have come to have a rematch of the test."

"Duwan?" The Leader peered into the darkness under the stranger's hood, saw the gleam of orange eyes, let his eyes fall to the newcomer's left side to see, to his disappointment, only emptiness.

Duwan pushed back his hood, smiling broadly. "Well, Leader, may I have my test?"

Belran felt like weeping. So the legend of renewal was false. If that part of the old tales was false, how could any of it be true?

"The longsword is no match for two," Belran said.

"Then we will make the odds even," Duwan said, sweeping his shortsword out from behind his back.

Belran's eyes went wide and he whooped. He

dropped his own sword heedlessly—and this action told Duwan more than anything else that Belran was pleased to see him—and slipped between Duwan's swords to embrace him. Duwan was laughing.

"Did you meet the Enemy?" Belran asked, pushing himself out of the twining of arms.

"I have met him," Duwan said. "The challenge is great, but the opportunities are greater."

"And does Du shine all year long? Are there many brothers? Is the Enemy strong? How does he fight?"

"Hold," Duwan laughed. "I have much to tell, and I don't want to have to tell it many times."

"You are right," Belran said, his hands feeling the hard muscles in Duwan's left arm. "Come, we must spread this news rapidly. We will have a gathering before Du slips below the horizon to the south."

"My father and mother?" Duwan asked.

"Well," Belran said. "Your grandmother hardens, but is also well."

"And the young one called Alning?"

Belran turned his face away. "She blossoms, and is well," he said.

It was at that moment that Jai chose to emerge from behind boulders and Belran's hand went to his sword.

"This is Jai, Drinker, once a slave to the enemy," Duwan said. "She, too, has much information to impart."

They spread the news through the villages as they walked the length of the valley. A growing entourage shouted, laughed, sang behind them. Minstrels flanked the moving mass of people, adding new verses of triumph to the *Song of Duwan*, for it had become a popular story since Duwan's leaving.

Duwan had known pain, the fear of death, wonder, sadness, the joy of grafting, but the emotions that came to him when he entwined arms with his father and then clasped his mother and the hard, old shell of his grandmother were the most powerful emotions of his young life. He was weeping shamelessly. Even his father's eyes were moist, and tears appeared, clear as dew, on his father's age-coloring cheeks.

His mother and his grandmother swept Jai away, leaving Duwan to accept the admiration and the questions of the growing number of warriors. The village square was soon filled, and still they came, from all parts of the valley. Now and then Duwan had a chance to look around, and he had not yet caught sight of the face that he wanted most to see.

When the last of the elders from neighboring villages were seated, forming a circle around Duwan and his father, with warriors massed behind the elders, Duwan rose and began his story. He told it quickly and simply, neither emphasizing nor playing down the dangers of the long trek to the south. He presented the Enemy as he had seen him, a potentially dangerous force grown weak with overconfidence and wealth. He spoke of the Enemy's evil, of death and murder and the eating of young, and hardened warriors shuddered and muttered. When he was finished with his story he paused, looked around, caught the eye of Belran the Leader.

"Only a handful of the Enemy, the royal guards, could make a contest of arms with even the youngest of our warriors," he said. "The time has come for us to reclaim our land. Under the wise guidance of our Leaders, such as my father and Belran, we can sweep down from the north and invest the northern cities and the settlements, capturing weapons that will then be distributed to the Drinkers, the slaves, of that land. As we use our training methods to teach our southern brothers the art of warfare, we will move southward and when the capital city falls, the land will be ours, and there will be only a matter of mopping up scattered points of resistance in the other Devourer cities."

A shout of excitement came from the younger warriors. So intent was Duwan on telling his tale that he did not see the shaking heads of some of the elders. During the feasting that followed Duwan was occupied in exchanging greetings with friends and then the visitors began to drift away. Still he had not seen Alning. He was about to sneak away when his mother came to him and took his left arm, feeling it, smiling, and weeping at the same time. "Now I claim your time," she said, pulling him toward the house. Inside, she guided him into the sleep room that she shared with his father. Jai and his grandmother were sitting in front of the fireplace, heads close together, the old one's ear close to Jai's mouth.

"While you were in your rightful place with the warriors," his mother said, "I have learned much from this female you have brought."

"There is much to learn about the Land of Many Brothers," he said. "It is a sweet and wonderful land, mother. It is our rightful land."

His mother waved one hand. "Oh, I am interested enough in this land to the south," she said, "but I am more interested, at the moment, in the glow that comes into the eyes of this female when she speaks of you."

Duwan felt his face grow hot.

"She has not *spoken* secrets to me, Duwan."

Duwan swallowed hard, fearing that he had caught her meaning.

"She is a strong, young female," his mother said. "I would not object to calling her my own."

Alarm jerked Duwan's head up so that his eyes met hers.

"You are my son," she said, "but you are not the same person who left here almost two cycles of the long light past. You have changed, and now you are warrior, mature, a son to give me pride, and to put the light in your father's eyes. But, Duwan, you are not the only one who has changed."

"What are you telling me, mother?" He leaned back, forced himself to give the impression of relaxation. "I think you're speaking indirectly of Alning."

"I take it that you have not seen her."

"No."

The look of feminine condemnation on his mother's face told him, but he chose not to believe.

"I don't doubt that she'd be reluctant to appear before you," his mother said. "You will find her in the new house, last on the northern side of the square before the yellow spring."

He rose. His heart seemed about to burst out of his chest. "I will see for myself," he said.

He walked slowly at first, lifting his hands in greeting. A group of small, young males surrounded him, clamored questions at him, and he told them that he'd repeat his story for them later. Then he found himself walking faster and faster until the bulk of the village was behind him and a new house, think vines showing an interesting design, appeared to him amid the mists of the yellow spring. He halted at the entrance and announced himself.

Her face sent a shiver of appreciation through him.

"Alning," he said.

No smile greeted him. Her face was as if frozen by the cold of the land of tall brothers.

"Not quite two times of the long light have passed," he said. "I have returned, and I am whole." He showed her his left arm.

"They said you would never return," she whispered.

"You listened to bad counsel."

"It is true."

"But now I am back," he said, wondering why she showed him only her face and did not ask him to enter.

"I am very happy for you," she said.

It was time to face facts. He knew, but he just

wasn't ready to admit that it was true. He bent, entered the house. She moved away, her back to him. In the light of the fire and the light vents left by the think vines she seemed different, more mature, but that was natural, for she would have filled out, especially during the time of long light when food was plentiful.

"Two cycles is a long time, Duwan," she said.

"True."

She turned slowly. In profile her stomach protruded mightily, suggesting that, perhaps, she carried twins. She had not even waited until the *beginning* of the second time of long light, much less the end, which had not yet come. Duwan felt a knife stab from the inside, and almost bent with the pain.

"Who?" he asked, his voice a croak.

"Noo," she said.

"A good match. Son of Manoo the Predictor."

"Oh, Duwan—" She took one step toward him, her legs wide to balance the front-heavy bulk of her body. She halted when there was movement behind them and a well built young male entered.

"Greetings, Duwan," said Noo, son of the Predictor. "I was moved by the recitation of your adventures."

"I have given my greeting to an old friend, a female that I tended in the young house," Duwan said. "I ask your understanding and forgiveness for entering your house in your absence."

Noo made a gesture of negation. "You are welcome as a friend of the family, and as our most famous warrior."

"May they be twins," Duwan said, nodding at Alning.

"The midwife thinks so," Noo said. He smiled. "A good way to start a family, is it not?"

Duwan walked north, skirted springs, found himself under the cliffs where, at a time that seemed both far distant and most recent, he had climbed into the rays of Du to thrust his left arm into the concealed maw of the rock sucker. He started climbing, soon felt the weak light as he clambered recklessly to the very top of the cliffs. At the top, with a cold wind sweeping across the barrens, he looked down on the steam and green of the valley and wept.

"Du," he said, "if this is punishment for my errant ways when I was among the enemy, then it is deserved." But, ah, it hurt. It hurt more than he had hurt when he'd lopped off his left arm to save his own life. It hurt so much that he remembered the story his grandmother had told him about the son who had leaped, or fallen, from the cliffs. It was tempting, for a moment. Then he looked again at the valley, saw the villages, the movement of Drinkers in the squares, remembered the intoxicating heat of Du in the far south. He had his duty.

He found Belran at the forge of a metal worker, stripped to the waist, wielding a hammer himself, forming a sweetly designed blade. He watched. That blade would taste enemy blood and help to return the stolen heritage of his people. Why, then, did he not exult?

"The fires of the forges will burn all winter," Belran said, as he dipped the glowing blade to the accompaniment of a hissing and metallic smelling steam. "There, that is all for today. We will let the spirit of the metal rest for a time." He wiped his hands on his garment and buckled on his weapons. "This royal guardsman you fought," he said. "Did you note well his technique?"

"Quite well," Duwan said. "He was the best I'd seen."

"Show me."

There was no audience. Longswords were padded. Duwan played the part of Captain Hata. His sword hissed and thudded against Belran's padded weapon. He felt the sweat begin to form, and the closest thing he would ever know to joy—or so, at least, did he think at the time—filled him as he faced a sword as skilled, possibly more skilled, than his own and demonstrated Hata's offensive techniques. Then he stepped back.

"I shifted to the left hand," he said, "after studying all his techniques. He was susceptible to a low, rising sweep, but he managed to counter it."

Belran came at him, and he found it more difficult to counter the left-handed blows. It ended, oddly enough, as his duel with Hata had ended. He felt the impact of Belran's sword on his head, was dazed, but felt the solid impact of his padded blade on Belran's toughened stomach at the same instant. He rose, shaking his head, and helped Belran to his feet. The older warrior was panting.

"Of course, the killing blow to the stomach would have been countered with the shortsword," Belran said.

"When we go south we will not fight by the Enemy's rules," Duwan agreed. "He is an abomination to the light of Du, Belran. It is given to us Drinkers to rid the land of him, to end the eating of Drinker young and the sacrifice of living entities of all brotherhoods, to bring freedom to the enslaved."

Belran clasped right arms with him, showed his teeth in a fierce grin. "It makes my flesh crawl to think of the Enemy's evil," he said. "We will fight side by side, warrior."

Why did being accepted by the great Belran as an equal not give him joy?

He ate with his family, hiding his heartbreak. Jai wanted to serve, but his mother insisted that she sit with the family and eat. His grandmother sat by his side.

"Thanks to you, my son," the old female said, as she toyed with her food, "I will become one with the earth when you lead us to our homeland."

"So be it, Grandmother," he said.

"To have eternal peace and warmth and to feed and grow on the goodness of the earth," she said.

"It is good," he said.

"You have heard the whispering?"

"Yes. Most of the time it is muddled, confused by many voices, Grandmother."

"This female, your Jai, says that she, in the end, could also hear the whisperings," his grandmother said.

He glanced at Jai almost guiltily. He had not given her one thought, much less a look, or a smile, since returning from the house of Alning and Noo. "She is, after all, Drinker," he said.

"Duwan, help me to survive the coming darkness," the old woman asked, pleading in her voice. "Promise me that you will not let me harden. Promise me that you will plant me yourself in some warm, rich spot blessed by the full rays of Du."

"I promise," Duwan said, taking her hand only to be surprised by the rigid, hard feel of her.

"There is much to be done," his father said. "I have called a gathering of elders. We must make our plans and our preparations. I have advised that all fertile grafting be discontinued during the coming darkness, so that we will have no new young to impede our journey."

"An excellent idea," Duwan said.

"I have spoken with Belran and the other village elders," his father said. "You will command the people of our village during the trek."

Duwan nodded, taking the responsibility not with joy but with a sense of duty settling upon his shoulders.

"Now you should rest, my son," his mother said. "You've been long on the march, and long awake."

When he awoke, the elders of all the villages were already gathering in the square. He was summoned by his father and went forth to see them, all the wise men of the Drinkers, seated on the good earth, looking up at him as he strode to the speaker's mound.

"My son knows the way to the south," his father said. "I and my village elders have put him in command for the duration of the trip. I ask that all other villages follow suit."

There were no objections.

"Now here is our chief warrior, Belran the Leader," Duwan's father said, "to make suggestions as to our preparations."

Belran took the speaker's mound. "I do not underestimate the difficulty of the journey. Duwan will tell us more, again and again, so that it can be implanted in our minds, as we prepare during the long darkness. When we leave, we must travel light. We will not be able, for example, to take our forges and anvils. Our loads must be weapons, food, water, clothing. When we have reached the lands of the south we must have spare weapons, the extra ones we will carry. We must, during the winter, have our metal workers convert all surplus iron into weapons. We will put emphasis on arrowheads, for our bows will be of great advantage to us. Duwan has told us that the bow is well known by the Enemy, but that it has fallen into disfavor. Since our supply of good wood for bows and arrows is limited here, we must carry only the pre-made heads, to be fitted to arrows made from the plentiful wood to the south."

An elder from a neighboring village stood and Belran politely stopped talking. "You are a respected warrior, Belran, but I think you presume too much," the elder said. "Our village has not yet voted."

Before the astounded Belran could speak, Duwan leaped to the speaker's mound. "Vote?" he howled. "This is not a matter of village politics. This is the destiny of our people."

He felt his father's hand on his arm and allowed himself to be pulled off the mound. His father spoke.

"Duwan is young, and he has seen the horrors done to living things by the Enemy." He nodded. "Yes, it is proper that we all vote."

The standing elder spoke. "The fires burn brightly in the young," he said. "Duwan fought well and slew the Enemy—a very few Enemy. Our questions are about the Enemy's vast numbers, his stone-walled cities that will be easily defended. We are few. They are many."

"And yet the population of enslaved Drinkers outnumbers their masters," Belran said.

Another elder stood. "We feel, in my village, that Drinkers who would allow themselves to be enslaved would make poor allies."

Duwan was at first amazed, then angered, then saddened, as objection after objection was voiced by the elders. It was pointed out that Duwan was the only living Drinker who had actually seen the land of the south, and that he was young, and, perhaps, incapable of accurate observation, that he based his case on having killed a few unskilled Enemy and one padded sword bout with a royal guard.

Alone with his father and Belran, Duwan was speechless.

"Duwan," Belran said. "You must take it upon yourself to visit each village, to speak personally to the elders and to anyone who will listen. Take the female with you. Let her exhibit the lash marks on her back. Let her tell of the sufferings not only of Drinkers, but of animal and fixed brothers."

Jai, although she was growing fond of Duwan's mother and grandmother, was more than eager to get away. She wore the neat winter garb of the valley, for Du had passed below the southern cliffs to be seen no more for long, cold, dark months. By firelight in village squares Duwan stated his case and then Jai told of life in the slave pens, causing gasps of fear and anger among those who listened. Making the round of the villages took time, and, meanwhile, nothing was being done in preparation for leaving the valley at the dawn of Du in the new beginning.

Properly, when spending sleep periods in the villages, Duwan bedded down with young warriors and Jai with unmated females. While walking from village to village, Duwan could not bring himself to be easy with Jai, for his heart still ached. While he was away Alning gave her mate, Noo, a pair of twin males, who were, with great ceremony (twins being quite rare) given to the earth in the village young house.

A dark period gathering was unusual. The call went out from Duwan the Elder, and from Belran the Leader, and the elders of the valley made their way through the darkness to the well lighted square of Duwan's village.

"If we are to move south with the new coming of Du," Duwan the Elder told the gathered wise ones, "we must begin our preparations. I have been told that many of you have voted. If it is your pleasure, we would know the results."

An elder from the village nearest the southern end of the valley rose. "First, know our reasons," he said. "We have heard Duwan, and we have heard the female, Jai. We listened closely to Duwan's plans which, we feel, rely too heavily on recruiting an army from the enslaved ones in the south. And yet, according to Duwan himself, and to the female, no slave rises against his masters, making us doubt their fighting ability."

Duwan, although his father tried to stop him, took the speaker's mound. "Before we proceed further, let me demonstrate that slaves can be taught to fight."

"If this can be demonstrated—although I see not how—we will be interested," the standing elder said.

"Jai, come," Duwan yelled and Jai, who'd been listening from the shadows outside the fires, came striding into the circle of light, weapons buckled at her waist.

"This is a female," someone cried.

"Yes," Duwan said, "and a slave, until she escaped." He drew his weapons and stepped into an open area. "At me, Jai," he said. "Show them how you have learned the swords."

"Hold," a voice cried. "Bare blades and the one who, obviously, taught her, and thus knows her every move will not be a test, but an exhibition."

"Do you call for a test?" Belran the Leader asked, and was answered by affirmative calls.

"We need an opponent," Belran said.

"You," someone cried.

"We will be fair," Belran said. "A young warrior newly trained."

A young male stepped into the light of the fires. "I," he said, "although I feel shamed to duel a female."

"Forget that I am female," Jai said, and she did not speak in the cringing tones of a slave. "Look on me as the Enemy."

Swords were padded and checked. Belran was to officiate. He stood between the male and Jai and, as was the custom for a test, stated the rules. As he stepped back, the young warrior spanked Jai across the backside with his longsword, chuckling, showing his contempt for a female opponent, and Belran started to bellow that he had broken the rules, making contact with the opponent before the proper signal, but the words were punctuated with a solid thud as Jai's longsword whistled, even with its padding, and landed against the young warrior's head.

"By Du," Belran roared, "no contact before the signal." But he was trying to hide a grin as the young warrior, stunned, was dragged away by two of his companions.

"We need an opponent who knows the rules," Belran roared.

Duwan stiffened as Noo, son of the Predictor, stepped forward, holding his swords out to be padded. "I know the rules," he said.

The ceremony began anew. Then Jai was crouched, waiting for Noo's move. He came forward cautiously and made two formal thrusts. Noo had not, Duwan remembered, been one of the most skilled trainees. He watched Jai's tense, waiting form and whispered to himself, "Now, Jai," and as if she heard she leaped to the attack and delivered a smashing blow that was barely countered in time by Noo.

Noo had more respect for the female now, and he fought carefully. Duwan started to worry, lest the bout go on so long that Jai's lesser strength began to work against her. He had seen three flaws in Noo's technique that would have been fatal had he himself been the warrior's opponent, and he was willing Jai to see them just as she lunged, feinted, slashed the padded tip of her longsword across Noo's chest and sent the shortsword stabbing into his belly. He sat down with a huff and it was over.

"An impressive exhibition," said the elder who had questioned the fighting ability of slaves. "How long, Duwan, did you train this female?"

Duwan would not lie, although he sensed the hostile intent of the question. "Through a winter."

"And will we be given that much time to train our army in the south?"

"Did you, during your stay in the south, influence a large number of slaves to join you?"

"How many of the so-called free runners joined your cause?"

The end of it became predictable. One by one, the chief elders of the villages rose and announced their decisions.

"We will not risk our females and our young in such a venture."

"Our home is here. We have been here for generations."

"While we sorrow for those who are enslaved, we must remember that our ancestors did not accept slavery, but risked all in coming to this valley."

"Our home is here."

Duwan the Elder rose sadly. Only his own village had not voted. He looked around, and Duwan was near enough to see that he had tears in his eyes.

"We are free," he said. "I respect your votes, while deploring your decision. I will not ask the people of my village to vote, for to take such a small number into the land of the enemy would be foolhardy. It has been decided by proper procedure that the Drinkers will not move south, will not retake the land of our ancestors. So be it."

Duwan wandered alone in the dark, stunned. He found a spring and lay on the damp earth, feeling the heat of the steam, his heart aching, his mind confused. He heard a sound and then heard his name being called softly. He wanted to be alone, but it was Jai calling, and she was unfamiliar with the ground and could, in the dark, fall and injure herself. "Here," he called, and her form emerged, a shadow in shadows, and he took her hand and pulled her down beside him. Neither spoke for a long time.

"This is a good place," Jai said, at last. "There is no cold. I hate the cold so."

"There is no sun, no eternal life. They have voted to let the ancient victory of the enemy stand, and it is not just the pongs of the south who will continue to be punished, but we, ourselves, for we are denied the bounty of the land, the Du-given right to go back to the earth after our time as mobiles."

"Don't try to contest their decision, Duwan," she whispered.

"No. They are free, just as I am free to do what I choose to do."

"What will that be?"

He mused for a long time. "I told Tambol I would return."

"He could well be dead by now," Jai said.

"I gave my word. If you think this is a good place, stay."

"I meant that it is a good place for you," she whispered.

"And not for you?"

"Your mother and your grandmother have been kind."

"Have others been unkind?"

She was reluctant to speak.

"Speak," he ordered. "Who has been unkind to you?"

"No one in particular. When I was with the young unmated females I made the mistake of exposing my bud point."

"So?"

"It's nothing," she said.

"Something was said?"

"You can imagine."

He could. In this valley a female's budpoint was unopened until her first coloration. He could imagine the talk among the females, for the word would have spread throughout the valley that this Jai, this outsider, had grafted and had no proper mate. He rose and took her hand and led her back to the village, entered the house of his parents and spoke, his face stern. "This is my mate. I speak for her, and I take her."

His mother leaped to her feet and embraced both of them. His father clasped Duwan's right arm with his own.

"We will make the announcement," his mother said. "A celebration enlivens things so during the darkness."

So it was done. The square blazed with light. Visitors came from several villages, as if eager to atone in some small way for the vote against going back to the Land of Many Brothers. Duwan moved unsmilingly through the ceremonies, spoke for Jai before many witnesses, and, to the cries and shouts and laughter of the gathering, carried his new mate into his father's house. Without light it was not possible to grow a new house, so they would occupy his old room until Du came again. He did not carry Jai to the room immediately. He waited until his parents and his grandmother came into the room and listened as the older women talked about the ceremony and the various people who had attended. When his father went off to bed his mother looked at him questioningly and he took Jai's hand and led her into the privacy of his room.

She came to his bed displaying some new shyness and he moved over to give her room. She lay on her back beside him.

"Wherever I am, if I am with you, I am happy," she said.

"Ummm," he grunted.

"Now I will be warm again as I sleep," she whispered, putting her arm across his chest.

"They have as little shame, my people, as those who live in the pongpens, and those who call themselves free runners but do not have the courage to fight," Duwan said.

"They fear the unknown," she told him. "Duwan, am I really your mate now?"

"Yes, of course," he said.

"Thank you," she whispered.

He felt her warmth against him and shuddered inwardly. His body warmed to her, begged him to relax, to turn to her and embrace her, but he was among civilized people now, and civilized people did not graft promiscuously as did the slaves and the enemy.

She was quiet for a long, long time, until he thought that she had gone to sleep. But then she whispered, "Duwan, was I wrong, when I fought Noo, to give him such a blow to the belly?"

"No, you were not wrong."

"I did it for you," she said.

"For me?"

"Because he took Alning from you."

"Ummm," he said.

"If it was within my power I would give her to you."

"Don't be stupid," he said.

"I know. You Drinkers have your own odd ways, but I wish that I could give her to you, put her in your bed. I wouldn't mind being your slave, and slave to your mate, not if it would make you happy."

He turned. There was total darkness in the room, but as his fingertips touched her cheeks he felt the wetness of tears.

"I understand. She is so beautiful, and she was the love of your youth. Just let me stay with you, Duwan, and serve you. That's all I ask."

"You ask too little, small fool," he said, for, suddenly, as if a cloud of steam had been wafted away by an errant breeze, leaving everything clearly visible, he felt the warmth and softness of her and drew her to him so fiercely that the breath was forced from her lungs. "You are more beautiful."

By Du, it was true. Jai had longer legs, a more sweetly proportioned body, and her face—he pictured it in his mind, and it was smiling and sunny and so dear that he kissed it and kissed it until, forgive him, Du, they were one.

3

Manoo the Predictor had said that the first feeble beams of Du would light the southern sky after a dozen more sleep periods. Duwan was at the forge, fashioning iron, barbed arrowheads. He looked up as someone entered, and nodded respectfully to his father.

"You spend much time making weapons," the Elder said.

"Yes."

"You'll go with the first light of Du?"

Duwan was surprised. He had not stated his intentions, not even to Jai.

"Don't you think we have known this?" his father asked. "Did you not say that you gave your word to a friend?"

Duwan tried to play it lightly. "Perhaps, if you try, father, you can talk me out of this foolishness."

The elder man laughed. "Yes, your task must seem impossible."

Duwan finished sharpening the point of an arrowhead and put it aside. He looked at his father. "If I go to my death I must go. Perhaps, after much time, I can train some few of them to fight."

"We can but try," his father said.

Duwan snapped his head around to look into his father's eyes. "We?"

"There was a Duwan with the Great Alon, when he led the Drinkers into the snows. He, too, made a promise. He, too, promised to return. He made this promise to Alon, it is said, before the great one hardened, here in this lightless place. It is time a Duwan kept that promise, and I will not let you do it alone."

"But mother—"

"She will go with me, of course. Will not your mate go with you?"

Duwan grasped his father's right arm. "We can go into the west," he said. "For I will not lead two Duwans to death."

His father nodded.

Four Drinkers, two of them females, would not be able to carry much. By the time the southern horizon was showing lightness at times, preparations were complete. Jai had accepted Duwan's decision without comment. She practiced her swordplay with Belran's young warriors. She had colored again, and they had, for the same reasons that had made sense during the last winter, abstained.

Duwan felt that he was no longer a part of the Drinkers of the valley. Somehow, what he had done and what he had seen in the Land of Many Brothers had made him a different Drinker. His own people seemed as alien to him as the Enemy now, and although he did not enjoy that feeling, he accepted it. There had been times when he'd suffered through periods of self pity and of condemnation for the Drinkers. Now it no longer seemed to matter. Each Drinker was the master of his own fate, and he had chosen his. He had made up his mind, after his father's decision to join him, to avoid Enemy population centers, to travel into the relatively unpopulated areas of the mid-continent, and there to live out his life with Jai, no longer withholding himself from her during her fertile period. There he would see his mother and his father, when the time came, return to the earth, and he would live near them in their fixed, honorable, immortal state to protect them from any chance enemy.

Only one thing troubled him, and that came to a head as Du's faint presence made a smear of light in the far south. His grandmother. He had promised her that he would personally plant her in a warm, sunny place in the south, and it was becoming more and more evident that she was entering the last stages of the hardening disease. She could not possibly make the hard, long journey to the south, or so at least Duwan thought. His grandmother had other ideas. She was not senseless, not yet. She noted the preparations, and she prepared her warmest garments and nothing else. Duwan saw her placing garments into a small, neat pack one day, as he and his father were making their last preparations, and his heart pounded. How could he tell her that she was to be left behind?

"You made me a promise, Grandson," she told him, when she saw the look on his face. "I hold you to it."

Duwan consulted his father about his grandmother's determination to accompany them. Duwan the Elder thought for a moment. "I have been anticipating this, and I think this way. Your mother's mother will soon harden, cease to be mobile, and then her heart will stop and she will be dead. It is true that the remaining time of her life could be spent in comfort here in this house, but when she hardened she would be just as dead as she will be if she perishes in the cold of the barrens or in the land of the fires."

Duwan lowered his head in sadness. He was about to speak when there was a call at the door and his father invited Belran the Leader to enter. The warrior stood stiff and silent for a moment, looking around the workshop to see the newly forged arrow heads, the newly polished swords.

"I had suspected that the younger Duwan would leave us again for the south," Belran said. "Now it appears that our chief elder is also contemplating a journey."

"Old friend," the Elder said, I was going to postpone that news as long as possible, but now I suppose it is time we talked. Yes, I will go with my son."

"Then count my swords among your number," Belran said, holding his chin high.

Duwan the Elder clasped Belran's right arm with his. "There is no Drinker I would rather have fighting by my side, but if you go who will lead these Drinkers who remain?"

"Many of the young warriors will choose to go," Belran said.

"And leave anarchy behind?" Duwan the Elder asked. "This one is my son, Belran, and he has given his word to those he left behind in the south. I, as you can see, must go, but you must stay. I know that it is much to ask, but both of us cannot throw over our responsibilities to our village. It is not yours to support the word of a son, as it is mine. You must stay, my friend, and, moreover, you must control your young warriors. If we bled off the strength of this village it would cease to function. It would be absorbed by the other villages. Can we be responsible for that?"

Belran's chin lifted even higher. "You speak the truth, but it is painful."

"I know," Duwan the Elder said.

"I will stay." Belran turned to Duwan. "I see something in you that was not there when you first left us. I see, I suspect, the quality that makes a Drinker a leader, and perhaps something else. When you begin to train your slaves, remember the lessons of Belran. Neither push them too hard nor allow them to be slack. And remember that you train the mind as well as the arms."

"I will, Leader," Duwan said.

Belran shook his head. "Two Drinkers to do the work of an army. I feel shame for my people."

"No," Duwan said, "there is no shame. This is their world now, and change is difficult. Change comes usually by outside agencies, and not from within, although that is not as it should be." He clasped Belran's arm. "We will send word. When we have proven that we can free the Drinkers of the Land of Many Brothers, when we have forged an army of them and have begun to retake our lands, we will send word and then perhaps the elders will choose to join us."

"I will wait with great impatience," Belran said. "My heart will be with you, and, some day, my swords."

As it happened, Belran's desire to leave the valley, to accompany the two Duwans to the south, was shared by others, and that, too, presented a problem. On the day that the journey began, when the Duwans and their mates emerged, laden, into the square, they were awaited by what seemed to be every aged member of the village, over fifty oldsters, and each of them was dressed warmly and carried a pack.

Duwan felt his heart sink. He knew, from talking with his grandmother, what wild hope beat in the hearts of those old, hardening Drinkers, and he quailed at having to tell them that they could not possibly make the trip, that four younger Drinkers could not be expected to tend to the needs of so many feeble old ones. Before he could speak, however, an old Drinker pushed forward. He was a warrior of note, had once been a Leader.

"Duwan the Elder, and Duwan the Son," the old Drinker said, "the mother of Sema, mate of Duwan the Elder, goes to the south to return to the blessed earth in the land of our fathers. We, too, will go."

Duwan swallowed and looked at his father, who was silent. "Honored old ones," he said, "someday, the

ones who grow old after you will have that right, or
so I pray. Now—" He opened his hands and stood
mute for a moment.

"We take the responsibility for ourselves," the old
one, Dagner, said. "We will not burden you. We
realize that some of us will die in the barrens, some
in the land of the fires, that not all of us will reach
the lands of the south." He drew himself up. "However, unlike some here in this valley, we will die
trying to reclaim our heritage."

Duwan whispered to his father, "They are weak,
old, and they will *all* die before we reach the land of
the fires."

"Death will find them, wherever they are," Duwan
the Elder said. "Give them their hope, son."

It was to become a matter of legend, a subject for
the minstrels, how the two Duwans, elder and younger, led the slow, sometimes reeling procession from
their native village, how the procession swelled as it
passed through the countryside, and grew by multiples as it passed the villages and reached the narrow
cleft leading out of the valley, how the first dead did
not even make it out of the valley, but fell in the
steams to return to the earth without hope, without
eternal life.

Duwan led the way out of the valley into the cold
winds of the barrens. It was still winter there, but the
thinking was that, fat and well fed, cells filled almost
to bursting with nutrition and energy, it would be
best to face iron cold at the beginning of the trip
rather than face it, as Duwan had, in a weakened
condition at the end of the trek. That decision was
not altered for the old ones, and the cold took its
toll, and the dead were left behind, to be buried by
the last of the winter's snows.

Duwan's mother, Sema, walked easily, strongly,
always near the front of the procession. Her orange
eyes seemed, almost, to glow in the dark. Beside her,

struggling resolutely along, was Sema the elder, her mother, Duwan's grandmother, bundled into all her clothing, lifting her feet in the deep snow with difficulty, but always, at the end of a march, when they dug down and made a place to sit in the snow, with them.

Jai and Duwan the Elder ranged from the front of the group back to the last straggler, encouraging, shouting, lifting some oldster to his or her feet. Oddly enough, the hardships seemed to put new life back into some of the old ones. By the time Du was a warming influence, and the smokes of the land of the fires could be seen occasionally, low on the southern horizon, Sema the elder was walking as if she were much, much younger, made more agile by having used up stored fat that seemed to accumulate under the hardening hides of the old ones. And some of the elderly warriors were now insisting on spelling Duwan in breaking a trail through deeper snow.

It seemed that those who were going to die had died by the time the snow began to melt and they walked on the ash and hard rock and felt for the first time the warming influence of both Du and the land of fires.

Duwan stood on a high place and looked back at the caravan. He saw his mother walking tirelessly, his grandmother at her side, walking stiffly but strongly. He saw Jai helping a female far to the rear and he hollered down to her. She waved. He worried that she was using too much of her energy helping the weak ones, but his father had said, "Her heart is great, Duwan."

He allowed them to rest well before entering the land of fires, and they fed on the pulpy stuff of the succulent fixed brothers of that place. Only one was lost in the land of the fires, an old female who stumbled and rolled down, down a cindery slope into a lake of fire, there to disappear in a puff of smoke.

The departure had been timed well. Du's warmth made it not simple, but not fatal, to cross the melting snow fields, to wade the muddy bogs of the tundra. They saw the first signs of fixed brothers while Du's face was growing warmer, and there were no storms as they entered the land of tall brothers and, for the first time, the old ones saw the life that awaited them, heard the whispers, called the fixed ones brother. There, since there was still time, a few chose to stay. They had crossed the tundra with the last of their strength and they chose to go back to the earth there, in that northern place.

Since there was time, and since the event was a significant one, Duwan called a rest, and they watched with wondering eyes as Du revealed his power and his mercy, for the newly planted ones showed alterations within hours of their plantings. Skin that had been hardening and flaking away hardened even faster, but clung closely to limbs and spread and soon it was not possible to see, except in bulging places, where there had been arms. The frondlike hair grew rapidly and became branches and when it became necessary for Duwan to lead the mobile ones away, the planted ones looked, from a distance, like that which they were becoming, fixed brothers.

"Farewell, farewell," came the whispers, clearly heard.

Dagner, the old warrior, walked beside Duwan. "As long as there is rain and sun you will be remembered," he said.

Duwan was silent, a bit embarrassed.

"And when we others go back to the earth we, too, will sing your praises," Dagner said.

"My friend," Duwan said, "you will not harden for many cycles. You will be active long enough to help us kill the Enemy."

Dagner laughed. "You joke, trying to cheer me,

when I need no cheering. But, yes, I would kill a few of the Enemy before I find my spot."

To Duwan's surprise, for there had been no Devourer settlements so far north before, he and Dagner walked directly into a clearing and stood face to face with more than a dozen of the Enemy. A nearby pongpen was crowded with slaves.

"You wanted a chance to kill Enemy," Duwan said, drawing his weapons. "You now have it."

Dagner sprang forward with a shout.

"Father," Duwan yelled, "forward with care."

He, too, leaped forward. The surprised Devourers met their rush with longswords and fell back before the onslaught of four swords wielded by as many hands, and then Duwan the Elder was among them, stroking and slashing mightily. By the time others of the older warriors came forward it was over and twelve of the Devourers lay dead.

Dagner, breathing hard, cleaned his swords on the tunic of a fallen enemy. "Praise Du," he said, "that I have had this opportunity to avenge, if only in a minor way, the past."

Duwan was looking at the thin, starved slaves in the pen. "These are Drinkers?" he asked.

"Judge them by the pores in the bottom of their feet," Duwan said.

He walked toward the pens. As he neared, the pongs began to fall to their knees and bow.

"Master," one of them said, cringing, as if expecting a blow. "Is it you? Is it you who was foretold by the holy man, Tambol?"

"Tambol, holy?" Jai asked. She'd come running forward, but too late to get in on the action.

"He teaches us," the pong said. "He tells of us a wise and big hearted one who will return from the north to free us. Are you he?"

"You are free," Duwan said. "I am no Drinker's master."

"With these you would make an army?" Duwan the Elder asked.

"Teach us, Master," the pong begged. "Teach us *how* to be free."

"On your feet, all of you," Duwan said, and the pongs leaped up. "Now, how did this settlement come to be so far north?"

"Master," the spokesman said, "the Devourers came here to extend the hunting range for the city of Kooh."

"Are there other settlements in these northern forests?" Duwan asked.

"This is the northernmost," the pong said. "There are others. We were many when we left Kooh, and many dropped off along the way to clear land and build way stations."

Duwan was thinking, *So, it is now time for us to angle off to the west, lest we encounter other Devourers.*

"How are we to be free, Master," asked a gaunt, half naked slave female. "It is said that you freed one female, and made her your follower. I would follow you, as well."

"Teach us the use of the Devourer's arms," cried a male.

"Tell us of eternal life," said another.

"Take down the bars from the fence that makes you a slave," Duwan said. He stooped and plucked a life organ from a fixed brother. "Then begin to feed yourself, thus, in the way of Drinkers so that you will be strong and then we will speak of teaching you the way of arms."

With a crack of wood the fence gave way. The ragged female who had been brave enough to speak fell to her knees in front of Duwan and plucked life organs from the low growing fixed brothers and stuffed them into her mouth.

"Bless this green, Master, so that I will live," she cried.

"Expose your skin to the healing, nourishing goodness of Du," Duwan said.

A few of them pushed back their hoods. One male bared his chest and looked fearfully up.

"Eat," Duwan roared. "If you won't eat of the sweet, growing goodness of the earth take yourself back into the pongpen there to remain a slave."

The female, her mouth full of green, her jaws working, tried to kiss Duwan's foot. He stepped back. "I am no one's master," he said. "I am Drinker. You are Drinker. And if you are to be free you must think and act like Drinkers."

"Teach us, teach us," came the cries.

Duwan made camp in the clearing. The pongs, stomachs bulging with green food, gathered fearfully around his fire. They eyed him expectantly.

"They will fight for you," Jai said.

"I don't want them to fight for me. I want them to fight for themselves, for their people, for their mates, for their sprouts."

"But they must have a leader, Duwan," she said. "Look at them. They are adoring you with their eyes."

"I am not a du," Duwan said.

"Speak to them," she insisted.

He rose. "One of you mentioned Tambol. Who spoke of Tambol?"

A gaunt male, his stomach looking almost comical, so distended was it with food, rose and bowed low. "I have heard the holy man, Tambol, with these ears, Master."

"And of what did he speak?"

"Of you, Master. Is it not true that you came to this land before, that you saw, and judged, and went back to the far north for your army?"

"My army," Duwan said, under his breath, looking around at the remaining old ones. "I came, I saw, and I went back to my home in the north. But you

cannot expect a large army to fight for your freedom. If you would be free of the Devourers, you,
yourselves, must fight."

"We will fight, Master," said the ragged female, "if
you will teach us, and if you will fight at our sides."

"Go," Duwan said. "Sleep. Rest. Tomorrow I will
speak with you again."

Duwan awoke late. Jai had guarded him, keeping
others away, keeping it quiet in the vicinity of his
fire. She gave him water and freshly plucked green
things. As he ate, Dagner approached. He was
panting.

"I've been working with some of these pongs, or
whatever you call them, Duwan," he said. "They're
puny and weak, but they're willing. I think when we
fatten them up a bit—they're going to strip the life
organs from every fixed brother around here if we
don't teach them the proper way to gather food—
they might just make warriors of a sort."

Other old warriors were showing pongs the proper
way to hold a weapon, using the swords taken from
the Devourers. Duwan strolled among them, Jai at his
side. His mother and grandmother joined them.

"Starving in the midst of plenty," his mother said.
"We cannot allow this to continue."

"Look," Jai said, "that one has a wicked thrust."

A pong lunged awkwardly at one of the old warriors and the thrust was easily parried.

"We go to the west," Duwan said.

"And these?" his grandmother asked, indicating the
pongs.

"They can go with us if they choose."

"Shall we not free the others, the ones in the way
stations to the south?" Jai asked.

"So, my warrior mate is now bloodthirsty," Duwan
asked.

"Look at them," Jai said. "Look at them. They're
free. They're fighting."

"An Enemy sprout could take all of them, one at a time," he said.

"Give them a chance. We can work with them as we move south. As they get stronger, eating and drinking Du, they will learn."

"And how do you feel about our new army, father?" Duwan asked, as he approached Duwan the Elder, who was showing a pong how to counter with the shortsword.

"I have looked, as you suggested, at the feet of many of them," his father said. "They *are* Drinkers, Duwan."

"It will take someone wiser and more patient and more skilled than I, even more so than Belran, himself, to train them."

"I have done some training myself," his father said.

"So be it," Duwan said, with misgivings.

At the next settlement ten more of the enemy died, two of them killed by pongs. Six of the pongs lay on the earth when the swift fight was over, however. More pongs replaced them from the pens, and the straggling, noisy, chomping, belching ragtag army moved southward to clear the forests of the new Devourer settlements. Duwan talked to his growing following nightly. He warned them to forage carefully, to spread out when they were eating, to take sparsely of the life organs of all fixed brothers, lest they take sacred life and, more immediately important to them, leave a trail that a Devourer army could follow.

He now found himself in familiar territory. The wide, deep canyon where he had wintered with Jai was not far ahead. They were in a climate zone, he knew, where the length of summer equaled that of winter, and the summer rays of Du were strong. With Devourer expansion to the north, it was important that he find a safe place for his grandmother to return to the earth, for the old female was failing rapidly now, and she spent all her time on the march looking for a suitable place for her return to the earth. Others among the oldsters were in the same situation, near the final, total hardening, and they, having seen the miracle of rebirth as a fixed brother, longed for the rest, the peace, the eternal satisfaction.

Duwan still had his doubts about the growing army of pongs, so he left them in the care of his father and Dagner, who now had no intention of returning to the earth until his blades had tasted much more Enemy blood, and Duwan led Jai and a group of twenty-one hardening oldsters toward the hidden canyon, being careful to cover his trail so that not even one of the supposedly loyal pongs could follow.

The canyon was in its peak of new green. The stream that had carved it and then diminished to a bright, sparkling, lively run over colorful stones was sweet. There was evidence, in the health of the green, growing things, that the canyon received plenty of sun, plenty of rain. Nowhere had Duwan seen such impressively tall brothers, boles as thick through as he was long, and healthy, and giving shade, and whispering, whispering.

"Yes," his grandmother said, when he showed her a little glade near the stream. "Oh, yes."

There was no prescribed ceremony for the return to the earth. Duwan planted his grandmother himself, kissed her, watched as her eyes closed. "I feel it, Duwan," the old female whispered. "I can feel the tendrils growing from my feet. I can taste the richness of this earth. You have kept your promise."

There was, in their cave, still signs of their occupation, rotting beds, dead embers. They refreshed the beds, slept by a bright, cozy fire, and spent the next day watching the swift, miraculous transformation of the twenty-one they had brought to the canyon. The newly planted could no longer speak, but there were, in their minds, sighs of contentment, and, "Farewell, farewell, thank you."

Voices blended into the background of the whispering brothers, none distinguishable until, after several days and nights—it was so pleasant to be alone that Duwan was in no hurry to rejoin the others, and he felt that he owed it to his grandmother and himself to stay with her until the transformation was complete—he went to the new grove of twenty-one growing brothers and squatted beside the thing, the tree, the brother, that had been his grandmother.

"It is a state not to be despised."

The statement came to him so clearly that he looked up to see if it had been Jai who spoke, but she was down at the crystal creek, bathing.

"In the time of the snows it is quiet and peaceful."

"Grandmother?"

"Yes, Grandson. You have chosen a place beyond compare for me to spend eternity. My peace will be complete—although I exact no promise, knowing that it might prove to be impossible for you to keep—if, when the time of my daughter and my son comes you would bring them here, and then, after a long, long time, yourself and your mate. It's peaceful and quiet in the winter and good in the summer. I drink the goodness, grandson, and I revel in it. I am one with the earth, and with all others."

"How is it that you speak with me so clearly?"

"It is my desire."

"And the others?"

"We are here, Duwan," came another voice in his head.

"The ancient ones. The wisdom of the ancient ones. Is it available to you?" Duwan asked.

"Some here were planted before the coming of the Enemy. The Drinker lands were far to the south. This has been a quiet, isolated place. Some rememɒer. Others choose not to, to feel only the wind, the sun, to dance in the winds and commune with Du."

"And the tall brothers at a great distance? Can you communicate with them?"

"A feeling," came the voice. "Nothing more. I sense, far off, that there is pain, and death, and evil."

"Grandmother, try to communicate with those distant ones. It would be very helpful."

"I will. Now you must go. Come back to me, Grandson."

"Yes," he said. "I will come. In this canyon I first began to understand the meaning of love, Grandmother. We will come when we can, Jai and I, and you will be in our thoughts when we are far away."

"Farewell, farewell, farewell."

4

For the first time in his life, Duwan delivered a blow to a living entity who was not the enemy. Another Devourer settlement had been destroyed, leaving more enemy dead. Now ex-slaves had seen their former masters vanquished. They had seen that the Devourers bled and died, just as pongs could bleed and die. There was noisy jubilation. Fires dotted the clearing and the surrounding forest. There was a babble of voices, for all the patience and authority of the valley Drinkers had not yet tamed a rabble of slaves into an organized force.

Duwan's surviving cadre of oldsters now numbered just under two hundred, and he never ceased to be pleased and surprised at the way the old Drinkers had risen to the occasion. Many of them, he would have bet at the beginning of the journey, could not have possibly survived the trip, much less survived to grow stronger and fight. It was, he suspected, the goodness of Du, for Drinkers marched and worked and fought as nearly naked as possible, the males clad only in a loincloth, to allow Du's kind and strengthening rays to caress every possible small area of old, hardening hide. He had broken the freed pongs up into groups, assigning them to the care of valley Drinkers, and training went on at all hours. The weapons captured from the enemy were meted out to the more promising pong males—and a few females who seemed capable of emulating Jai—and it had been discovered that there were a few workers in wood among the pongs so that these skilled craftsmen were now being instructed in the art of making bows, of finding straight shafts for arrows and rounding them true.

According to the pongs, two settlements, each one larger than those already taken, lay between Duwan's force and the northernmost city, Kooh. Duwan hesitated to move on the settlements, although he was being urged to do so by Jai and others. He knew a rabble when he saw it. He'd never fought in nor had he even seen a pitched battle, but he knew the legends. He knew that a well ordered force of only a few men, such as the royal guards he'd seen in Arutan, could rout his slave army, and he did not want to discourage his own people and the slaves by suffering a defeat. The way ahead was long, and would require much patience.

He was making the rounds of the various camps, consulting with his sub-leaders, seeing with some satisfaction that a few of the pongs were beginning to show some little skill with the bow. As he walked through a dense copse of tall brothers his nostril hairs quivered at an unpleasant stench, and he detoured to come upon a group of pongs in a small clearing, ten of them, male and female. They had taken a cook pot from a Devourer hut and a part of the stench that insulted Duwan's nose was coming from it.

It was the scent of cooking flesh.

He was not seen, for it was growing dark and he moved silently, and he stood in the edge of the clearing just long enough to see a pong male butchering a Devourer female's body and tossing bits of flesh into the pot. The female's haunch was roasting on a spit over the coals of the fire, and from that piece of burning flesh came the worst of the stench.

He had traveled far, and he had had many disappointments. He had lost his first love—although that no longer mattered, for Jai had become his mate in every way—and he had been deserted by his own people. His hope of achieving his goals rested on his own good sword arms, his father, a relatively small number of aged Drinkers, and a rabble. And now Drinkers, people of his own race, where flaunting Devourer evil in the midst of his blood, the stench of their unholy feast floating to the noses of his mother, his mate, his father.

With a roar, with both swords in hand, he leaped into the firelight and kicked the cooking pot over, spilling boiling liquid and flesh onto the ground, and, still roaring his anger, his disgust, he began to flail around him with his weapons. He used the flat sides of the swords, leaving in his wake bloody heads, aching backsides.

"Fools," he roared, punctuating the roar with a blow here, a kick there, as the pongs scrambled to escape. "There will be no abominations in my camp," he yelled, as he kicked the backside of a wailing female, crawling for the cover of the forest.

He stood, alone, in the flickering light of the fire, his chest heaving, tears streaming down his face. He had now reached his adult height, and his body had filled out impressively. His strongly muscled arms hung at his sides, the tip of his longsword on the ground. His legs were parted, and his trunk-like thighs showed the muscles, the strength, that had carried him over so much of the good earth. And he wept. He lifted his face. Through the branches of the tall brothers he saw the twinkles of the sky's night lights.

"Du," he whispered, "help me. I cannot do it alone. It is too much for me, Du. Guide me, inspire me, tell me your will. Am I being arrogant in hoping that I, one Drinker, can make a difference, that I can change this evil that soils your land?" He sank to his knees. His tear-stained face was still lifted. Although Du was resting, and the sky was dark, he knew that he was heard. "I am tired, Du, and I despair. Is it your will that I lead those who are mine into the uninhabited areas to the west? I am sick of blood and death, Du, and I pray for your guidance."

At first he thought that it was the whispering of the tall brothers, the spirits of departed Drinkers, for the words were indistinct and came, seemingly, from a great distance. And then he began to hear, or feel, or sense, and a feeling of awe pushed his head low, until his forehead rested on the hilt of his shortsword, the sword's point on the earth.

"South. Go south. South. My people—" And in his mind were pictures of the sufferings of the enslaved, the stench of burning flesh was in his nostrils, and the roar of battle in his ears. A death scream pierced him, left him trembling, and his muscles quivered as if from great strain. And then, clearly, the voice of his grandmother, echoing in his head.

"You have come too far to turn away, Grandson."

"I hear," he said without speaking.

"Have patience with them, for they have suffered much."

And that other voice, hollow, distant. "They are of me and for me and you are the chosen one."

"Who?" Duwan asked, aloud.

"Question not," his grandmother said. "Listen. A day's march to the south is another settlement. There are many Drinkers there. Free them. The settlement is but lightly guarded, and the Devourers are lax. From the southwest a stream will give you access to the settlement so that your approach will not be noted. Go swiftly. And tarry not there, but move immediately to the last, and southernmost settlement, where you will face your first severe test."

The other voice. "Let my people carry the load."

"Who, Grandmother?" Duwan asked.

"I know not. Farewell."

With the coming of the light, he gathered them, Drinkers and ex-slaves, and he stood on a rise and looked at them, seeing masses of rags, gauntness, only a few with weapons. They were whispering among themselves. He raised his right hand and there was silence, only the luffing breeze and the stir of the leaf organs of the nearby tall brothers breaking it.

"We are of a people," he said quietly, but his voice carried well. "Today we march to the south." A cheer went up and he waited for it to quiet. "Today I give you a choice, for no longer can the Drinkers of the valley carry your load. Now you are free, as we are free. Do you value this freedom?"

A roar was his answer.

"Then here is what you must do," he said, his voice rising. This is the law of Du. There is one Du and you will honor him, and obey his laws. You will live in brotherhood with all things, except the Enemy, who has dishonored Du and usurped his lands and his people. You will not take a brother's all, but will share only that of his substance that will not cause him harm. You will honor and obey those chosen by Du to lead you and instruct you, although you are free. You will eat of the green, growing brothers, and drink of Du and honor him by exposing your hides to his goodness."

He paused. There was a gentle murmur of sound from the assembled people. "Mark those laws well. You are a member of the Army of Du, and the breaking of Du's laws will bring punishment. If you choose not to abide by these laws, then now is the time to state so, and leave. You are free to go. Now. If you choose to leave us you will not be punished, nor condemned. Go, if that is your choice."

Again he paused. A growing sound of voices came to him. He watched, half expecting the crowd to melt away in front of him. Instead, they pressed closer, until he could smell them.

"So be it," he said. "Now, there are also rules of common sense. A clean body is a healthy body. Water washes away the sweat and soil of the day, and a scouring with sand cleanses all. Water also takes the stench from your garments, and does not harm them. When we march to the south I do not want to smell you."

Laughter.

"Nor do I want an enemy, downwind, to scent out our presence," he said, smiling, hearing more laughter.

"I want all bowmen to join my father there," he said, pointing. "You will be our shock force. You will have first crack at the enemy. Work hard, my friends. Hone your skills so that not a single arrow is wasted. Swordsmen, there," he pointed to another area. "This will be a day of practice, for you will finish what the bowmen start. The coming battles are yours. Will you be prepared?"

A roar told him of their eagerness, but he was still doubtful. He kept that doubt until, wearing freshly washed rags and smelling only of fresh sweat, pong bowmen cut down all exposed enemy, after approaching the settlement in the cover of the stream's swath, and pong swordsmen, with few losses, cleared the settlement of surviving enemies.

Night. Flickering firelight. Duwan sat, a robe over his shoulders, gazing into the fire. Jai and his mother were preparing food. His father and Dagner, who seemed to grow younger, rather than older, sat on either side of him.

"They fought well, my warriors," Dagner said. "And we recovered all but five arrows."

"They are in high spirits," Duwan the Elder said.

"Yes," Duwan agreed. "We move with the light."

"I will fight with them next time," Dagner said.

"No," Duwan told him.

"There is a garrison of soldiers at the next place," Dagner said.

"Conscripts," Duwan said.

"But well armed." Dagner pointed out.

"The conscripts have not much more training than our most experienced troops," Duwan said. "No, this is their fight."

"It seems to me," Dagner said, "that you test them, Duwan."

He remembered the voice, the distant, hollow voice. "Yes, it will be the first test," he said.

"But—" Dagner began, and was silenced by the glare of Duwan's orange eyes on his.

"I know you want to fight with them, Dagner. You are still our finest warrior. But what if, by accident, you are taken from behind? Who, then, will train our new recruits? We Drinkers have the knowledge, the skills. We must survive, at all costs, to pass this knowledge and our skill along to an army. We have no more than two hundred, male and female, and to reclaim this land for Drinkers, all Drinkers, we must have multiples of that, thousands, hundreds of thousands. The enemy will always be better armed, for we have not metals, nor metal workers, nor mines. We must overwhelm him by numbers, and to have numbers we, Drinkers of the valley, must lead." He put his hand on Dagner's arm. "There will come the time, my friend, when you can wet your blades with Enemy blood again. Meantime, patience."

"At times I forget that that young, still green head of yours contains so much wisdom," Dagner said.

On the way south a northbound caravan fell to an advance party of Duwan's army, and there were more dead enemies, more weapons, and more pongs to be

added to the army. Many of the pongs in that caravan were woodsmen, and their cutting tools were
turned into weapons and distributed to pongs who
had received some training. The sharp blades and
long handles of the cutting tools made them effective in hand-to-hand fighting, even though they would
be no match for the blade of a trained swordsman.

Duwan, with Jai at his side, scouted the last and
largest settlement north of Kooh. They climbed the
limbs of a tall brother and looked down over a make-
shift stockade intended more to keep pongs in than
any enemy out. Soon, Duwan knew, the news would
trickle back to the Enemy cities that for the first time
in generations there was sudden death for Devourers roaming the forests of the north, but, judging
from the activity within the settlement's stockade, the
Devourers suspected nothing as yet.

The stockade was roughly circular, and covered a
large, grassy area bounded on two sides by forest,
and to the west and south by sparsely treed plains.
The garrison, conscripts dressed in dull, plain uniforms, had huts surrounding a central compound.
Pongpens lined the walls of the stockade. Two gates
stood open. He estimated that there were no more
than fifty soldiers, armed with longswords, but there
were probably two hundred Devourers, male and
female and young, living in the settlement.

"After this they will know," Jai said.

He looked at her with a frown. There were times
when it seemed that she could get inside his head.
He had been thinking the same thing. There were so
many of them that it would be a miracle if, in the
confusion of the attack, at least one did not escape to
carry the news of warfare in the north to Kooh, and
thence to the capital at Arutan.

"We will lose many here," she said.

He nodded grimly. "The first test," he said.

He planned the attack after consulting his father and Dagner. It began at dawn. Female pongs—Jai had become a powerful role model for the females, and they begged, insisted, that they be made a part of the Drinker Army—had crawled to lie against the stockade walls while it was still dark. Just before dawn they kindled fires at points opposite each other on the circular stockade, fanning them and adding dry material until the flames reached high and began to eat at the logs of the stockade.

Inside the stockade an alarm was shouted and Devourers began to pour toward the fires. While their attention was on the fires, agile young Drinkers scaled the stockade wall, dropped inside, and opened the gates, and from two sides Drinkers ran silently, gained the gates without alarm, and spread out inside the compound.

Duwan ached to be with them, but he knew that he and the less than two hundred oldsters were not going to be able to conquer the might of Arutan alone, that, in the final analysis, freedom for the Drinkers of the Land of Many Brothers depended upon the inhabitants of that land. He knew, as he watched from the same tall brother from whose limbs he had first scouted the stockaded settlement, that he was running a great risk. If his rabble—he could not yet call them an army—failed, if they were defeated, the word would spread and the pongs would hesitate to rebel at the risk of being peeled, would no longer seek to escape their masters and join him. But if they won—ah, then that word, too, would spread, and he would be in a position to send out a call to all pongs to rise, to escape, to join in the fight for freedom and the retaking of their lands.

The first silent onslaught caught the Devourers inside the stockade totally by surprise. Many went down. Jai, clinging to a limb at his side, put her hand on his arm and felt him tense as he saw pong warriors slay females and young as willingly as they smote the Devourer males.

An officer rallied the Devourer conscripts and about thirty of them formed a defensive square in the central compound. "Bowmen," Duwan muttered, although there was, of course, no chance of his being heard. But he had given his orders clearly, and the group leaders among the pongs began to shout their own orders so that a line of bowmen formed and the iron-tipped arrows began to take their toll of the Devourer soldiers. Then, with a screaming, wailing, nervous cry the swordsmen rushed forward and Duwan could hear the clash of iron on iron.

"They've done it," Jai said, blood-hunger making her voice hoarse. "They've done it!"

Organized resistance was at an end. The pongs dispersed, each male seeking out hidden Devourers, and as females and young began to be dragged from huts, as fire was applied and the settlement began to burn, and the freed pongs from the pens were milling, shouting questions, some screaming in fear, Duwan turned his eyes away and began to climb down from the tall brother. He and Jai joined Dagner and Duwan the Elder, at the head of the reserve force, and marched into the burning settlement.

Duwan was growing accustomed to speaking to newly freed slaves now, and he stood before the assembled pongs confidently, seeing that, as usual, they were emaciated and weak. He spoke the usual things to them, and, as always, he found that word of his coming had gone before him. Finished, he gazed at them, wondering if there would be among them a male of leadership quality, for that was his most desperate need now, pongs who could assume the role of sub-leaders.

"Well, you're a skinny bunch," he said, spreading his hands and smiling, "but Du's goodness and the sweet things of the earth will soon have you looking as fat and sleek as these." He waved his hand at a group of freed slaves from his forces who had been filling themselves for a long time on the things that were natural Drinker food.

"There is one here who is not skinny," a voice called out.

"Step forward," Duwan said.

A tall figure in dark, all-covering clothing stepped forward. It was a male, and he walked toward Duwan and fell to his knees.

"Master," he said.

Duwan pushed back the Drinker's hood and the fat one looked up, smiling, tears in his eyes.

"I knew you would come, Master," said Tambol, as Duwan pulled him to his feet and clasped arms with him and Jai ran to his side to join in the greeting.

Duwan sent scout parties, under the command of the more agile valley Drinkers, to the south, to try to capture or kill any who had escaped, for he still feared that word of the uprising would be carried south to Kooh, and then to Arutan. He called a conference of his Drinker leaders and sat Tambol at his side.

"This is the Drinker," he said, his hand on Tambol's shoulder, "who has been preparing the way for us. "Tell us, Tambol, of the things you have done and the things you have learned and seen."

"Master, since you traveled to the north I have walked this land, and I have told of you in almost every village, every city."

"With some very inventive embellishments," Duwan said, with a smile.

"I have told only the truth as I have seen it and heard it," Tambol protested. "I have told them that you came from the earth, as it was foretold, and that you are mighty and have the blessings of the one Du."

"So be it," Jai said.

"I have made others believe," Tambol said, "and now they, too, spread the joyful news. There is not a pongpen in this land that does not have one who believes in you, Master, who constantly reminds all that you are to return, that freedom will be theirs, and plenty, and peace in the end."

"I'm sure this news has reached the ears of the Devourers," Duwan said.

"Without doubt, master," Tambol said. "But they, in their arrogance, do not believe. They look on the stories as the vain hopes of the pongs and laugh." He raised his stern face to the sky. "By Du," he said, "soon they will not be laughing."

"No signs of preparation?" Duwan asked.

"None, Master," Tambol said. "There has been no increase in the strength of the royal guards. Males are conscripted only to guard far-flung settlements, such as these that you have destroyed, and that not against any possible enemy, but merely to assure that there is an adequate guard force to prevent escape from the pens."

"So," Jai said, "if we now attack Kooh, they will not be expecting us?"

"Unless some escaped to carry the word they will be feeling snug and safe behind the walls of the city," Tambol said. "The new High Mistress is more concerned with her own pleasures than with any possible dangers."

"High Mistress?" Duwan asked.

"Yes, Master, the old High Master, Farko, is dead. His daughter, Elnice of Arutan, rules in his place, with the guards captain you once dueled at her side."

"This should make our task easier," Dagner said, "if this country is ruled by a female."

"Don't underestimate this one," Duwan said, "or she will feast on your bud.

"Du's face," Duwan the Elder said. "You jest."

"No," Duwan said. He turned to Tambol. "You have traveled much, and you seem to have access to the pens."

"Indeed, Master. I go disguised as a priest of the minor du, Tseeb, he of the clear skies, the du of hope for the pongs."

"Can you enter Kooh without endangering yourself?"

"I come and go as I please. The Devourers are delighted to have me teach the pongs that their role is to obey and to await their reward in Tseeb's clear-skied paradise after death."

"Go, then," Duwan said. "Return to us when you have determined whether or not word of our warfare here in the north has reached the city. We will be there." He pointed to the west. "I think you can track us by the swath we leave in the green."

"West?" Dagner asked.

"West," Duwan said.

"Kooh is to the south," Jai said.

"My warriors fought well today," Dagner said.

"Against a few conscripts, traders, females, and children," Duwan said. "There is a small garrison of guards in Kooh, and there are the walls. We will march west, training our forces as we march, and only when we can field a disciplined force of at least two thousand will we attack Kooh."

"And if the enemy learns of us and brings more forces into Kooh?" Jai asked.

"Then Du will guide us," Duwan said.

On the westward march, the freed pongs of several villages swelled the ranks. The corps of bowmen was growing, with new weapons being made constantly. The great shortage was of swords. Dagner worked out a system of using axmen and swordsmen in a flying wedge, and, in theory, it was devastating. The freed pongs fattened on the bounty of Du and the earth.

At last, Duwan called a halt and a camp was set up.

Now bow and arrow making was intensified. Now the training went on from the first to the last light of Du. The days were growing shorter, the change of season nearing. Jai and Dagner kept reminding Duwan that if Kooh was to be taken, it had to be soon, before the snows came and made marching difficult.

The nights were growing quite chill by the time Tambol returned. He came walking alone to find Duwan standing on a knoll watching the entire force of his army make a simulated attack on a walled city, the city represented by a rising wall of natural stone. Over a thousand pongs made the assault, using ladders of wood laced together by vines to climb the rocks. There were accidents. Pongs fell and were injured. Duwan was pleased with the progress of the training, but highly doubtful about the chances of this partially trained force against Kooh.

Tambol waited patiently until the exercise was over, the leaders had dismissed the various contingents of the army, and the evening campfires were beginning to make their smokes.

"Master," he said, "Kooh goes about its business. There is a garrison of a hundred guardsmen, and they are not the elite of the guards, but lesser ones, who consider the assignment in Kooh as exile from the pleasures of Arutan."

"Are you saying that none escaped the settlements to carry word?"

"To all appearances, yes," Tambol said. "There have been no alarms. No urgent messengers have left the city for the south. A pong who serves in the guards' barracks heard that, soon, a force will be sent north, to find out why the settlements there have not started sending flesh and hides to Kooh. There seemed to be no hurry about this. So, as it stands, an attack in the next few days would come as a surprise."

"We are ready," Dagner said, with an outthrusting

of his hardening chin. "We must not lose the advantage of surprise, Duwan."

"There will be help from inside the city," Tambol said. "I spent several days and nights in the pens. At a signal, pongs will break down the fences and open the gates."

Duwan frowned. He still felt it was too soon. He had been thinking in terms of moving farther to the west, making winter camp and using the cold time for training and building his forces.

"Master," Tambol said, "they are waiting. They believe. They hunger for you."

"Pongs who have no training, who have never known freedom, they will risk peeling to open the gates?"

"Master, those who have heard me, and believed me, teach day and night. Yes, they will open the gates. And when we have Kooh!" He looked to the sky and muttered a prayer. "When we have Kooh the word will spread like wildfire when the rains fail. They will rise in Tshou, and in Arutan, and in the southern cities. We will march in triumph the length and breadth of this land!"

"I will think on this," Duwan said, rising. He walked away from the fires, left the camp behind him, scarcely noticing that Jai was following. He sought a high place, sat on a night-chilled rock, and searched the lights of the night sky for an answer. Jai, silent, sat with her back to his, giving him of her warmth, until, still without speaking, he rose and went down from the high place into a grove where there were whispers. He lay on the earth and opened his mind. The whispers were faint, massed together into a languorous murmur.

"Grandmother," he said without words. "Grandmother."

But there were only the distant, meshed, indistinguishable whispers of the old brothers and no word came to him, no sign, no guidance. He prayed, listening for that odd, hollow, faraway voice, and there was only the silence and coolness of the night and the faint backwash of massed whispers.

This decision would be his and his alone.

"You say go," he stated to Jai.

"You are our leader," she said, "but my heart and my head say go."

"As say Dagner and others."

"We will obey, whatever you decide," she said. "But consider this. Even if we are repulsed at the walls, and I don't believe this will happen, we will have sent a message to all who are still in the pens. We will be saying, look, we are here. We are free. We are strong enough to threaten a Devourer city. Join us."

Duwan took her hand and led her back. Dagner, Duwan the Elder, others of the valley Drinkers and a few of the pong sub-leaders were listening to Tambol as he taught the miracle of Duwan, how he had come from the earth, how he had the ear of Du, himself.

Tambol fell silent when Duwan and Jai walked into the light of the fires. Duwan stood, tall, an imposing figure, the light gleaming redly on the hilts of his swords.

"We will go to Kooh," he said.

"Du has spoken," Tambol hissed, in awe.

"No," Duwan said, somewhat angrily, "Duwan has spoken, and he prays that he has not made a bad decision."

"The city is ours," Dagner said.

"We will go. We will take the city. We will destroy it. We will raze its buildings and its walls, and we will water the earth with the blood of Devourers," Duwan said. "And then we will march to the west, far to the west, and there we, ourselves, will establish a defensive position from which we will, after the snows have come and gone, raid the countryside, building our army. After Kooh there will be no more surprises for the enemy, for he will know, and he will mobilize himself, and there will be no standing against him in open battle, not for a long, long time."

"We will send teachers to all cities, to the pongpens," Tambol said. "We will instruct the pongs to slow down their work, to do damage when they can do so without detection, and this unrest in the pens will force the Enemy to use more of his conscripts and order keepers to watch the pens. Each one detained in this manner will be one less we will face on the field of battle."

Duwan spent the next two days making his plans, remembering clearly the layout of Kooh, and its approaches. He went over and over his plan of attack. This time the various units would be led by their valley Drinker leaders. This time he, himself, would fight. The four gates of Kooh would be attacked by four strong units, Duwan with the force at the main, southern gate, Duwan the Elder at another, and Dagner at the third gate. The fourth gate, a lesser gate at the west, used mostly for entry by the gatherers of firewood, would be attacked by a smaller force, and that attack would come first, with a delay to pull the guards garrison toward the Wood Gate.

If all went well, the other three gates would be opened by pongs from the inside. The attack would come at first light, giving the night to move the army into position unseen.

Now with the scouts out front, the army was on the march. It moved through the western forests like a multi-segmented, long, deadly snake. It did not move in silence. Although there were many among the force who were becoming skilled with weapons, it was, Duwan knew, still more rabble than army. Ideally, his army would have been as well trained, as dedicated, as disciplined as the army of the great

Alon. Alon had but to nod, said the legends, to send a fast moving strike unit into action, with all units coordinated as if by magic, but, actually, by training and discipline.

Once more Tambol went into the city, moving ahead of the army as fast as he could walk. As Duwan positioned his forces for the final nighttime approach, Tambol found his way back to Duwan's camp to report that the pongs of the pens were ready, and that the gates would, surely, be opened from the inside.

"To be sure," Tambol said, "I am going back into the city. I will personally lead one group, the one to open the main gate, Master."

"You have risked enough, my friend," Duwan said.

"Then give me a sword and I will fight at your side."

"And how much training have you had with the sword?"

Tambol lowered his head.

"My friend," Duwan said. "You have done more than any other. You have done your part. Thanks to you we have this army. Thanks to you there is hope for the enslaved. I would not lose you now, doing something for which you are not trained, for your leadership, and your teachings, will help us to multiply the size of this force. In that way your talents will be best utilized."

"As you will, Master," Tambol said.

The signal to those inside the city's walls that the attack was beginning had been arranged by Tambol, and it was a huge bonfire on a hill that was visible from within the city. The fire would be lighted when Du first showed the edge of his face over the eastern horizon, and by that time the four attacking forces had to be in position.

For once the army moved in silence. Duwan, with Jai at his side, positioned his group in the southern forest, a hard run from the main gate, and watched the signal hill. Since those on the hill were at a higher point, they saw Du first, and it was in pre-dawn darkness that Duwan saw the first smoke, then the glow of fire, and heard, in response, the faraway shouts of the force attacking the western gate. He moved forward, hugging the earth, taking advantage of cover, getting near enough to the wall to hear shouts from inside, to know that his plan was working, for there were sounds of running, and shouted orders to tell him that the guards were moving to the Wood Gate. He stood and signaled Jai to give the order for the force to advance, and they began to emerge from the forest on the run, swordsmen first, then unarmed men carrying wooden ladders for use in case the gates were not opened from the inside.

As the first swordsmen drew near he heard sounds from behind the tall, strong, wooden gate and then a creaking as the gate began to open.

"Now we fight," he yelled to the first swordsmen to reach him. "Go, go, go!" They streamed past him, yelling, swords raised, pouring into the opening gates. He could hear faint shouting from the eastern gate, and he was elated, for it was going well. The crucial moment had come when his men ran toward the gate, exposing themselves, but the pongs from the pens inside had done as Tambol had promised, and now his army was pouring into the city and it was, for all practical purposes, his. Not even a trained unit of royal guards could stand against the human tide pouring through the gates.

Jai had run to his side. "Come," she said. "We will miss the killing."

"There will be enough blood for all," he said grimly.

One third of his group had entered the gates and the rest were crowding, yelling, pushing to enter the relatively narrow opening when he saw the gleam of Du send light to flash from the bared swords of a running, silent mass of Devourers in the blue of the guards.

They fell onto his force from the right rear, and they came in trained formation, each Devourer's flank protected by a companion in arms, and their blades began to bring havoc to the slave army.

"Turn, turn," Duwan began to shout, leaping into the melee of pongs pushing to enter the gate. "Turn and face your rear."

5

Duwan was never to know the exact course of events that had resulted in a rear-flank attack on his main force before the gates of Kooh, but he had been prophetically right in warning others not to underestimate Elnice of Arutan. She had made a decision, in the face of some amusement from her male advisers, based on the report of one Devourer male. This one, a hunter, had been afield when the first northern settlement had been attacked. He had returned toward the settlement, laden with the pleasing results of a good day in the forest, to hear the screams of the dying. He came near enough to see, to his astonishment, that pongs could fight, and he was so traumatized that, for a day and a night, he hid near the destroyed settlement, then entered to walk among the bodies of the dead and to sift through the ashes of his hut.

Still in shock, he headed south, promptly became lost, and when he found his way again he arrived at the next settlement to the south in time, once more, to witness the bloody signals of a vast change. He saw females and children put to the blade and the fear sent him running to the south, bypassing all settlements, for he was convinced that the entire land swarmed with the bloodthirsty pongs. He lost his way again, discovered his approximate position when he was to the south of the coastal city, Tshou, and, walking on the last reserves of his strength and fear, reached the capital city and collapsed. It was days before he came to his senses again and began to try to get someone in authority to listen to him.

When, at last, he was admitted to the presence of the High Mistress, he saw her dressed in a flimsy, clinging, ankle-length garment of the richest material, seated upon the throne of Arutan, a handsome, tall, well-built captain of the guards standing at her right side. Given permission to speak, his story began to be blurted out in sometimes almost incoherent half-sentences, so that the captain became impatient and told the guards to remove this idiot.

"Hold," the High Mistress said. "We will hear what he has to say."

He told, tearfully, of finding the body of his female and his two children in the ruins of the settlement and then became involved in a confusing account of his arduous journey all the way from the northern settlement to Arutan.

Elnice listened patiently. She asked questions.

"Are you expecting us to believe," the captain asked, "that pongs killed swordsmen of the master race?"

"Hata," Elnice said harshly, "hold your tongue."

When she had heard all, how this male had witnessed the total destruction of two major settlements, she dismissed him with instructions to put him in the care of the healers and keep him near for further questioning.

"He's mad," Hata said. "It is not unusual for the loneliness of frontier life to destroy reason."

"I have a report from Kooh that states that there has been no return, in the form of flesh and hides, from the northern settlements," Elnice said.

"I heard the report," Hata said. "It takes time to clear the virgin forests, to establish routes."

Elnice was silent for a time. "Have you also heard the reports of decreasing production from the pongs?"

"I ordered that their food allotments be reduced

until the work begins to produce the usual results,"
Hata said.

"Have you heard, as well, the whispers of a new
Master who will free all pongs?"

Hata laughed. "The teaching of the sect of Tseeb.
Yes, I have heard. I, myself, spoke with a priest of
Tseeb. He was a fatuous fool, wanting to spread his
message in the pens of this city, and I gave him
permission. To have hope of something in the not
too definable future keeps the pongs working. To
believe in a du of mercy, who will give them freedom
and eternal life in the afterworld, allows them to
endure their otherwise intolerable condition."

"I wonder," Elnice said. "Send a spy into the pens.
Have him name two or three who seem most excited
by these messages of hope. Have them peeled slowly,
giving them plenty of time to talk. Meanwhile, acti-
vate all guard reserves, and conscript enough males
to form a full conqforce."

"A conqforce?" Hata gasped. "High Mistress, there
has been no army of that size in existence since the
days of the conquest."

"If the male who came from the north is mad,"
Elnice said, "we will use the conqforce to sweep through
the western mountains, to eradicate for all time any
vestige of runaway pongs."

"It will be a severe drain on your treasury," Hata
said.

Elnice laughed. "You still have hopes, I see, that I
will relent and make you my consort. Never fear,
Hata, should I decide on that course, there will be
enough left in the treasury to assure that you will
live well."

Elnice could not say, nor, being High Mistress, did
she have to, what prompted her to march out of
Arutan at the head of the largest force that had been
gathered since the days immediately following the
Devourer migration from the humid, hot lands of

the far south. Perhaps it was nothing more than a desire to see some of the land that she ruled. Perhaps, deep down, not realized even by herself, there was uneasiness at the continued silence from the new northern settlements.

"We have invested good treasure in those settlements," she told Hata. "I think it is time we found out why we are not yet getting a return."

She marched by easy stages to the north, spending a pleasant few days in the coastal city, giving her subjects there a chance to see her, her splendid body hinting of its beauty through her thin garments, giving the residents of that city a reason for pride with drills and reviews of the well trained conqforce. The change of season forced her to leave Tshou's pleasant beaches, for if she was going to travel past Kooh, to the first of the settlements, and return before the snows, she could not afford to waste any more time.

Actually, Hata found that being in command of a full conqforce was an exciting experience. He had no illusions, he felt, about a threat in the far north. Pongs were inferior, and incapable of fighting. But it was glorious to give commands to so large a force, and he took full advantage of the opportunity to exercise his military skills. He set problems for the traveling force, and sent out scouts just as if there was an enemy army lying in ambush in the vast northern forests. Thus it was that two of his scouts almost blundered head-on into Duwan's main force moving toward Kooh.

"Have you been at the cup?" Hata demanded, when the breathless scouts came to his tent and reported a large force of armed pongs moving toward the city. He felt first a chill of apprehension, then elation. No Devourer officer had faced combat in generations. All his life he had been a soldier, and aside from peeling a few pongs he had never had a chance to exercise his skills. He summoned the High Mistress and had the scouts repeat the story. Then he sent others and, during the night, reports came back that astounded him. Four separate groups of armed pongs were closing on Kooh, the largest moving toward the main gate, the southern gate.

"We will attack at dawn," Elnice said. "Spread your forces, captain, to destroy all four of the forces that dare to threaten my city."

"Your forgiveness, High Mistress," Hata said. "One of the most fundamental rules of warfare is never to split your forces in the face of an enemy of unknown strength."

Elnice frowned. "Then what do you suggest?"

"We will first wipe out the larger force of enemy, the force that is getting into position in front of the south gate. Then we will move to destroy the others forces one by one."

"And if the other forces flee at the first appearance of our troops you will have to hunt them down one by one in the forests. Dus, Hata, these are pongs. Do you fear them?"

Hata drew himself up. "I bow to your wishes." He gave orders to split his forces, to have four separate groups move into position. He doubted that they could move fast enough to reach the eastern and northern gates before first light, but he had to admit that Elnice's reasoning was good. There could be no serious threat from pongs, and he didn't relish having to spend the winter chasing them one by one through the snows.

When Duwan saw the advancing lines of enemy guardsmen, his heart leaped. He had not felt right about this attack, and now he had learned a lesson. He had learned to trust his intuition.

"Turn, turn," he shouted, leaping among the pongs who were rushing to enter the city through the southern gate. "Protect your rear." He managed to turn most of his force. As he faced south, he saw pongs dying. To his great pride they did not run. They turned from the walls and faced the lines of iron, giving forth their shrill battle cries, meeting iron with iron and not dying in vain, for guards died, too. But they were being forced back. Duwan began pushing his way forward. Jai was at his side.

"Go to the rear," he ordered. "Send messengers to my father and Dagner. Tell them to abandon the attack and form a defensive line just north of the city to give us a place to fall back upon."

"Duwan—" she began.

"Go," he roared.

He pushed his way ino the front ranks, both hands filled with iron, and his swords began to take a toll. A group of his soldiers rallied around him and the advance of the guards, at that point, was halted, but to his left and his right the pongs continued to fall back.

"Give way," he shouted, "pass the word to give way slowly. Fall back. Pass the word for the men on our flanks to pull in toward us."

His longsword split the helmet and the skull of a guardsman, and he took a few steps backward before another leaped forward to challenge his iron.

From a small rise Elnice and Hata watched the battle. "Look," Elnice said, pointing. "See that one with two swords who rallies them to his side." There was, she felt, something familiar about that figure.

"He anchors the line," Hata said. "We will account for him." He sent a group of his reserve to attack at the point where Duwan was rallying his troops. The fresh guardsmen began to push back the middle of Duwan's line. Seeing the situation, he passed orders to those near him to fall back, for the flanks to hold and then to slowly begin to fold in toward him.

"He gives ground," Hata said, laughing, as the center began to fade. Then he was screaming warnings as the flanks began to fold slowly in on his reserves, but it was too late. The fresh guardsmen were surrounded and, with Duwan leading, his two swords flashing, the pong army began to decimate the surrounded Devourers.

"Fall back, fall back," Hata was screaming. He sent a messenger to pass that information, but it was too late.

The small victory gave heart to Duwan's force, and he had difficulty in getting them to follow his orders. They wanted to pursue their advantage, but Duwan had seen ranks of guardsmen, their bright uniforms flashing through the forest, moving toward the site of battle. His orders were finally relayed and the pong army began to fall back, managed to disengage totally before the new force of guardsmen was in position.

He found his father engaged in a heated little battle before the eastern gate, and his attack on the rear of the Devourer force resulted in many dead. Inside the city the pongs who had entered the gates were creating devastation, but the enemy inside had managed to stand, to hold the central square. Duwan sent messengers with orders to fall back. Many pongs inside the city did not get the orders. Left behind as Duwan moved to the north to join with Dagner's force, they perished as the enemy inside the city rallied.

The smaller force of pongs at the Wood Gate to the west had already begun to withdraw, with panic among some, and as Duwan retreated toward the north stragglers began to join him. He called a forced march. Rearguard scouts reported that the enemy forces were consolidating to the north of Kooh, and that there were many of them.

Duwan marched his troops for most of the night, called a halt, ordered a cold camp, and with the first light of Du was making the rounds of his various units, calling for an accounting. To his sadness, he estimated that a full third of his force had been lost, dead, too severely wounded to march, strayed, captured. He called his leaders together.

"Forgive us, Duwan," Dagner said. "We gave you bad advice."

"There is no blame," Duwan said. "The enemy will be counting their dead, too. Now we must march, and march fast, to the northwest."

"They will move to the west," Elnice said, her face grim as she listened to the various unit commanders report their losses.

"To the north," Hata said.

"Into the snows?"

"My High Mistress," Hata said. "I have spent my life studying military matters. I advised you not to split our forces, and we count many dead as a result. Had we had our entire force at the southern gate none would have escaped to join the others. I advise that we move north, and quickly. They are pongs and they cannot match the endurance of our trained soldiers. We can head them off by marching past them to the west and meeting them in the forests where their bows will be ineffective."

"Well, my military genius," Elnice said. "This time I will listen to you, although it seems to me that you were the one who told me that pongs could not fight."

The experienced guardsmen set a fast pace. Lashes were used to speed up the stragglers. It was true that the pong army could not match the pace of trained Devourers, not so much from physical conditioning—Duwan's forces had learned to fatten themselves off the land—but because of the superior organization of the Devourer force and the ruthless way that the officers drove their soldiers.

Scouts reported to Duwan, on the third day of the retreat, that the leading elements of the enemy army were to the west, blocking the route in that direction. Duwan, himself, went forward and saw the enemy moving in strength at a half-trot. To continue to the west would bring a head-on battle. He altered his route northward. Meanwhile, Hata's scouts had located Duwan's army, and Hata had ordered even more speed of movement, to put himself between the pongs and the great, dense, northern forests.

The chase continued for days. A captured Devourer scout, tortured without Duwan's knowledge by pongs, gave him a word for the enemy army. Conqforce. Conquering Force. An army, the invincible formation that had driven the Great Alon from the Land of Many Brothers. Thousands strong, the enemy seemed tireless, and as the days passed the Devourer force spread out in a long line to the west, with the lead elements forcing Duwan's course into a northeasterly direction. If that continued he would be pinned against the sea.

Now the destroyed settlements were being passed, and the sight of the devastation gave new strength to the enemy. Hata marched his guardsmen and the conscripts past the settlements, giving them time to see the decaying remains of those who had died. "No prisoners," he said, and this order was issued until every guard and conscript muttered it under his breath as the settlements were passed.

Duwan knew that the snows would fly soon, and his plan was to use the snow as cover to move his force into the deep forests. He was in familiar territory. Ahead was the wide, sheltered canyon where he and Jai had wintered, where he had planted his grandmother and the other oldsters. He had mixed emotions. He knew that the valley would be a fine place to make a stand, and it was becoming apparent that he could not continue to outdistance the enemy.

And yet to fight in the valley would risk the death of the relatively newly planted old ones.

It was the enemy who made the decision for him. A fast moving column crossed the head of the canyon to the west and positioned itself to the north. To the east the canyon tapered off and ended in high hills.

"Here we will stand," he told his leaders. "If we hold them until the snows come, they will be exposed, while our forces will have the shelter of the canyon. A winter siege will favor us, for we have food in the canyon, while they will have to hunt for theirs, or have it transported from the south."

He set up his headquarters in the cave where he had spent such a wonderful winter with Jai. The enemy could come at him from only one direction, the west. He positioned his bowmen behind tall brothers, behind boulders, with orders to fire and fall back to join the main force in defensive positions in front of the small grove where his grandmother lived on. In the following days, the enemy engaged them in probing actions. Devourers came down the steep sides of the canyon in small groups and were killed or forced to scramble up for their lives. A large force probed toward the east to find that the narrow confines of the canyon there, the steep, almost impassible hills, favored the defenders too greatly.

"There is only one way in," Hata told Elnice of Arutan. "Up the canyon from the west. The one who leads the pongs has chosen well. He can match our numbers in the confined floor of the canyon, but we will wear him down by repeated attacks."

Hata, himself, led the first probe directly up the canyon and he came face to face with the tall leader he'd watched at the battle before the gate of Kooh. He tried to fight his way to where Duwan was holding, a stack of dead guardsmen before him, and got close enough to see the face of his adversary.

"You will be interested to know that an old friend of yours anchors the center of the pong line," he told Elnice, after he'd ordered a withdrawal, leaving more of his own dead on the field than he liked to admit.

"A traitor?" Elnice snarled.

"Tomorrow, when we attack, you will see for yourself."

Elnice, surrounded by her personal bodyguard, made her way near enough to the battle line to catch a glimpse of the powerful warrior who anchored the pong line and killed her soldiers with dismaying regularity. She again felt that he was familiar, so she pushed closer. She was in no danger, for the pongs made no attempt to advance. They had established positions where the bowmen could take a toll, and the swordsmen could fight from the advantage of a small rise in the canyon floor.

"Duwan," she gasped, when she finally got a glimpse of his face in a moment of violence, as he threw back his head to avoid a thrust and then lunged forward to slay still another of her guardsmen.

"I want him taken alive," she told Hata, that night, when, once again, many dead littered the field of battle. "I took him into my bed and now he betrays me. He will be peeled so slowly that he will howl for mercy."

Next day the line gave, but did not break. Little by little, the enemy pushed it back, back, until a new set of defensive positions were reached and hidden bowmen caused a temporary panic among the enemy, a panic that was halted by officers cutting off the heads of a few fleeing conscripts and lashing the others back toward the line of battle. And so it went for ten days, then fifteen.

Each day was the same. The attack began shortly after first light and continued as wave after wave of fresh troops replaced those who had taken their losses in attacking Duwan's positions. At Duwan's back, now, was the grove, the young grove of growing brothers where his grandmother lived. His losses had been severe. Each day saw fewer experienced swordsmen at the line. Worse, the supply of arrows was running out, for it was impossible to retrieve more than a handful after each battle. Pongs had died trying to retrieve arrows, for Hata had noted the arrow gathering activity after each battle and had taken steps to stop it, placing fresh troops behind the battle line to ambush the arrow gatherers.

Duwan knew that defeat was inevitable. He prayed for the snows. He tried to communicate with the tall brothers, and his grandmother, but it was as if the presence of the enemy in the valley muted the whispers. He was still alone, and the hard fighting had not only depleted the pongs, it had taken its toll among the old valley Drinkers, as well. Males he had known from his first mobile days had been buried, or lay, unrecoverable, on the field of battle.

After a long, hard day of fighting he called his surviving leaders into council.

"The snows are tardy, and even if they come now it is too late," he said. "Our only choice is to try to salvage a portion of our remaining forces. They have fought well. They can become a cadre to form other fighting groups. It will avail us nothing if we all die here. With us will die all hope."

He outlined his plan, and, as she heard, Jai felt her heart pound painfully. Dagner protested. Duwan the Elder rose, his face grim.

"I see the wisdom of your plan, my son," Duwan the Elder said. "I question only one aspect of it. I will stand at your side."

"Father," Duwan said. "You must protect my mother. You must do as I say, or we have fought and died for nothing. Dagner, you have regained youth here in this land, and you must use your skills to train other fighters. You must all trust me. Many will die tomorrow, and perhaps I will be among the fallen, but I will die with my heart at ease knowing that you have obeyed my wishes, that the hope will not die with us who remain on the field of battle."

"Do not ask me to desert you," Jai said.

"I don't ask, my love, I order," Duwan said. "And if you don't obey me I will have you tied hand and foot and carried."

"Duwan," she wailed.

"No more," he said, and she was silent until, with the ordered movements made during the night, she lay by his side with the lights in the night sky putting a dim glow on his face.

"Let me stay," she begged.

He held her closely. "I do not plan to die. I will hold until you are safe among the hills, and then I will follow."

"Let me stay. Life without you would be more pain than pleasure."

"And to know that you die at my side, would that give me pleasure?"

She wept silently.

6

With the coming of darkness Duwan's army began to dissolve. Small groups began to make the difficult ascent of the steep walls of the canyon at its narrow, eastern end. There were quiet but tearful leavetakings, promises to meet again in the west, in the land of the free runners. The groups had been assembled carefully, with a male of fighting experience in each.

Duwan made the rounds of his camp, speaking to as many as he could. "On you rests the hope of tomorrow," he told them. "You have faced the enemy and you know that in his veins runs blood, and that that blood can be spilled. You must be my cadre, my teachers, until I can rejoin you. You must spread the word that Drinkers can and will drive the enemy from this land."

He found Tambol speaking to a large group of males and females and he halted in the darkness, outside the glow of the campfires, to listen.

"Of you, much is asked," Tambol was saying. "I, myself, shudder to think of going back among the enemy, but I will go and if it is your desire, you will go. There you will spread the word. Be cautious, my friends. Speak in whispers and in the protection of the darkness in the settlements, in the cities, anywhere you can find a slave to listen, and tell him of his true heritage. Tell him of the Master. Say that our battle here was not a defeat, but a victory, a victory marked by hundreds of enemy dead, a demonstration of what we can do if we all stand together."

When Tambol was alone Duwan approached and was greeted with an arm clasp and sudden tears from Tambol.

"I had counted on you to consolidate them in the west," Duwan said. "Yet I hear you speak of going back into the cities."

"I will do as you wish, Master."

"Then guide a group to the west," Duwan said. He'd given up on trying to prevent Tambol's using the exalted title in addressing him. "Tramp the hills. Gather the scattered elements together. Be my voice, Tambol, and gather others to you until the army numbers in the tens of thousands. Tell them to listen to the valley Drinkers, to my father, to Dagner, and the others, and to learn their lessons well before making another attempt to meet the enemy head-on. He is warned now, and he will be prepared."

"Master," Tambol said tearfully, it is you they follow, you who gives them the strength to die. Let me fight the holding action. You go and lead them into the west."

Duwan smiled and put his hand on Tambol's shoulder. "My friend, I have seen you with a sword. Your tongue is your weapon. Use it well."

Duwan climbed with his mother and father and the small group chosen to accompany them to stand on a high place and look down on the camp. The few who were left were kept busy adding wood to the hundreds of fires that were kept burning to prevent the enemy from suspecting the mass escape from the canyon. He saw Jai working among the others and his heart filled. For one painful moment he considered going to get her, taking her and fleeing with the others.

"Don't stay too long," Duwan the Elder said. "We

will have the hours of the night. It is the enemy custom, as you well know, to attack at first light and then to pause at midmorning while fresh troops are moved up. When that pause comes, take the opportunity."

"That is my plan," Duwan said. "Now, father, please wait here while I bring my mate to you. Guard her and my mother well. Find a warm cave in the western hills and save a spot near the fire for my bed."

No further words were spoken as they clasped arms and his mother embraced him. Then he went down the canyon wall and found Jai carrying wood for the fires.

"It is time," he said.

"Oh, Duwan—"

"Come." He took the firewood from her, tossed it to the ground and took her arm. Once again he climbed the steep wall, pulling her along with him, until they stood just below where his father waited.

"If you do not come to me," she said, clinging to him, "I will arm myself and seek out the nearest enemy and send many of them ahead of me into death."

"You will stay with my father and mother," he said sternly. "You will help train the army. You will teach newcomers the way, the proper foods, the truth of Du. In that way you will honor me best." He shook her, both hands on her shoulders. "Promise me this."

"Yes, yes," she said. "I promise. But promise me that you will not die just for the sake of stubbornness, because you do not wish to flee from the face of the enemy. Promise me that you will escape when the enemy pauses in his first attack."

"Yes," he said. He held her close and then pushed her up the steep hill. But he held onto her garment and pulled her back. "Once before I sent you away," he said, "and you came back. What do you hold most sacred?"

"My love for you," she whispered.

"Then, on that love, I want your word that you will not come back into the canyon. Promise me that, regardless of what happens, you will not come back. If I am to die, and that is not in my plan, I do not want the sadness of knowing that you threw your life away as well. Promise me."

"On my love, I promise," she whispered.

To Duwan's surprise, he slept. Around him those who had volunteered, who had begged to be allowed to fight at his side, slept or gazed at the fires, anticipating the morning. They were few, only enough to man the defensive positions in the very narrowest part of the canyon. Duwan awoke with a hand on his shoulder.

"Master, the sky lightens in the east."

He rose. He chewed tender life organs from a fixed brother, drank from the steam which, fortunately, came from the east and was, thus, not stinking with the blood and rot from the dead as it was farther down the canyon to the west. He saw to the positioning of his bowmen. They had the last of the arrows and they had been selected for their skill with both bow and sword, so that when their few arrows had been fired they could take up the blade and fill the gaps in Duwan's thin line.

Gradually the darkness faded. And then Du appeared over the eastern hills and from down the canyon they heard the grunted, guttural marching chant of the enemy. The bright uniforms of the enemy were soiled, but still impressive as the first elements emerged from a dense forest and passed near the young grove where Duwan's grandmother lived on. Then the enemy force began to be constricted as the canyon narrowed. Some marched in the shallow stream, slipping now and then on the rocks. Duwan stood, straight and proud. He had

come to know the insignia of the various units of the
enemy conqforce, and he recognized the markings
of the elite Arutan home guard. It was Hata's own
unit that was making the initial attack. He looked for
Hata and saw him, near the center. More then once
they had seen each other on the field, but had not,
as yet, come face to face.

Shouted orders from Hata halted the unit at a
distance calculated to tempt Duwan's archers into
wasting arrows at extreme range. Duwan stood motionless. There was a brittle air of expectancy in the
morning chill. No one moved. All was silence. When
it became obvious that Duwan was not to be tricked
into wasting arrows, there were more orders from
Hata and enemy soldiers began to advance in stag-
gered formation, running, swerving from side to
side.

"Hold," Duwan ordered, lifting one hand toward
his archers. He saw several of the archers notch
arrows and half-draw the bow, and he kept his hand
up, holding them back. "Swordsmen," he bellowed,
"take these few. Archers, hold!"

The tactic had been used against him before, and
he was ready for it on that last morning. He had
positioned his archers high, so that they could fire
over the heads of those engaged in sword to sword
combat below them. His swordsmen met the running, weaving advance and the clash of iron on iron
rang and echoed from the canyon walls. He did not
hear, but saw Hata give the order for the main
advance, as the enemy began to fall to the swords of
his best bladesmen. He waited until the mass of
Hata's force was in fatal range of the bows and then
lowered his hand and saw the arrows flash darkly
outward and heard the grunts, moans, screams of
agony as they found their marks.

"Fall back to your positions," he shouted to the
swordsmen engaging the first advance below him

and his warriors disengaged and scrambled back to find their assigned places between trees, behind boulders, places chosen to make it impossible for more than one enemy at a time to face them. Duwan's usual place was at the center and he met the rush of an enemy with an almost casual thrust and then kicked the quivering body aside to make room for another. And then the morning became endless repetition. The clash of metal. The moans and screams of the dying. Duwan protected his position with a fierceness and rage that piled the dead in front of him, leaving, at times, a blank spot in the enemy line, since none cared to face him. He smelled the battle, the sweat, the blood, the acrid stench of fear, and he heard the thunder of the enemy captains' voices, and the shoutings of his own leaders.

Sweat rolled into his eyes and he wiped it away with the top of his shortsword wrist while parrying a thrust by an enemy. Blood smeared from the contact, not his own. The enemy leaped forward as if eager to impale himself on Duwan's shortsword and was given his desire and then Duwan was moving to his left where a swordsman had fallen. Now the battle reached a peak. Hata's own unit was a prideful group, and for many days now they had been repelled by a force of pongs. They had come with Hata's harsh words burning in their ears, words of reproach and shame, and they were determined not to leave the field with a single pong standing.

One by one the defenders fell, and there were several times when Duwan felt that all was lost, when screaming guardsmen breached the line and threatened to fall on the defenders from behind. But each time his warriors rallied, threw themselves into the breach, pushed the enemy back.

The enemy pullback began at the center, where Duwan was the anchor, and spread until there was no longer the sound of sword on sword, only the moans and cries for aid from the fallen. Duwan saw Hata standing at a distance, his arms crossed over his chest, glaring hatred. Now was the time. Now was the time to pull his own remaining warriors back into the trees, to send them climbing up the steep walls, taking their last chance for escape and for life. Now it was time for him to follow them, to lose himself in those dense stands of tall brothers in the hills and slowly and carefully to make his way westward, there to rejoin his family and Jai.

He looked across the body strewn battleground to see Hata still standing, still glaring at him, and at Hata's side there appeared Elnice of Arutan, dressed in a crimson copy of the guards' uniform. He looked at her for a moment, then turned to give his orders to begin to fade back into the trees. At that moment a shout of warning came from his rear and he ran back to see a sprinkling of color on the steep walls of the canyon.

His heart leaped in alarm, not for himself, but for Jai, for his mother and father, for the enemy had come to his rear in force and were now sliding and slipping down the canyon walls. They had not tried that since the first days, when they had lost many men. To get into position to come at him from the rear they had had to move during the night. Had they known of his plans? Had they come upon the small groups who had left the canyon and destroyed them one by one? No, surely he would have heard had that happened. He could only hope that they had not started their movements until late at night, that his mother and father and Jai and the others were safely away.

Now he heard the battle chant of the enemy from his front. A few of his warriors were running to meet the enemy scrambling down the canyon walls. He lifted both his swords and shouted, "To me. Form

on me." Except for isolated individuals already engaged with an enemy who had come down the steep
walls, they came to him and he stood among them,
so few of them now, and he said, "It is not Du's will
that we escape this time, my friends. We make our
stand here."

"It is better to die fighting than fall into the hands
of the enemy," someone shouted, and Duwan nodded.

"Let us show them how Drinkers can fight," Duwan
shouted, as the enemy began to reach the floor of
the narrow canyon and advance and he heard the
sound of the chant and the poundings of many feet.

The guardsmen who had come down the walls
fared rather badly, for they were winded by their
march and their efforts. They found that pongs could
fight well and they died, their bodies littering the
ground. Then, from the west, Hata burst into the
field at the head of fresh forces.

Each one of the enemy came toward the concentrated melee with the words of their High Mistress
ringing in their ears.

"Remember this well," she had told them, time and
again, "I want their leader, this Duwan, alive. If he is
killed not only will the one who killed him be peeled,
but each surviving one in his unit."

Thus it was that Duwan had to seek engagements,
and was surprised at the ease of his victories. Many,
seeing him coming toward them, ran, often straight
onto the sword of another Drinker. But one by one
the Drinkers fell. Surrounded, in the open, the out-
come was inevitable.

At last he stood with the only other surviving de-
fender, an ex-slave whose back was to Duwan's as a
ring of enemy closed in them.

"Master," the one who was soon to die said, "we will
meet again in Du's paradise."

A surge of guilt swept through Duwan. "Du," he

prayed silently, as the enemy closed, swords extended, "if I have used your name in vain, forgive me." For he knew that he had been presented by Tambol and Tambol's followers as, at the least, favored by Du, and, at best, as Du's own representative on the earth. It was true that he had often denied divine origin, but he had not been firm, had even, he guessed, as death closed on him, been willing to let the ex-slaves believe in him in order to make them fight better.

"Forgive me, Du," he said aloud, as he lashed out and his sword swept aside a blade and brought blood from an enemy who fell back, screaming. At his back he heard the clash of metal and felt his last companion lean suddenly against him, then slide to the ground.

"Come then," he shouted, "let me take a few of you with me."

Surprisingly, the enemy backed away. He rushed toward them and they slipped out of his path, but always he was surrounded by a wall of uniformed, armed Devourers.

"Fight," he hissed, making a lunge that was avoided by an enemy officer who actually turned and ran into three soldiers, sending them sprawling.

"Fight, cowards," Duwan roared, as he stood, swords hanging down, panting with his efforts.

"It is over," he heard, and he spun around to see Captain Hata standing, sword in hand.

"We fought once, Hata, with padded weapons," Duwan said. "There is no pad on my blade now."

"Nothing would please me more," Hata said.

Duwan crouched and began to advance toward the captain, but he halted when Elnice pushed forward and stood by Hata's side.

"You will not find an easy death in battle, traitor," she said. She turned to Hata. "Take him."

"I have never killed a female," Duwan said, stalking

toward Elnice and Hata, "but when she represents evil—"

"Will you take him, or will you let him walk forward and kill me?" Elnice asked, her voice calm.

"Take him," Hata thundered. "Take him alive, or, by the dus, you will all be peeled."

Hopelessly, the front ranks of the soldiers began to close on Duwan and his blades flashed and enemy died and then, lest they all die under his iron, they screamed and pushed forward without their weapons and in blood and screamings bore him down by sheer weight until his swords could flash no more, until his breath was forced out of his chest by their weight and he was helplessly screaming his rage and anger.

"Bring him, and any living wounded, to the camp," Elnice ordered.

He was carried, tied well, by four of the enemy. He fought against his bonds until he was exhausted, and then he closed his eyes, prayed to his Du, and tried to commune with the tall brothers, but all was silence from them. They tied him to the bole of a tall brother in an area where all green had been ruthlessly cut away. From where he stood he could see the grove of his grandmother, and he prayed that the enemy would do what he was going to do and leave the canyon before harm came to those new immortals, who had grown rather impressively since the plantings and were no longer recognizable as Drinkers.

Elnice stood before him. She had changed into something more comfortable than her uniform, a loose, short gown that showed her bud point and the shape of her legs clearly.

"Not that it matters, traitor," she said, "for all your deluded followers are now dead, but I will know your thinking, your methods, your lies that you told to the those doomed pongs. Talk."

"I am Duwan the Drinker," he said. "Since I am not of you, how can I be a traitor?"

"You told me you were a wanderer," Elnice said. "But you were more. A Drinker? That is a word that means nothing. You are either pong or master. Which is it?"

"I drink of the sun, just as I have taught many to drink," Duwan said.

"He has exposed his head to the sun and it has addled him," someone said.

"Silence," Elnice said. She whirled to Hata. "Clear this area."

Within moments only Duwan, the High Mistress, and Hata were in the clearing.

"How did you know that you could drink energy from the sun?" Elnice asked.

"By the grace of Du," Duwan said.

"And you eat of the green, growing things. How did you first know they were not, as you were taught, poisonous?"

Duwan started to answer, but he closed his mouth. He had led an army, had slain many foes, and the enemy was now alert and, perhaps, in spite of the victory, a bit frightened. He would not give this female enough information to alert her to a population of Drinkers in the far north. He doubted that Devourers could survive the journey, and find the way through the land of the fires, but he would say nothing to put his own people in the valley at risk.

"I asked you a question," Elnice said.

"I am tired of talking," Duwan said, with a little smile.

"They, the pongs we have peeled to get information, say that you came from the earth," Elnice said, "that you are a god, a new master. Did you come from the earth?"

It was safe to say, "We are all, we Drinkers, of the earth and for the earth."

"Don't prate superstition at me," Elnice snarled. "I can give you a quick death. That much I will do if you will tell me how you managed to convince pongs to bare themselves to the sun, to eat green."

"Death, fast or slow, produces the same end result," Duwan said. "I will say that you will have ample opportunity to study the problem, for something has started in this land that you will not be able to stop, Elnice. All pongs know the truth, now, and if some are still fearful, they will come to believe. They will drink of the sun and they will eat and grow strong and then they will drive you and all Devourers back to the southern jungles from whence you came."

Elnice leaped at him and slashed his cheek with her nails, leaving three welling streaks of blood. Then she turned to Hata. "Bring the wounded. Show him what he faces."

A wounded pong warrior was dragged to the clearing. He was peeled quickly. Skilled Devourers used sharp knives to make a circle around the pong's left arm, his uninjured arm, and then the hide of the arm was seized in powerful pincer tools and ripped off, leaving raw, unprotected flesh welling blood as the pong screamed in agony and became unconscious. The hide was like a glove, complete with fingers and thumbs. Elnice picked it up gingerly and slashed it wetly across Duwan's face.

"Your treatment will be slower," she said.

He closed his eyes as seven wounded were peeled, first the arms, then the legs, then, in strips, the hide from the back, belly, ribs, hips. Death and the smell of it surrounded him, and the moans of it, for careful peeling left a raw, bleeding mass of flesh that lived on, often for more than a day. Fortunately for those who had been peeled, many were near death from their battle wounds so soon only two lingered, screaming in pain.

"I will give you death," Elnice said, standing over

one of the screaming masses with sword in hand. "Tell me of this Duwan."

"He is the Master," the dying pong gasped. "He came from the earth. He is the appointed one of Du, the one Du. He gave us magic to eat the green and to drink of the sun."

"How many eat of the green?" Elnice asked. That question had been asked many times before of dying pongs.

"Tens of thousands," the dying one said. "And more each day."

"Liar," Elnice screamed, bringing down the sword to finish the pong's agony. The last survivor died as she asked her first question.

Duwan wept. Even in death the warrior had been loyal. "Tens of thousands," he had said, and it was, as Elnice had said, a lie, for there were mere hundreds, and no one knew how many of them would survive to reach the doubtful security of the western wilderness.

"I want this one peeled with the greatest of care," Elnice told the two guardsmen whose specialty was shown by the oddly shaped knives they carried. "He is strong. Peel him in tiny strips. I want him to live for a day, perhaps two. Then we will see if he has had enough talking, or if he will be eager to talk, will beg to be heard, in exchange for the release of death."

A peeler came to stand beside Duwan, knife in hand, made a cut at Duwan's shoulder.

"No," Elnice said. "Start at his feet. You should know that he will last longer if you start there."

She sat in a chair beside the tree and watched with slitted eyes as Duwan's left foot was lifted and the knife made an incision and the sole of his foot was peeled away. She looked up at Duwan's face, contorted in agony.

"Some find that screaming helps. It seems to use up energy and hasten death," she said. "Will you scream?"

He screamed, loudly and lustily, as the knife sliced and the hide was peeled from the arch of his foot and down off his horned toes.

The clearing was now surrounded by soldiers. Some lay on the ground, heads cocked to see the show. Others sat, kneeled, stood. They drank their rations of wine and made wagers on how long Duwan would live once he'd been fully peeled.

It happened slowly, slowly. Little by little, strip by strip, his lower legs were bared. Flesh oozed blood. The pain of peeling made his senses reel. He screamed. And the peeled, exposed flesh burned with the slightest movement of wind, burned with a pain unlike any he had ever felt, a pain more severe than that he'd felt when the rock sucker was draining all his blood and he had cut off his own arm.

When he was without skin to mid-thigh he began to pray to Du for death. He didn't care if anyone heard him, he prayed aloud, almost screaming the name of his Du, and the High Mistress laughed.

"Pour wine on his exposed flesh and see if his du can stop the pain," she said.

Duwan screamed and writhed against his bonds as liquid fire attacked his exposed legs.

"Your du is not on duty today," Hata said, laughing.

"So he came from the earth," Elnice said. "Let us return him to the earth. Peel him to the waist and then plant him to mid-thigh in the earth. Let us see if that will awaken his du."

Jai, of course, had not obeyed Duwan's wishes. In the darkness of the night she had whispered to Duwan the Elder, "I go. Don't bother to follow me. Take care of your own." Then she was gone, and Duwan the Elder could only continue, for he had the responsibility of his mate and others on his hands.

Jai lay hidden high on the side of the canyon. She had, by sheer good fortune, chosen a place where no

enemy came down, and she watched the last battle
with wild, desperate tears. More than once she jerked,
almost making the move that would send her down
the wall of the canyon to join the dying remnants of
the once great pong army, but, although she had
broken part of her promise, she could not bring
herself to betray Duwan's orders totally.

When, at last, Duwan stood alone and then was
taken she was in shock, incapable of movement, save
for her eyes, and they followed him as he was carried away. She regained movement and crept along
the side of the canyon to see that he had been tied to
a tree and she could hear what was said. She ground
her teeth in anger as the wounded were tortured
and then she almost screamed with Duwan when his
first agonized wail came to her.

He was going to die. She did not want to live with
him dead. She gathered her limbs to leap to her feet
and go charging down the hill to, hopefully, surprise
the enemy and get within swords' length of Elnice of
Arutan, to take that evil with her and Duwan into
death. She was poised to move when she heard, "Stay
as you are, daughter."

She looked around, frightened, for she had been
very much alone in her hiding palce. And she was
still alone.

"You have given your word," the voice said, and
she realized that it was in her head, not her ears.

"Who?" she whispered.

"I, too, know his agony," the voice said, "and he is
my grandson, but you have promised him. You must
not die with him."

And, in spite of her efforts, she could not stand.
When Duwan screamed again she hid her face in her
hands.

She had to look. She saw the torture proceeding
slowly and, although he still writhed and screamed,
she knew that he was dead, for he was peeled to the

waist and no one could survive that. A silent wail of grief filled her, and the voice spoke, and it was laughing.

Laughing?

"The fools give him to the earth, daughter."

He returned to the earth, buried up to his hips in an upright position. He knew a new agony, for as the soil was shoveled and packed around his raw legs it was as if he'd been dipped to his hips in the molten rock of the land of the fires.

They braced his back against a post and tied his hands above his head so that the peelers could reach the tenderer hide of his underarms.

Between each strip, the peelers rested, and Elnice, seated comfortably in her chair, taunted him, promised him that he would talk, would answer all her questions. And in her hiding place above, Jai died a little with each strip of hide removed from Duwan.

When, as the day grew long and Du sank low, there was only the skin on his face left, he had screamed so that his sounds of agony were now nothing more than a hoarse croak.

"Leave the lips," Elnice ordered, as the peelers began on the face.

His eyelids were removed carefully. Now his orange eyes seemed on the verge of popping from his head and he stared without seeing at the smiling face of Elnice.

"You've stood more than most, already," Elnice said. "It is not that I believe you have any secrets worth knowing, it is just that you *will* talk. Tell me, if nothing else, of your childhood, my lover."

"The curse of Du be on you," Duwan said. "The agony you have given me will be returned to you in multiples."

"Take the fool's lips," Elnice snarled, leaping from

the chair, her skirts swirling as she walked regally
away.

Night. A light rain came, cold, not a great hardship to the camped enemy, but new horror for the
peeled Drinker, with each drop striking like acid
fire. He could no longer moan, for his throat was
swollen closed with his screaming, and his breathing
was difficult. There was no time. The rain stopped
and he knew that death was near. He did not know
how long the night had gone on, whether for an
eternity or for an hour. He determined to live until
Du came, to look upon Du's kind face just once
more.

His sight was blurred by the blood that ran over
the lidless balls, but he saw a lightening in the east.
He lifted his head to agony. He had been in a semi-
conscious state of shock, and the movement seemed
to awaken his mutilated body to fire. But there was
Du. He could not blink to protect his eyes from the
brightness.

"Du," he tried to say, and managed only a croak,
"take me. I can stand no more."

And then the red, fiery circle was fully exposed
above the hills and he set his lidless eyes on it and
prayed until the rays began to burn his sight and
blackness came slowly, slowly.

Elnice was in her uniform. Around her the conqforce was making preparations to move out. She
stood and looked down upon the raw, bleeding body.
His head was hanging on his bloody chest. His lungs
had ceased to function.

"I had hoped," she told Hata, "that he would last at
least until the heat of midday began to cook him."

"He died just after dawn," Hata said, "with one last
prayer to his du."

"So much for dus," Elnice said. "I am ready."

She did not look back. The last of the conqforce
was out of the canyon by midday, leaving behind a

feast for the scavengers of the earth and the air, and a weeping female who knelt before the dead one. In her nostrils was the stench of the newly dead and the long dead, for the enemy did not bury his own, much less dead pongs.

"You could have come with us," Jai whispered to dead ears. "You could have left during the night, and we would now be marching to the west and you would be alive. You could have, you could have."

7

Sema, mother of Duwan the Drinker, put fresh, dry wood on the fire. The cave was an ideal place, for there was a small vent at the very rear that allowed the smoke to be drawn straight up and out. She looked up as her mate entered.

"More have come," he said.

"Is there word?"

"None," he said. "Save that the enemy marches south and does not pursue any toward the west."

"And of Jai?" she asked.

Duwan the Elder shook his head. "There is one of the newcomers who has an infected wound."

Sema rose, reached for her bag of dried healing herbs.

"I will tell you immediately if there is word of either of them," Duwan the Elder said. "Go now, for the warrior is in pain."

They had joined Tambol and a growing group of Drinkers who had found their way into the hills of the west. The last stages of the journey had been made in snow and sleet and cold. Many wounded died. A few of the old valley Drinkers had chosen a pleasant valley in the foothills to go back to the earth. Now the cadre of valley Drinkers had been reduced to less than ten, and Dagner, as if the defeat in the canyon had taken away his seemingly new-found youth, was hardening and had spent the first few days in the hills looking for his chosen place to return to the earth.

There were, counting females and the few young, just over three hundred of them in the valley they'd chosen when a band of free runners came. Duwan the Elder went out to meet the runners, marveling at their wasted condition in the midst of plenty. There were evergreens and plenty of dried fodder, enough food to make a Drinker sleek and fat.

"If you must make your presence so blatant, with fires and noise," said the skinny spokesman of the runners, "you will leave this area and go further west, lest you draw the masters down on us."

"Who gives me orders?" Duwan the Elder asked.

"Farnee, Eldest of the free runners."

"I see only a fool who starves with Du shining and good food everywhere," Duwan the Elder said.

The group of runners, thirty strong, reached for weapons. Duwan the Elder clapped his hands and the group of runners were quickly surrounded by swordsmen, healthy, fat swordsmen who, except for their ragged dress, looked like masters. Farnee yelped and tried to run and two strong Drinkers seized him by the arms and brought him back to face Duwan the Elder.

At that moment Tambol appeared and Farnee, seeing him, cried out, "Traitor, you have led them to us."

"Be quiet, old one," Tambol said. "We are Drinkers, all. We have killed the enemy, and we give you one more chance to join us."

"I see the new mounds of earth where you have buried dead," Farnee said. "If you have killed the enemy, why are you here, hiding as we hide?"

All during the march to the west Tambol had been trying to come up with an answer to just that question, and others like it. There had been long days and night when he walked in miserable muteness, when he knew the blackest despair. From the beginning Duwan, the Master, had been the heart of it.

He had come from the earth to fulfill the ancient prophesy, that coming witnessed by his mate, Jai, and he had killed the enemy and taught others how not only to kill, but to live. Tambol could not delude himself into believing that things would be the same with Duwan gone. During those first grim days, when everyone was fearful that the Enemy was just behind them, he could not muster enough faith to believe that Duwan could escape the canyon of death. He knew that Duwan had accepted death, in exchange for a greater chance of escape for his followers.

Try as he might, Tambol had never been able to hear the whispers from the trees, trees that Duwan called brothers, trees that, said Duwan, were the spirits of Drinkers. His entire faith was based on the Master. He had seen the evil in the pens, and he had heard others weep and pray to many dus. Emotionally, the concept of one Du, an all-powerful, merciful Du who was the Du of the Drinkers, appealed to him. Intellectually, he doubted during those days when it became apparent that Duwan had died in the canyon and would never rejoin them. He felt hypocritical when he told others, "This is the way of the Master. He left us once before, to attend to the business of Du. He has left us once again, but only temporarily. It is up to us to honor him and what he has done for us by carrying on his work. In the days of final crisis he will return to lead us into the last battles."

As for the freed slaves, never having had anything in which to believe save some nebulous dus who seemed always to favor the stronger, the Devourers, they seized on Tambol's teachings and spread them.

So, although Tambol, himself, knew doubt, he also knew the worthiness of the cause, and he still had some small hope that Duwan's ultimate goal, freedom for all, could be achieved under the leadership of the Master's father. So he was ready for Farnee's question.

"We will not regain the lands of our ancestors and rid ourselves of the Devourers without loss," he said. The Master guides us, speaking to us through the spirits of our ancestors. He calls out to all to join in the battle." He drew himself up and looked at the free runners, his face majestic, grim. "And these are the words of the Master. All who are not with us are against us."

Duwan the Elder seized upon that thought. He had been told that there were hundreds of male runners, and that number would partially replace the losses to the army.

"We will waste no time on those who equivocate," he said, "but we will shove them aside, treating them as we would treat the enemy, lest they stand in our way or betray us to the enemy."

"The choice is yours, Farnee my father," Tambol said. "Join us, accept the ways of Du, live a good live eating and drinking of the bounty of Du, or risk our wrath. The sight of you reminds us of what we were before the Master taught us to be Drinkers, and that we cannot abide."

Farnee looked around nervously at the bared blades of the swordsmen. "What would you have us do?"

"Eat," Tambol said. "Fatten yourselves, and then you will be assigned to a unit for training."

Farnee swallowed and then said, "Can we not simply leave you, go farther to the west where we will not offend you?"

Duwan the Elder motioned with his hand and the swordsmen moved closer to the group of runners. "You are with us or against us," he said, borrowing Tambol's words. "Eat."

Farnee was handed leaf organs from an evergreen. He glanced around, in panic. Seeing no other course, he ate. In the days that followed it became a challenge not to get the free runners to eat, but to keep them from stripping all green in the immediate area.

Runner males began training. The surviving wood wokers began to replace lost bows and arrows, and, in the absence of metal, experiments were made in accordance with ancient legends of the making of arrowheads from stone.

"It is time for me to go," Tambol told Duwan the Elder, on a day when the first severe storm of winter threatened, when the sky to the northwest was purple-black and Du's rays seemed to be already weakened. "I will try to outpace the winter to the east."

Winter overtook him, however, and he walked through snows and winds and when, at last, he reached a settlement he was weakened, looking very much the part of a wandering priest of Tseeb. He was given shelter in the pongpen and began, that first night, to talk of the Master.

Winter had come to Arutan. The conscripts among those who had served in the conqforce were sent back to their homes. All was quiet in the pongpens. Elnice had ordered a few random peelings, with questioning, to determine if word of the abortive slave rebellion in the north had reached the pongs of the capital city and she was pleased to hear no hint of it from the screaming, begging victims. She had ordered a quarantine of the city of Kooh. It was enforced by a large force of her guards. No citizen or pong was allowed to leave Kooh to travel to the south.

As the cold closed in and made her luxurious quarters seem even more cozy, Elnice consulted her wise men with Captain Hata present.

The eldest of her advisers was speaking. "It is my opinion, High Mistress, that there is no present danger. The future? That is another matter. It took our ancestors three generations to wipe from the memory of the relatively few native survivors of the conquest the knowledge of the special abilities of these people. Now that knowledge is once more afoot. We know that there are escaped slaves in the west. Your own people say that many escaped death in your last battle in the north. We can be assured that those who escaped will continue to spread the word, and that, High Mistress, is the danger."

"I see no danger," Hata said. "A few pongs were deluded by a rabble-rouser. He is now dead."

"Do you read the priestly writing, Captain Hata?" the old adviser asked. Hata shook his head. "Perhaps you should have read to you the records of those who came to these lands first. It is not widely known that our ancestors narrowly escaped being pushed back to the south, in bloody defeat, by peoples who, until our arrival, knew nothing of weapons or killing. Tell me, did the pongs fight well? Did you not have losses?"

Hata made a gesture of dismissal, but Elnice said, "Their losses were greater, but the bones of our dead litter a canyon in the north. And one of them fought better than any warrior I've ever seen."

"So it was in history. Once they learned, they fought savagely. And," he squinted and looked around with a wry smile, "this will ruffle the pride of many, but it should be said. Warrior for warrior, equally armed and equally trained, they were superior, those early people who called themselves Drinkers."

Hata started to protest.

"Captain," the old adviser said, "can you march for one change of the moon without rations? Can you live, in winter, on dry leaves and grass? Can you expose your skin to the sun and use its light to make energy? They can. Another thing. Have you seen figures showing the total population of pongs in our cities, in our settlements, in the single establishments in the countryside? We have, to sustain our lifestyle, allowed our slaves to outbreed us, to actually outnumber us."

"There is a simple solution for that," Hata said. "Kill them all."

The old adviser spread his hands. "Are you willing, captain, to cook your own food, to carry your own wood, to clean your own house? Are you willing to take your turn in the mines, in the fields, in the workshops? Our entire way of life is based on our slaves, captain. To eliminate them would require vast upheaval."

"Well, all is quiet now," Hata said.

"Yes. It is winter," Elnice said. "What of the spring?" She looked at the old adviser. "What are your suggestions, old one?"

"Slow change," he said. "Little by little we must require more of our own people, our idlers. We must make it a requirement that each of our young learn a trade. We must limit the breeding of the pongs, allowing only enough of their young to survive to maintain a solid pool of breeding stock. Slowly, without letting it be known to the general population of pongs, we begin to reduce their numbers. This can be done easily in the cities. A pong, or an entire family, simply disappears. It happens often. Pongs are sold or traded. It will take years, perhaps ten, to make a significant reduction in the pong population without causing panic among them, without disrupting our economy."

"So be it," Elnice said. "Will you assume responsibility for starting this program?"

"I will, High Mistress," the old adviser said. "There is one other thing. You have begun to dismantle the army you put together. That process should be halted. Instead, you should build several forces, not as large as a conqforce, and train them well, have them ready to move instantly to any trouble spot in the land. As soon as the weather permits, the strongest force should be sent west to comb the hills. I would also suggest that you send emissaries to the western land, across the great, inland mountains, to see if there has been trouble there, to warn them if there was not."

"They would laugh at us," Hata said heatedly, "if they knew we had lost warriors to pongs."

The old adviser shrugged. "A small blow to pride, considering what is at stake."

"Let them laugh," Elnice said. "What I want to know is how this Duwan came to be a leader. He was pong. I saw the pores in the bottom of his feet. How did a pong rise above his station and influence thousands?"

"You killed the only possible way of knowing that in the canyon," Hata said.

"He could not have spread the word alone," Elnice said. "I want spies sent into the pens. I want to know who among them carries the messages of sedition." She rose. "Hata, begin to build the armies. You, yourself, will lead the force to the west in the spring. I want a daily count on the number of pongs put to death not only in Arutan but in all other cities. Upon consideration, I think it wise to exterminate the entire pong population of Kooh, and all surrounding settlements. If not all at once, at a rate in multiples to the exterminations in the other areas, for the pongs of Kooh saw an attack force kill masters in their city. That news must not spread."

"It will be done," Hata said, his eyes on Elnice's shapely backside as she swept from the conference room.

So it was that when Tambol came to Kooh, in the dead of winter, he came to terror and death. The days were filled with fear and wailing as entire families were taken from the pens to disappear forever. Not a day passed without several public executions in the square for offenses that, in the past, would have brought nothing more than a mild lashing. Tambol was shocked to find that fully a quarter of the population of one pen had already disappeared, or had been killed quickly—there were so many executions that peeling was too time consuming.

A sense of panic filled Tambol. Many of those whom he had taught personally were gone. Only a few real believers remained, and they were filled with fear and doubting, so that his urgings for hope, for action, went unheeded. When the edict came down to the pens that there was to be no breeding, there was a general wail of despair.

"It is evident," Tambol told a selected group, "that the Devourers' intent is to wipe out all knowledge of what happened here. They are going to kill all of you, so that no one will be able to tell others that here pongs fought and killed their masters. There is only one thing to do. We must help as many as possible to escape. This will be possible in the confusion, for so many are being killed that a few more who do not return, for example, from their work outside the city walls will not be missed."

Singly and in groups of two to five, those who saw the hopelessness of staying in Kooh began to move toward the west. In their desperation, knowing that they faced certain death if they stayed in Kooh, they ate as Tambol had instructed them to eat. Most lived to survive the winter march, and many found the valley where they were welcomed by the growing force under the command of Duwan the Elder.

If the Master was dead, and Tambol began to believe that he was, his dream was still alive, not burning brightly as it had burned when an army marched and slew the enemy, but flickering, nevertheless.

Winter had also come to the northern canyon where Duwan had made his last stand. The snows were deep there, and, although the canyon floor was shielded from the worst of the cold winds, the stream was frozen and the tall and other fixed brothers were laden with snow and ice. Jai had accumulated firewood and food in the cave where she had wintered with Duwan before they had made the trek to the valley of the Drinkers. There she had her memories. She had intended to leave the valley before the snows, but another change, a puzzling one, had kept her there.

When the change first began she had screamed out in horror. She had noticed it first on the second day after Duwan's death. She'd spent the night in the cave, shivering with loss and the cold, too tired to build a fire, and she'd made her way to where he was standing, planted in the earth, shortly after sunrise to see that *things*, living *things*, were attacking his thighs just above where they disappeared into the earth. The *things* seemed, actually, to be growing in his dead flesh, absorbing the congealing liquids that had seeped from his exposed cells. She screamed and reached out to jerk them away, but she could not bring herself to touch that mass of horror. That was Duwan, his remains, but it was not the Duwan she'd loved. His orange eyes, now burned to a dull rust by the heat of the sun, were no longer the eyes into which she'd loved to gaze, picking out the little individual flecks of color.

She could not see the things growing, but by the end of the second day they had extended upward a full handspan on his thighs. She was led to remember the think vines, the living green that could be directed by the minds of the valley Drinkers to form their huts. She had seen Duwan's grandmother and many others of the valley oldsters return to the earth. In fact, as chance would have it, Elnice of Arutan had chosen an opening in the very grove where Sema the elder grew. Was this, Jai wondered, the earth reclaiming her own? Was Duwan to become one of those whisperers?

She lay on the cold earth before him and watched

as, little by little, his peeled flesh was taken by the thick growth of tendrils. The growth spread as it reached upward, and there formed a moss-like fuzz, an all-covering blanket that gradually began to obliterate the shape of separate legs and arms.

With the coming of the first serious snow Duwan's body was no longer recognizable. It was a fuzzy mass, rounded to a point at the top, an odd growth, but a part of the earth, so much so that birds landed there to preen themselves and once she saw a small ground creature standing on its rear legs nibbling at the moss-like covering. Then the snow began to hide the mass, drifting against it, lodging on it, and soon there was a white pillar standing there in the grove.

She had conflicting emotions. She felt a need to be away from the reminder of her sorrow, but, when she thought of going, the emptiness inside her grew and engulfed her so that she would go into her cave, curl into her bed of boughs by the fire and weep until she fell asleep.

Then the snows were too deep, the weather too cold, to consider traveling, so she settled in and would not leave the cave for days, for she could supply her need for water by eating the snow that drifted into the entrance. In the quiet winter nights, with the cold so brittle that the smallest sound seemed to reverberate throughout the entire canyon, she relived every moment she'd had with Duwan and as she remembered there were the whispers, indistinct, distant but comforting. To her knowledge she was the only one, other than valley Drinkers, who could hear them now that Duwan was dead. The whisperings renewed her speculation about what had happened to Duwan. Had the earth claimed him? Other dead bodies moldered, rotted, were eaten by scavengers. (It was more pleasant in the valley since the snows, for the grisly reminders of death were, at least temporarily, covered by a blanket of pure white.)

Was he, like the ancestors and those oldsters from the valley, alive? She could not understand how. His heart had stopped. When Sema the elder and the others went back to the earth they had been living, if hardening. No, she told herself, he was dead, deprived even of that doubtful existence as a tall brother.

She had not yet accepted that aspect of being a Drinker. To think of half-burying oneself in the earth to become a tree seemed almost as horrible as being killed and left to become a part of the earth through decay. But now that Duwan was of the earth, she began to wonder, and, as she heard the confused, indistinct whispers, she told herself that, when her time came, she would return to the canyon and join Duwan there, to be by his side for—how long? Forever? Did the tall brothers die? She'd seen them killed by Devourers, cut for their wood. How could anything, even a tree, live forever?

"What follows forever?" she asked, aloud.

"Eternity," came the answer, clearly.

She jumped, startled. She came to her knees on her bed of boughs and looked around. The fire had burned low. She threw on dead branches and the light flickered. The entrance was almost totally blocked by snow.

"Who?" she asked. "Is it you, Sema? Speak to me. Tell me of Duwan."

Silence. Massed whisperings.

With the morning she went to the green pillar that had been Duwan and brushed away snow with a fresh bough. The moss-like covering was denser, and seemed to glow with life. She touched it. It was not unpleasant to the touch.

"Duwan," she whispered. "Do you live? If you live tell me, and I will join you now."

The silence activated her pain and in a frenzy she began to dig away at the snow until she reached the frozen earth and broke fingernails trying to dig a hole into which she would plant herself.

"Peace, daughter," the voice said inside her mind. "It is not your time. Rest. You will go with the coming of the change of seasons."

She kept her vigil through the coldest months. There was no change. The green pillar did not grow. Was that to be his last and final form? She asked and received no answer.

"You're hateful," she told the whisperers, one night when she'd called and called and prayed to Duwan's Du without answer. "You can speak. You can tell me, and you won't. You are cruel. I will leave this place with the first thaw."

When it came, the change of season, it came suddenly. She awoke one morning to find that she was not, as usual, shivering with the cold. There was a sound of dripping water. Since the cave was dark, lit only by the fire and a slit for ventilation at the top of the newly banked snow, the coming of morning meant nothing to her, and she slept, often, until midday. She saw a trickle of melt water running down the inside of the snowbank at the entrance to wet the dry floor of the cave. She pushed an opening through the snow and looked out to see a wet, bright, dripping world. A mass of snow fell from the laden bough of a tree and made a wet, soggy sound. She went to the green pillar. Its snow covering was melting, too, exposing the rich, dark green color. The sun had a hint of warmth. She bared her arms and drank of it. Soon, she told herself, she would set out for the west.

There was little preparation to be done for leaving. She would carry only Duwan's swords. They had been cast aside by the enemy and she'd stored them in the cave, keeping them bright during the winter by rubbing them with sand.

On a day that dripped a new layer of melting snow, snow deposited by what she felt would be the last of the late winter storms, she buckled Duwan's swords to her hips and emerged from the cave to take one last look at the valley and the green pillar. The sun was just beginning to light the top of the canyon's sides. She walked to the pillar and stood there, remembering.

"I go now, Duwan," she said. "I will come back, someday."

"It is not yet time," the voice in her mind said.

Anger flooded her. "Now? Now you speak?"

"You will go when Du warms the earth so that the new, green grass comes."

"I will go now," she said. "Why must I wait?"

There was no answer. "May the dus curse you all," she shouted, and her voice echoed back to her. She fell to her knees and faced the green pillar. "Duwan, Duwan, they torment me so."

She would have spoken more in complaint, but her eyes fell from the pointed peak, where his head had once been, from the point where once his fiery eyes had flashed, down to a point not far above the ground. A small movement had drawn her eyes. She gasped. The mossy green covering split before her eyes and she saw one finger. A finger! And it was not raw, or decayed. It had pale green, healthy, living skin.

"Duwan," she screamed, reaching for the spot, finding that the mossy covering was tough, so tough that she could not tear it.

"Peace, daughter," said the thought voice of Sema the elder. "Do not disturb him, for he still sleeps."

"He's alive?"

"He is with us. Be patient, daughter."

8

"It is not a full conqforce," Dagner told Duwan the Elder. The old Drinker had not weathered the winter well. He moved with difficulty. The hardening had reached past his hide and was affecting his joints, his flesh, his bones. "The scouts have all returned, and fresh ones have been sent out. They estimate that there are more than two thousand armed men, with a support group of more than two hundred slaves guarded by lightly armed conscripts. Their movements indicate that they are making a methodical search. They send out groups of about one hundred in various directions, surrounding a given area, a valley, for example, and then sweep all toward the center. One of our scouts was thus encircled and did not escape."

"Was he a good warrior? Would he have talked?"

Dagner shrugged wearily. "Who can say what a Drinker will do or say when he is peeled rapidly? We must assume that he talked. Du knows that I probably would if they were taking my hide."

Duwan the Elder nodded gloomily. He could field an armed force of less than a thousand warriors. He was not ready, and he had feared the coming of the thaws and the warm, sunny weeks that followed. But he had no choice, or, at best, some doubtful choices. During the winter he had questioned the free runners who were now a part of his force. He had learned that to the west were the impenetrable, high, always snow-capped mountains. To the southwest, the desert. To the north, he knew, were the dense forests and beyond them the tundra. He could not move west. He could not move to the south. Should he move to the north?

"We will attack the separate groups," he said.

He called in his group leaders. "To kill the enemy, to prevent him from chasing us down here in these hills and throwing all his strength at us at once, we must move quickly."

A young leader moaned. He remembered the grueling training marches of the winter, through the snow and cold, when Duwan the Elder had pushed them to the limit of their endurance and beyond by reminding them that it was the enemy's mobility that had trapped the army in the canyon.

"The enemy moves swiftly," Duwan the Elder said, "but we can move even more swiftly. We will move as a body, and attack as a body. Behind us will come the females, the young, and those who do not, as yet, have arms. Their function will be to strip the battle-field of all weapons, all scraps of metal. We kill, they salvage, and as weapons are captured, our force will grow."

"Run, run, run," a young warrior complained, as the first elements of the army left the western valley. "I'd rather fight than run. Run all day and all night and then fight. Does he think we're dus?"

"He thinks you are Drinkers," an officer bellowed. "Save your breath for the running."

The encirclement was made with some units at a full run so that they arrived at their assigned points panting, out of breath, dripping sweat. The unit that had had to run faster and farther met the enemy first, a group of just over eighty well disciplined guards, and in their exhausted condition they took quick losses until Duwan the Elder, driving his unit hard, closed on the enemy's rear and the swords were aimed at enemy throats from two sides. It was quickly over. Leaning on his longsword, realizing that he was not as young as he once was, Duwan the Elder stiffened when a scout came pounding onto the battlefield.

"Two escaped," the scout panted. "Come, you can see them."

Duwan the Elder followed the scout to a sheer drop, a precipice of faulted stone, and looked down into a river valley to see two blue uniforms, dim dots in the distance, moving rapidly. He had to look harder to see Drinkers in pursuit, so far behind that it was hopeless, for in the distance he could see the massed blue of the main enemy force.

He summoned his leaders. Old Dagner was grunting with the effort of walking. "They know we are here," Duwan the Elder said. "Now our only advantage is that we can pick our own ground."

He chose well. At the western end of the valley the stream had eroded its way down through native rock to form an outlet. On either side the slopes rose steeply. The slopes were stony and barren of heavy growth near the valley floor, slanting upward to a tree line where a dense evergreen forest offered protection and cover.

"We will be outnumbered," Duwan the Elder told his leaders. "We will have to kill two for one. We will entice them to us by exposing ourselves on the barren slope and falling back gradually, making them fight uphill until we are in the tall brothers, where their formation will be broken and the action will favor us. Our bowmen will be concealed in the trees, and will choose targets of opportunity as we draw the enemy near."

The Devourers advanced in two columns, coming up the valley on either side of the stream. Their scouts had seen Duwan the Elder's battle formation

on the barren slope and they were advancing at
quick pace, their guttural chant reminding veterans
of the nortern fighting of the sounds of a charging
conqforce. Duwan the Elder, noticing the nervousness among his force, strode back and forth in front
of the formation.

"Our withdrawal must be orderly," he shouted.
"Keep the lines straight. Keep your eye on the warriors on either side of you. Should there be a break-
through, close up and cut off the enemy. Fight as
you back up slowly. Remember that you are Drinkers, and more than a match for a Devourer. Those
of you who kill one enemy on the slope will have
only one left to kill in the melee among the tall
brothers."

And, as the enemy reached the foot of the slope
and, chanting, swung into a broad front, an attack
formation, he yelled, "For Duwan, for Du, and for
the land of our ancestors."

Duwan the Elder had no way of knowing that this
force of guards that he faced had been hand-picked.
They were all veterans of the northern fighting, and
they'd undergone the most intensive training that
Hata could organize. Moreover, before their departure from Arutan the High Mistress, herself, had
addressed them, and had told them that their expedition was more than an effort to punish escaped
pongs. She had, against the advice of Hata, told the
guards of the special abilities of the pongs, who
called themselves Drinkers, had given them a short
lesson in history, and, perhaps most effective of all,
had promised a bonus to each man based on the
number of pong killed during the campaign. There
had not been a more motivated force of Devourers
in the field since the days of the conquest, and it
showed as the enemy came charging up the hill with
dismaying speed and energy to strike the formation

of Drinkers a blow that sent them reeling. So fierce
was the assault that there was no question of a slow,
orderly retreat. The Drinker line began to give way
rapidly on the left, and Duwan the Elder shifted
strength there only to see the center crumbling.

"Fall back," he bellowed, fighting for his life as two
snarling enemy pressed him hard.

Panic struck on the left, and Drinkers turned their
backs, and ran. Many died as they were overtaken.
Screams and the clash of blades filled the air. Dust
billowed up from the dry, rocky soil. Duwan the
Elder's vision was limited by the dust so that he
didn't know what was happening to his far right.

"Fall back to the trees," he bellowed, fighting as he
backed up the slope, leaving enemy dead behind
him. But once more he was reminded that he was
not a warrior in his prime as his longsword arm grew
weaker and weaker with fatigue and he found himself relying, dangerously, on his shortsword.

There would be many who claimed to have seen
the miracle first. It came from the left, where the
panic had begun and where the Drinker line was
dissolving.

Two figures emerged from the tall brothers, moving down the slope not in haste but with long, pur-
poseful strides. The taller of the two uttered a
powerful cry as he launched himself at the enemy
flank and his blades sang and hissed and thudded
and caused a ripple in the enemy line, then a pause,
and then the shout began.

"The Master!"

It came from someone on the left. It was repeated.

"The Master!"

"The Master has come!"

"Rally round the Master!"

Fleeing warriors halted, turned, struck down their
pursuers or were struck down. A mass of Drinkers
converged on the left and this movement was seen

dimly by Duwan the Elder. He saw a knot of enemy surrounding just two Drinker warriors and was astounded to see that the two were more than holding their own.

"The Master! The Master!" The word was shouted, whispered, screamed, and the Drinker line wheeled and converged on the battle that had formed on the Drinker left.

"No, no," Duwan the Elder shouted, knowing that to stand in the open would be fatal. The odds against them were too great, but he, too, kept hearing that word, "Master," and he, too, seeing that it was impossible to restore order and continue the withdrawal, began to fight his way to the left.

Without orders, the archers in the trees bolted toward the battle. The enemy, trying to engage the Drinkers, who were congregating at the left, was milling in confusion, only a few of them in actual contact with Drinker swordsmen. Their rear was riddled by the arrows from the archers. Stone arrowheads were not as effective as iron. Some shattered without wounding deeply, but they took their toll.

In the valley, Captain Hata saw the surprising turn of events and shouted. "Reserves, to the right, come on them from the right, from up the slope." And his two hundred reserve swordsmen began to run up the hill, skirting the battle to gain the advantage of higher ground.

By all logic, being outnumbered, the Drinkers should have formed a defensive square, limiting their exposure to the more numerous enemy. Instead, they charged. They charged in the direction of the thickest fighting, where blades caught the rays of the sun, flashed, and dripped blood. All formation was lost on both sides, and it became a confused, dusty, screaming mass where it was often difficult to distinguish friend from foe.

Gradually, out of the chaos, a wedge-shaped formation grew, with two at the head, fighting side by side, swords meeting the best that the enemy had to offer and leaving carnage behind them. Twice this wedge carved its way through the milling, sweating, dying masses of warriors, taking a toll of the enemy. And now all the surviving Drinkers were a part of it, and the split enemy flowed along the sides of the wedge with clashing swords. Enemy captains bellowed, trying to bring order, to get their warriors back into formation. And from the valley, Captain Hata saw that his numbers were thinning much more quickly than those of the pongs.

"Formation," he screamed, "form a double line."

But his voice went unheard. In desperation he led his two staff officers running up the slope to join the fighting and for a moment it seemed that his presence would turn the tide as guardsmen began to rally to him and seek a disciplined line. Just as it seemed that he had control, the pong wedge turned toward him and came rolling down the slope, leaving dead, blue-clad warriors in its wake and those who had rallied to him turned and ran, some of them falling and tumbling down the slope.

Hata found himself almost alone, with only two of his officers and three guards at his side. He moved to avoid the rush as the wedge broke, pongs yelling, "After them. No prisoners. For the Master."

The battle rolled past and Hata stood, panting, looking on the carnage. Much more blue than the colorless garments of the slaves was on the ground. And below there were footraces as pongs ran down guardsmen and killed them from the rear.

Still he stood and now, below, there was only silence. A wounded man moaned. A light breeze cooled his brow. He saw the pongs turn and start slowly up the slope. And at their head was—

"You!" he said, his voice breaking, as Duwan the Drinker halted a few paces in front of him, swords dangling, blades bloody, face smeared with blood, his body nearly naked, and that, too, smeared with blood that was not his own. "But you're dead," he said.

"*They* are dead," Duwan said, pointing with his shortsword to the litter of bodies.

Hata's sword jerked into readiness. "I killed you once," he said. "Now, apparently, I must do it again, or have you the courage to face my sword alone?"

"At your pleasure," Duwan said.

Hata had noticed that the one who had fought so well by Duwan's side was a female, but now he had eyes only for Duwan as he moved cautiously down the slope.

"Two swords against one?" he asked. "When we dueled in the square at Arutan you put aside your shortsword."

"That was sport," Duwan said. "I will show you as much mercy as you and your ancestors have always shown to Drinkers."

He moved swiftly up the slope, met a thunderous downswing of Hata's longsword and, without regret, with no desire to prolong the fight, plunged his shortsword to the hilt in Hata's breast.

Duwan the Elder had pushed through the crowd of drinkers to see the last encounter. He didn't wince as the remaining Devourers were put to the sword, but then he was blinking as he stared into a pair of fiery, orange eyes.

"Duwan?"

"Father."

"Du is great," Duwan the Elder said.

"Greater than you could have ever imagined, father," Duwan said, clasping his elder's bloody right arm with his own.

"I, too, am here," Jai said.

Duwan the Elder looked into her face, embraced

her. Pushed her back to look at her again. "I never thought to see either of you—how—"

"There will be time for that, for there is much to tell," Duwan said. "Are there other enemy units in the west?"

"Not within scouting distance," Duwan the Elder said.

"How many more warriors do you have?" Duwan asked.

His father smiled grimly. "You are looking at our entire force, alive and dead."

Females and young had begun to search the battlefield, coming away with swords carried like firewood in their arms.

"Your mother will be happy to see you, my son," Duwan the Elder said.

"And I her," Duwan said. He was watching as the wounded were being treated. Here and there a Drinker or two knelt beside a warrior too severely injured to be moved, waiting for the end.

Duwan the Elder turned to his leaders, who had formed behind him and were gazing at Duwan in wonder. "Form them up." he ordered, "and we will move toward home."

But the march was delayed by the arrival of a panting scout. "Leader," he shouted from a distance, "there come ones with whom you will wish to speak."

There were five of them, escorted by another scout. Their bellies were bloated and distended in the manner of those who were eating their fill for the first time in their lives.

"And who are these?" Duwan asked, as the ragged group came toward the leaders, looking to the left and right in some fear at the sight of so many dead.

"We are from Kooh, Master," said a male, bowing.

"Good," Duwan the Elder said. "I will detail some to march with you and show you the way, since you will have difficulty keeping our pace."

"Master," the male said, bowing ever lower. "There are others behind us."

"Excellent," Duwan the Elder said. "I will leave some to guide them, too." He turned to pick out a warrior or two to leave behind. As an afterthought he asked, "How many are coming?"

The swollen-bellied male bowed again. "There are too many to count, master, as many as the leaves of the trees."

Duwan, who had been staring moodily at the Drinker dead, jerked his head around. "What did you say?"

"Master, they were killing us by the dozens, by the hundreds. Every day they were killing us, and when we finally began to believe the words of the wise priest of Tseeb, we rose. We slew our masters, or at least many of them, and we left behind us a burning city."

"Du!" Duwan breathed. Tambol had once estimated for him that there were over twenty thousand slaves in the city of Kooh. He turned his burning orange eyes on his father. "There is our army," he said. "Now if they will only give us time."

"We will make the time," Duwan the Elder said.

The momentous news filled Duwan's head, almost making him forget something that had been on his mind. He did not hear his father, at first, when Duwan the Elder made a suggestion. When it was repeated: "Duwan, I will stay with the rest to escort the hordes to our valley. Go ahead, with your mate, to greet your mother."

"Yes," Duwan said. Then he remembered. "It has been said that the Devourers have a method of recording on lasting material the spoken word. Is that true?"

A former pong nodded. "That is true, Master. It is the priestly writing. They use a colored fluid to make marks on material pressed into thin sheets from the pulp of a certain plant. I have seen this writing."

"Do you practice it?" Duwan asked.

"No, Master. That is for priests and certain temple pongs who are trained in this magic."

"Find me, among those who are coming from Kooh, one who can both record words and recite them back," Duwan said. "Bring him to me as quickly as possible."

"It will be done," the pong said.

9

This is the word of Duwan the Drinker, who was dead but now lives, son of Duwan and Sema, Drinkers of the Valley, led into the homeland of my fathers by the wisdom and grace of Du there to be captured and peeled by the enemy and to be returned to the earth in a spirit of irony by the High Mistress of Devourers, Elnice of Arutan.

As I died, Du lifted my spirit from my body and I looked down upon our earth from the blackness, where the lights of the night sky sang with mighty voices of crackings and whistlings and odd growlings.

And Du said, "Look on my works."

And there was, near at hand, a huge ball of molten fire that shot out from its cauldron streamers of light, and below me was a ball showing the colors of blue and green and I could see whiteness covering the land and the waters and gleams of reflected light from the snowy wastes of the northland.

And Du said, "There I created you."

For we and our earth are not the center of the universe. The ball that is our earth spins and travels far through blackness and is warmed only by that molten fire.

"Du!" I said.

And Du said, "None have seen my face, much less those who in the past ignored my teaching and flaunted my word, for that which you see is nothing more than one of my lesser creations, set there in the emptiness to give life to you."

"Teach me, Master," I said, "for I am in Du's paradise."

And Du said, "When I saw a need to fill the emptiness I made the sun and the earth and those other suns and earths that you, in your ignorance, call the lights in the sky. I gave you the earth, and its goodness, I gave you the succulent green, growing things and the fresh waters and there was none to come against you. I taught you a reverence for life, and I put upon that earth the small, furred animals and the farls of the forests and others that you know not. And I made you the greatest of all living things, keepers and eaters of the green grass and the fruits and the myriad of other growing things, the vines and the small flowers, the towering trees and the growing shrubs, and of the animals I gave you custody, to see, and to admire, and enjoy."

And I came to know that all is a oneness, that all life is kindred, whether it be mobile, fixed, or animal. And I said, "Master, how did we err?"

And Du said, "One tasted flesh and ignored the warnings of my spokesmen. Others tasted flesh and then I brought against you the Enemy, the Devourers, and for generations I have punished you."

And I asked, "How, Master, can we atone for the sins of our ancestors?"

And Du said, "A few were faithful to my word, and I led them out of the land of death."

And I asked, "Do you speak of the Drinkers of the Valley?"

And Du said, "But they, too, were weak, and began to see my face in the disc of the sun, forgetting the teachings of my spokesmen. Yet there was a certain devoutness that remained, and I relent."

And I said, "Du is great. What have I to do, Master, now that I am dead?"

And Du said, "My son, you sleep only, for you are my instrument. I have regretted my own creation, and you will be my instrument of punishment for those who have for so long oppressed my people."

And I asked, "When I awaken, Master, how will I know the proper course?"

And Du said, "I will be with you. I will form your words

as you teach my people, and I will provide helpers for you. Those you will instruct as I instruct you."

And I said, "Teach me, Master."

And Du said, "You will not take the all of any living entity, except in doing my work against the Devourers. Even then you will be merciful, for there is room for all. You will respect the rights of all brothers, neither taking nor desiring that which is theirs. You will obey me in all things, for I live, and I am unique. You will honor your old ones, and see that they have choice earth where they will await my call to paradise. You will honor the family unit, and cleave to your chosen mate, and teach your offspring the word of the one Du. You will heal the scars made upon my earth by the devourers, for their building is not my wish. You will spread my word to the far corners of the earth, and release others who are in bondage."

And I felt myself falling and saw no more. "Master," I cried, "I am but one Drinker."

And Du said, although I heard not, but only sensed it, "One can change a world when he believes."

And I cried, "Master, there are questions. Have I sinned in loving my mate, in being with her for pleasure only?"

And Du said, "Have I not made you as you are?"

Then I heard no more, save for the whispers of those who await Du's call to paradise, and I awoke. Now all living things combine in a oneness. Now I know that the sun, whom we have called Du, is but one small creation of the one Du and his gift to us. Now these words will be copied and recopied and those who copy and read will teach others to copy and read and if we learn, and obey, and keep the laws of Du this land shall be ours once more in oneness.

Thus it was told to me. Thus it will be.

—The testament of Duwan the Drinker, Chosen of Du.

10

Duwan watched from a hill as Kooh burned again. He had come to a half-dead city to find only a few Devourers. Below him, moving south, there was a large group of females and young, for he had been merciful, giving orders to spare those who did not fight against Drinkers. He had had to be firm with that order until a Drinker leader, from the ranks of those who had led the last uprising in Kooh, smiled and said, "I see your plan, Master. Dead, the females, the young, the weak and the ill are a burden to no one. Alive, they will strain the resources of the city of Tshou, where they will surely go."

Duwan was content to let them believe that he had motives other than mercy. But Tambol understood, for he had studied the writings that Duwan had dictated to a former temple slave. And there were others, too, for Duwan spent much time in teaching, and those he taught multiplied his efforts.

Even as he watched the Devourers move to the south he saw them passed by a smaller group of Drinkers, and to his sadness there was killing and maltreatment until a unit of his army arrived and stopped the violence. He did not know how they found him, the ex-slaves who flocked to his army with each passing day. The horde that he had led out of the western hills had almost doubled, with ex-slaves from almost all of the Devourer cities, and they reported hardship among the former masters, and resistance to the order by Elnice of Arutan for total mobilization.

Nevertheless, there was a Devourer army before the coastal city of Tshou. The climactic battle was fought on the beaches, and the receding waves carried with them severed limbs and white foam turned green with blood.

Now, behind him, lay Tshou, walls dismantled stone by stone, buildings laid waste. Already the creeping green things were climbing, growing, covering the mound that had been a city.

"Where will we live, Master, when we destroy all the buildings, all the huts, all the homes?" it was asked.

He set the few remaining valley Drinkers to searching out the think vines that grew wild all over the Land of Many Brothers, then to teaching their cultivation and their control. Some learned quickly, and began to teach others. All along the route from Tshou to the south Duwan left growing villages, peopled largely by females, young, and the old.

Before Arutan, Duwan said farewell to Dagner, whose hardening was so severe that he had to be carried. He was returned to earth with ceremony, with noble words spoken by Tambol, and there was gladness, for now it was known that Dagner joined those who lived on, waiting for Du's call to paradise.

Arutan fell only after long siege, and it was discovered that the High Mistress, Elnice of Arutan, had fled to the south upon the approach of Duwan's army.

To the credit of the Devourers, few males survived, choosing to fight to the death. And from the growing horde of Devourer females Drinkers took mates. This disturbed Duwan, at first, until he reread his own testament to find the words, "All life is a oneness." Could that not be applied to Devourer females, so long as they choose to abide by the teachings? To his relief, all offspring of Drinker-Devourer matings had the pores of the Drinkers on their feet.

Now, one by one, the remaining Devourer cities fell, and were returned to the earth. Survivors marched to the south and were escorted into the heated, jungly lands from whence they had come, although many chose to stay, to adopt Drinker ways, once they were given the choice at Duwan's orders. Nor was there any slavery, although many clamored for it as a revenge for their generations of oppression.

Five years from the time that Duwan lived after being dead, he marched toward the north, accompanied only by one, a sleekly beautiful Jai. From the great mountains of the west to the sea, and south to the sodden, fever-ridden jungles the Land of Many Brothers was Drinker, and he was tired.

Although it had been a long time, he found the canyon without problem. Once they had made bough beds and built a fire in the cave he fell asleep immediately and slept through the night and into the next day until the sun had already sunk below the rim of the canyon. He roused himself, washed in the stream that had long since purified itself of the carnage of battle, and with Jai at his side sat in the center of the grove of his grandmother. The trees had grown impressively in the years since the plantings. As darkness fell he mused and listened to the whisperes. No word was distinguishable.

"I have returned, Grandmother," he said, aloud.

The whisperings did not change.

"Does she hear?" Jai asked.

"I believe she does, but she is nearer to Du than we, and not concerned with the things of our lives now."

"Do you think she knows how things are?"

"Yes. When I was in the earth, and she and the others sent tendrils to nourish me with their own substance there where times when I was almost wakeful and could sense, or feel, events at a great distance."

"Tell her, Duwan," Jai said.

"Yes." He nodded, and it seemed, as his head dropped, that he was sleeping. He did not speak, but Jai heard, and was frightened, at first, for she had not experienced that form of closeness to such an extent, having heard only a few distinct whispers from ancestors, never the thoughts of the living, but then she was not surprised, for he was Duwan, and she was his.

"In the end, Grandmother, all living things were one, and they combined to overcome the enemy. Tall brothers dropped limbs upon them in the forests. Vines writhed and tripped their warriors at crucial times. The grass bled of its substance and made itself slick under their feet, and even the tiny spores of the green, living things flew into their eyes to impede their vision."

For one moment it seemed that all the whisperings combined into one long, hissed sound. "Sooooooooooo."

In the cave, Jai nestled against him, he talked to her gently, telling her of his love, begging her to forgive the years when he could not devote himself to her, and she, weeping happily, turned her face to him.

"A Duwan fighting to free our land, a Duwan so occupied with his duties that he has time only to speak to me once a year is better than any other," she said. "But now we are here, alone, and the first snow will come soon. I will be selfish and keep you to myself for a long, long winter."

"That is a threat that I will face gladly," he said.

"And you will not think, and this is an order, my master, about crossing the western mountains to free the slaves there. Nor will you think of going to the north to bring your valley Drinkers to join us. Is that agreed?"

"Well, perhaps I will not think of those things too often."

"There is," she whispered, "another matter that I want you to consider." She pulled up her tunic and placed his hand on her budpoint. He felt the sweet heat and smiled. Then he jerked his head down and looked at her in the flickering firelight to see that she was blooming.

"It's early yet," he said.

"That's so our son will be well formed by spring and you will not be tempted to drag me on a long trek to the north."

"Humm," he said, drawing close so that his nostrils were filled with the flowery smell of her.

Author's Note: All writers of imaginative fiction are familiar with the difficulty of creating environments or lifeforms that bear as little as possible resemblance to the endlessly astounding variety of life on our own planet. When I first conceived the idea of having the Drinkers convert sunlight directly into energy, I felt that I had come up with, at least, a new slant on life. Then, in recent months, I read of the work of the Chemist Pill-Soon Song and others at Texas Tech, who, it was reported at the annual meeting of the American Society of Photobiology, had discovered a blue-green protozoan, *Stentor coeruleus*, that uses photosynthesis to create adenosine triphosphate (ATP), the chemical used as energy for all cells. Thus, without chlorophyll, using the photosynthetic pigment protein stentorin, *S. coeruleus* uses light to make energy, and the one Creator makes fiction, once again, merely a reflection of life.

DAW

**THEY WERE THE ULTIMATE ENEMIES,
GENERALS OF STAR EMPIRES FOREVER OPPOSED—
AND WORLDS WOULD FALL
BEFORE THEIR PRIVATE WAR...**

IN CONQUEST BORN
C.S. FRIEDMAN

Braxi and Azea, two super-races fighting an endless campaign over a long forgotten cause. The Braxaná—created to become the ultimate warriors. The Azeans, raised to master the powers of the mind, using telepathy to penetrate where mere weapons cannot. Now the final phase of their war is approaching, when whole worlds will be set ablaze by the force of ancient hatred. Now Zatar and Anzha, the master generals, who have made this battle a personal vendetta, will use every power of body and mind to claim the vengeance of total conquest.

☐ **IN CONQUEST BORN** (UE2198—$3.95)

DAW

A GALAXY OF SCIENCE FICTION STARS

- ☐ **TERRY A. ADAMS Sentience** — UE2108—$3.50
- ☐ **MARION ZIMMER BRADLEY Hunters of the Red Moon** — UE1968—$2.95
- ☐ **JOHN BRUNNER More Things in Heaven** — UE2187—$2.95
- ☐ **A. BERTRAM CHANDLER Kelly Country** — UE2066—$3.50
- ☐ **C.J. CHERRYH Cuckoo's Egg** — UE2083—$3.50
- ☐ **GORDON R. DICKSON Mutants** — UE1809—$2.95
- ☐ **CYNTHIA FELICE Double Nocturne** — UE2211—$3.50
- ☐ **C.S. FRIEDMAN In Conquest Born** — UE2198—$3.95
- ☐ **ZACH HUGHES Sundrinker** — UE2213—$3.50
- ☐ **CHARLES INGRID Solar Kill** — UE2209—$3.50
- ☐ **TANITH LEE Days of Grass** — UE2094—$3.50
- ☐ **BOB SHAW Fire Pattern** — UE2164—$2.95
- ☐ **E.C. TUBB The Temple of Truth** — UE2059—$2.95
- ☐ **JACK VANCE The Book of Dreams** — UE1943—$2.50
- ☐ **A.E. van VOGT Null-A Three** — UE2056—$2.50
- ☐ **DONALD A. WOLLHEIM (Ed.) The 1987 Annual World's Best SF** — UE2203—$3.95

Write for free DAW catalog of hundreds of other titles!
(Prices slightly higher in Canada.)
